E. Grandon

MY PRIDE, MY FOLLY

My Pride, My Folly

BY SUZANNE BUTLER

Little, Brown and Company · Boston

Published simultaneously in Canada by McClelland & Stewart Limited
PRINTED IN THE UNITED STATES OF AMERICA

For my mother,
to whose stories of Denmark
this tale owes
part of its inception,
and
for the friends
to whose
encouragement and insistence
it owes its completion

I   TWO years before he laid eyes on her, Michael Shea believed he knew exactly how Kirstina's marriage had been arranged. She had been then only fourteen, but she had a dowry of ten thousand kroner, which could be translated into American money at roughly five thousand dollars. The man named Aage Nordrupp was a well-to-do innkeeper from Boston. He took passage on the ship commanded by Michael's uncle with the intention of revisiting his village in North Jutland to pick himself out a wife. On the journey he enjoyed explaining the reasons for this undertaking and said repeatedly that he was not going to look for a young girl. His business had grown beyond his singlehanded control, and what he wanted was a woman to take charge of the kitchen and the maids. To return to Denmark was costing him money but he knew that there he could find the woman he wanted: one who would be honored at his notice and would recognize the importance of the trust he was prepared to repose in her.

The *Kronborg* was a very small ship and Herr Nordrupp her only cabin passenger. He and Captain Erik Warre sat smoking and talking together every evening and agreeing that Nordrupp was wise and farsighted in not taking an American wife.

Michael Shea, who acted as his uncle's mate, kept out of their way.

At the end of the summer Nordrupp came on board again at Aarhus and he was still alone. Michael was curious enough then to stay around and hear what had happened.

Kirstina Brandt had ten thousand kroner, said Nordrupp. Was not that ample excuse? But the very size of the dowry excited suspicion and he knew it and was frank. The girl was illegitimate and her stepfather wanted to be rid of her.

"I know," said Nordrupp, "that it is not what I went for. I have been persuaded to change my plans. But I am also doing the people a service. Where in their own village will they find a husband deserving of the money who will marry a girl like that?"

He would have brought her away with him at once had it not been for the village pastor, who insisted she was much too young. Ridiculous—such a fine, upstanding girl as she was, as tall as a man already —and very hard indeed, said Nordrupp, to expect him at his age to wait two years. He arranged now that when the time came Warre should bring her out—her, and her dowry and linen, and a friend to keep her company. Nordrupp would pay.

Michael Shea heard all this and much more. He was twenty, and he lay awake at night in his bunk and thought about Kirstina Brandt. He recalled Nordrupp's voice full of the smug businessman's satisfaction with a plain matter of business, and the Irish half of him stood uppermost until he refused to believe that a girl in full knowledge would have taken part in so infamous a bargain. He wondered how she had been coerced and if she were still child enough to have been easily bribed. His imagination was stirred by her youth and her ill fortune so that even if he had been told she was cross-eyed he would still have expected to find some attraction in her.

Then through the intervening two years he was busy with other things. He did not altogether forget the story he had heard, but neither did he have any time to waste in dreaming about it.

He saw her at last in September 1844, when the *Kronborg* put in to Aarhus to take her on board. She stood on the wharf while her trunks and bundles were being unloaded from a dray. It was a moment of bustle and movement, with her stepfather being greeted by the captain and her friend beside her pirouetting and staring about; but Kirstina Brandt was composed and still, standing alone as if she let nothing excite her until she chose. She was a very tall girl. Her gray dress molded her figure in severe simplicity. She wore no bonnet and her hair in the bright sunshine was corn-yellow.

Michael moved up to the ship's rail and leaned there. Behind her was the line of old houses, soft, red-brown brick, mellow and warm under the blue sky. There on the cobbled wharf she was all gray and gold and yellow. The yellow hair was in an arm-thick braid that slid down over her breast almost to her knees. He was close enough to see the light red flush on her golden cheeks.

The sun beat down on his head and he remembered vividly the dark nights two years before, and everything he had ever heard or thought about Kirstina Brandt. He remembered Nordrupp. He did not forget his uncle's best interests. But deep inside him he began

8

to laugh with the joy of knowing that he had found something he wanted, and that he meant to get.

Kirstina had said good-by to her mother at the farm. Neither of them had cried: each had understood the other too well. Kirstina did not cry now. Her stepfather kissed her and petted her and fussed about the appointments of her cabin; he admonished Helga Brunker, her companion, to be a good girl. When at last he was gone, and Helga Brunker had followed him up on deck, Kirstina looked about her, not exactly with relief or exultation, but with an emptiness that would presently be filled with both. She took hold of her braid of hair and rubbed its smoothness against her cheek and thought, This is myself; I am here; it has begun.

She had been waiting much longer than the two years, for since she had been a small child she had lived with the knowledge that she could depend only upon herself.

All her life, and at times with startling clarity, she was to remember a scene that took place when she was five years old. It was winter and early evening and she and her small brother were sitting on the floor near the porcelain stove. The farmhouse was very old, with walls that were several feet thick and small windows with immovable panes of glass. It was warm in the room and very quiet. She played almost noiselessly with her wooden doll and Johannes was on the point of going to sleep. Suddenly the door opened and a draft swept in and her mother was there.

"Kirstina," she said, and held out her hand, "come and see what I have for you."

Johannes awoke and scrambled up but their mother just stood there, watching and waiting.

Kirstina got to her feet shyly and went and gave her hand to her mother, who drew her out into the cold passageway and across it into the small, square room that Hans Brandt used as his office. Hans was not there, but on his big heavy table stood a box—a small, wooden, iron-bound chest.

Johannes reached the table and climbed up on a chair to get at the box. Their mother moved quickly and smacked him aside, so that both children's mouths fell open in utter surprise. Jan was too astonished even to howl, and while he still stared Maria Brandt picked up Kirstina bodily and plunked her down on the chair and said, "There. For you alone. Not for Jan."

Kirstina shivered with excitement while her hands explored the lid of the box; she felt the smooth, blackened wood, the cold iron corners. With her eyes on Maria's face she lifted the lid and pushed it back. When she looked down she saw that the box was full of round gold pieces.

Jan pushed his head under her arm to see and plunged his acquisitive little fists in among them. One slid out upon the table and Kirstina picked it up. It was smooth and shiny. She ran her fingers over the man's head on one side. Her brother butted her elbow and her coin went flying; she slid down under the table after it and groped on her hands and knees.

While she was down there she heard her father's voice, very sharp, and her mother's, once again butter-smooth, in reply. She came out slowly and they were standing there together, watching each other.

"I gave it to you to use," murmured Maria.

"It belongs to the child."

"So I have told her."

Her mother had already left the room, with Jan trundling after her, when Hans looked down and saw Kirstina still holding the single gold piece in her hand. He took it from her and put it back in the box, and closed down the lid. She stayed and watched while he opened his strongbox, in which he kept the deeds to his land, and he put her box in there and locked it away.

Hans Brandt was twelve years older than his wife Maria. When he had been a young farmer, she had been still a short-skirted little girl chasing about her father's fields. By the time she had grown up to become queen of the village, he had been already too old and too dull to please her. Maria was a silver beauty, whose hair when she let it hang loose was like moonlight on water rippling. She had reminded Hans of the ice maidens in the old tales who came to live in a man's house through the winter months and then melted away with the spring. In the end she had tired of all her village flirtations and had gone to Copenhagen to be maid to the daughter of a noble family. For two years she was away. Then one morning Hans Brandt's housekeeper had interrupted his breakfast to tell him dryly that Maria Svensen was back and at least six months with child.

He had not hesitated to take what he wanted when it fell into his hand. Before the baby was born he had married Maria, and he expected to reap a double harvest in gratitude and love.

What finally broke this illusion was the money. Maria turned over to him her box of Copenhagen gold, saying, "Add it to whatever my father paid. It is of no use now to me." She did not even know how much was there. But Hans counted the money and as he did so every coin fomented doubt, until he began to see himself as ridiculous. Where could be the sense in looking to her for recognition, when she had already enjoyed all that he would never be able to give her?

"Tell me," he had ordered, "where I can send this back?"

It was the one thing she never would tell him.

So long as Kirstina was little, she was sent daily to the pastor for lessons, and Hans continued sending her there when she was much older than was usual. He was kind and did his best to protect her, but in time she learned to keep her mouth shut and bear insults in secret rather than to keep running to him for comfort. Eventually her regard for his affection came to be tinged with contempt for its helplessness. She listened more and more to Maria, for, though she did not love her mother, she knew it was with her that the only help lay. "You have the money," Maria reminded her. "When you are a little older everyone will remember that." Occasionally they would take out the box of gold and Maria would open it and let the child handle the money and count it.

By the time she was fourteen Kirstina knew exactly what was due to a girl with a dowry the size of hers. She looked about her with appraising young eyes and discovered that there was not a man in the district whom she would want her money to buy for her. Then she remembered how her mother had gone away, and her dreams and all her thinking became colored with the vision of escape.

What Aage Nordrupp said on the *Kronborg* was truthful insofar as it went, for he did not know that it had been Kirstina Brandt herself who first saw the chance he offered her. Hans had been shocked when she told him. He had harped on her age and said he loved her and did not want her to be snatched away. Maria was far more practical. "What else are you going to find for her?" she had asked. "She is too young, but when she is sixteen will there be anything better? She knows what she wants and I understand her." Maria had said she would go to Nordrupp herself, whereupon Hans gave in and went—and when he was there, his very dislike of the proceeding made him drive the best bargain he could.

The *Kronborg* was a world Kirstina could not have imagined.

The first day out Helga Brunker took to her bed, but Kirstina was up with the dawn and ate her meals with appetite. She had not been twenty-four hours at sea before she knew that it was Michael Shea who was god on board the ship.

The captain paced soberly beside her on the deck and told her long tales, but meanwhile Michael stood at the wheel and it was he whom she covertly watched. His short, waving brown hair was little deeper in color than his tanned skin. He grinned widely, showing very white teeth. His blue jacket was usually unbuttoned. He stood at least six feet tall and he carried his shoulders as if he owned all he saw. The sailors on the *Kronborg* were friendly and smiled at Kirstina and answered her questions, but when Michael shouted his orders they left her and jumped to obey, and this was something she liked to see happen.

At Bremen the German emigrants came on board. Michael moved among them after the fashion of a young and well-intentioned host. He did not speak German fluently—his uncle and some of his crew were far better at that—but he had the trick of making people trust him on sight and turn to him for help. He went between decks with the ship's carpenter to have partitions put up and he carefully allotted space for each family according to its numbers. He had his men stack the baggage with due regard for balance and convenience. He took pains to make clear that the captain carried no emergency rations beyond ship's biscuit and potatoes, though fresh water and fuel were included in the price of the fare. He called the women together and explained the system of relay that would be employed for cooking meals, and he had the two immense ranges on the foredeck uncovered while he demonstrated their use.

As the result of his concern for his passengers' welfare, he received from them all the co-operation he could wish. The women listened to him with maternal affection; the men puffed on their pipes while they nodded agreement and began calling him *der Junge*.

Owing to the great number of people on board, the cooking stoves were very rarely out, and in the evenings everyone but the youngest children would come up on deck and gather near them to sing. The music was solemn rather than merry; the Germans clung to their rhythmic Lutheran hymns and the deep voices of the men outweighed those of their wives and children. Kirstina knew the tunes and sat following them with words in her own tongue. Forever after the scene was imprinted in her memory: the fading light, the ship lifting and falling and moving always into the west, the fires on deck, the soberly clad crowd of figures that sat about them and on up into the bow of the ship. Slowly the faces and forms seemed to merge into one, until only the glow of the ranges, and the little points of fire that were the men's pipes, remained distinct.

At last one morning she woke to discover that the fine weather they had enjoyed so far had broken. Helga was again moaning and retching in her bunk and Kirstina did what she could for her, with the capable and healthy kindness of those who are never seasick; then she hurried away to get up on deck. She came out there on the starboard side, in the lee of the deckhouse and sheltered from the southwesterly wind. In the cabin she had felt the ship heaving and laboring beneath her feet, but here in the open air the *Kronborg* seemed to be swinging forward to meet the waves. The dark, bluish clouds lay fold upon fold and the dull-shadowed water slipped by ominously fast. Kirstina was delighted to see that there were no other passengers on deck. The hatches were closed and the emigrants ignominiously stowed below.

For a while she stayed where she was. Then she started forward to see what was happening on the other side of the ship. A seaman in the bows caught sight of her and waved her back, but she paid no attention to him. She came in view of the wheel and of the helmsman braced there with Michael Shea beside him. Michael also saw her and waved as the other man had done. She lifted her chin and took another step, and in that moment the gale seized her skirts and halted her and drove the breath back down her throat so that she gasped and put out her hands and was sent staggering to one side.

Michael ran up and caught her round the waist and guided her back out of the wind to the starboard rail.

"You silly girl," he said, "didn't you see me wave?" But he knew quite well that she had and he grinned at her.

She stopped gasping in order to protest, "I didn't know the wind would be so strong."

"Next time you be ready to take a man's word for it—or I may not be in time to save you."

"I would have saved myself."

"Would you that?" he said. He took his arm away and stayed beside her, watching her face. He had never until now had the opportunity he had wanted, to talk to her alone, and the longer he had waited the more curious about her he had become. Suddenly he said, "There's one thing certain—no one could have been more mistaken than I was in what I used to think about you."

"What do you mean?"

"I had you such a poor little thing—such a poor little thing that could be sold away without a thought! Nice to be kind to and to cuddle a bit. And from the start I meant to spoil old Nordrupp's fun for him. But how was I to know it would be yourself? A tall, proud, queen of a girl, with a way with you like a queen to hold everyone far off?"

He was still smiling at her, quizzical, only pretending to be perplexed. Kirstina turned her head away and stared out over the sea. She made her voice blank and quiet, and asked, "Who told you?" though she knew very well who it must have been.

"Nordrupp, the old goat!" said Michael promptly. "He should have been ashamed, snapping up a little girl in short skirts! But it was the money that counted with him, and that he couldn't keep quiet about! I can hear him now, telling my uncle, 'Born in wedlock she'd have had nothing but the dowry of a farmer's daughter. Why shouldn't I be glad of what is my good luck?' By God, but I was angry at him!"

He had no idea of the full import of his words, no idea of the fond hope he was cruelly shattering. Kirstina had been blissfully happy on the *Kronborg* because it had seemed to be the world out of her dreams, in which no one knew anything about her except what she would wish them to know. Now, while Michael spoke, the old humiliations and shame clutched at her, and dragged her back. She had a physical sensation of breathlessness and desperation that surged through her so that she choked and felt ill, and it was a mighty relief when this first shock passed and was succeeded by rage—rage that swept up and engulfed her and that she could direct at the man who stood beside her rather than at her own ugly fate.

She gave him no warning, but lifted her hand as she broke away from the rail and turned and slapped him. "You know about me!" she shouted, and then again, "You know about me!" The wind carried her voice back at her. Suddenly the tears poured down her face. She lost all reason and slapped at him again and clawed his cheek before he managed to grab her arms and hold her off.

He was as excited as he was astounded. If she had not been so fierce he would have tried to kiss her, but while he held her she was still fighting to come at him. Then she stopped struggling and they

14

stared at one another until she wrenched herself free and got to the companion hatch and was gone.

For the rest of that day Michael went about whistling, his scratched cheek bothering him not at all.

The wind that had nearly blown Kirstina off the ship increased by evening to gale force, piling up the seas before it. Next morning the ship was pitching uneasily between villainous waves. So long as her head was kept into the wind, she pierced the waves with her bow and they slid over her knee-deep, doing little damage. But it took two men to hold down the wheel and again and again she would veer, and then broadsides sent her rolling far enough to ship water over the starboard rail.

Just before dark a great wave came rolling in over the port bow, caught one of the steersmen off balance and hurled him away. The ship swung. There was no time to bring her about before a second great wave reared up, pushing the ship sideways, towering over her whole length until it finally broke and crashed its weight upon the deck. Michael had the breath wrung from him and felt his body almost torn from his arms, but the thundering, murderous water passed over and like a miracle the ship came upright again. Each man let go what he had been clinging to. The steersman who had first been swept away lay by the rail with his skull cracked. A second man, caught farther astern, had a broken arm. Every water cask that had been lashed on deck was smashed.

By morning the gale had begun to travel away, but with half their water supply lost the captain decided it would not be safe to continue. He was glad that they were not yet beyond the Irish coast and altered course so that they could put into Cork for new casks.

On the short journey there Michael saw Kirstina only twice. She would not look towards him and her face was stiff and unhappy.

He had been into Cork many times before and had friends there. The cooper to whom he went could not supply the casks all at once and said it might take as long as a week. Erik Warre was not pleased but Michael soothed him and went back on shore.

After the storm the weather had turned fine again and the passengers were glad to get out in the air. The men stood smoking on the wharves or strolled into the town, curious about the wild Irishry whom they knew were all Papists and under the thumb of Spain. The women went to bargain with wordless obstinacy in the market place for fresh meat and fowl, then returned on deck to cook it for the hungry children who had been chasing on the beach. Even Helga Brunker recovered enough to come out and sit in the sun, which banished a little of the green from her thin cheeks.

The third afternoon Michael came back from town to see Kirstina standing with a group of children at the near end of the wharf. He walked straight up beside her and before she could guess what he was about had clamped his hand on her left wrist.

"Now," he ordered, "you come with me."

He knew her well enough already to be sure she would make no outcry, and he was right. Willy-nilly she followed him away.

He led her along by the wharves and ships' chandlers, up past the cooper's shop and then into the little yard beyond it, that was piled with the seasoning lumber and cask and barrel hoops, and casks new and old and falling to pieces. One fat keg stood handily before a tower of new planks. He pulled Kirstina over and sat her down on it. Then he took his hand from her wrist and stood squarely in front of her to say, "Now tell me just what it is that I have done."

She stared up at him sullenly and brought her right hand to rub the wrist he had loosed. After a while she said again the thing that haunted her.

"You know about me."

"And what is there that I should not know? Didn't I tell you that it had made me angry for you? I hated that man until I could have strangled him, with his air of a good bargain he had made and his talk of human beings as if they were no more than a piece of goods! That was two whole years ago. The poor little thing that I spoke of —that I thought then you would be—her I would have pitied and tried not to frighten. But to you there is so much I need to say and why should I hide it and not speak?"

Kirstina said flatly, "I know I should not have been angry. I am sorry I hit you."

Then he began to laugh at her, the ridiculous golden creature who was so slow to rouse and would not learn what he meant.

He asked her, "Don't you know what I am talking about? What do words matter, or anything that happened days and days ago? You scratched my face and I wanted to kiss you. You stood on the wharf at Aarhus and I fell in love with you. Kirstina Brandt, look at me. I am the one you are going to marry."

She was looking at him. A deep, warm flush rose up her neck and cheeks. Her lips parted a little, and the sunlight showered down on

16

her hair. Michael moved quickly and took her in his arms and kissed her. When he lifted his head she gave a little sigh; he drew her to her feet and they kissed again.

Presently he said, "My uncle shall marry us as soon as we're at sea."

"Your uncle?"

"Yes. He is able to, once we're at sea."

"But I'm betrothed to Herr Nordrupp."

"I know it. Christ! To think he might have married you."

"He will marry me," she said.

She was still standing in his arms. As he had done on that other occasion, he took hold of her and held her away.

"What do you mean?"

She repeated it. "Herr Nordrupp will marry me. That is why I am going to America."

"But now everything is changed. I love you."

"Everything is not changed. It is all arranged for me and I want it the way it is arranged."

It was Michael then who was out of his depth. "Listen—you don't care for old Nordrupp. And he hasn't treated you right. He promised you he would keep quiet and then he told your story to everyone he met."

"No," she said, "he did not promise me that. I see now that I was foolish to hope he would do so. But we are betrothed. You are not Danish and so you do not understand, but a betrothal is very like a marriage. We have exchanged rings and the pastor was there and I signed the contract."

"Yes—I know all that! I am half Danish. But it amounts to nothing. You are not married to him."

"I am promised."

"Look, girl! What is it you want?"

"There is my dowry. That is promised him also."

"Let him have it."

"And he is paying to have me come to him."

"My uncle can give him back his money."

She was white with her alarm and her perversity. He was no longer touching her and she stood alone, clinging to what she knew. "I want what is arranged for me! I want to go to America and marry Herr Nordrupp. I don't want anything else."

"Kirstina, darling, I love you and I want you to be happy. But you will not be happy if you do as you say."

Watching him, she cried out, "Don't kiss me again! I don't want you to kiss me! I never let anyone kiss me before . . ."

Michael kissed her, and she struggled and submitted, and then begged him for more. Until he said, "I shall take you back to the ship. Tomorrow we can talk of this again."

Next day, when he sought her out and took her ashore, he found to his delight that she was ready to flirt with him. She cast him side-long glances as they walked. In a shop near the cathedral she let him buy her a black, carved wooden pin, and use it to fasten the shawl she wore hanging back from her shoulders. Her yellow hair hung in the rope he longed to take in his hands.

"Were you born in Ireland?" she asked, fingering the bog-oak pin.

"No. I was born in Boston. It was my father came out from Ireland. He did sail from Cork itself as an emigrant."

"Like ours?" she asked, taking possession of the *Kronborg*.

"No indeed. My father would not have thought much of our good Germans with their bundles and preparations and prayers. My father went on board with a pair of dice in his breeches pocket, and a parcel of food that might have lasted, with luck, for a week."

"But how—Why did they let him on the ship like that?"

"Why should they not—since his passage was paid beforehand? This was more than twenty years ago and in those times no one troubled himself much over a half-dozen corpses buried at sea. And my father did not starve, though the voyage lasted forty-two days. I did hear that at the end of it he was selling their potatoes back to the men he had won them off, and giving them away to the women and children."

"Did he tell you that himself?"

"My uncle told me, and he had it from the captain of the ship my father sailed on. The captain said he never saw another man so sure of his luck as was Brian Shea."

"What did he do when he reached America?"

"He joined his elder brothers that were there before him. And he married my mother, who was Erik Warre's sister. And he died of the cholera when I was two."

He was aware of the drama of this ending, and Kirstina was shocked and said soberly, "So after all he was not lucky."

"I think he was. He never knew he would die so young and because he believed in his luck he took every chance he was offered while he was alive."

He took her for dinner to an inn where the landlady was his friend. They were shown into a private parlor beyond the taproom; it was very small, with a window that gave upon a garden which in turn sloped gently down to the west branch of the Lee. The landlady provided them with a hot fish stew, a game pie and an apple tart, and a bottle of red wine. The queer excitement that possessed Kirstina would not let her eat much. She drank the wine that was poured for her and watched Michael and let her gaze slide over the room.

Presently they went out into the garden, which about the house was messy and untidy, with few flowers and with traces of chickens. But farther on it became orchard, with unpruned apple and pear trees sweeping their branches to the ground and thick grass growing between. Along the river bank at the end was a brick wall; they leaned on it watching the water and Michael went on telling her about things that had happened long ago.

His mother also had died, when he was only just old enough to remember her. It was his Danish uncle and aunt who had brought him up. His numerous Irish cousins in Boston were the children of his father's two brothers, who had three families between them since one of them had married twice. They lived all together in a house much too small for them, with children spilling out of the door. The children thought Michael an oddity because he was one alone, but they welcomed him in among them and when he grew bigger and stronger than they he became the natural leader of their tribe.

Once, when he was still only about ten, after a violent dispute with his Danish aunt, he had run away to live with his Uncle Patrick and refused to return home until Erik Warre arrived with strong methods of persuasion. As he remembered it now, he had not been in the least comfortable in Patrick Shea's house. He had had to sleep in a bed with three cousins, his clothes had been allowed to fall into holes unattended and he was seldom required to wash. But the exploit had retained a certain glamour in his mind, and thereafter he had always been able to reduce his Aunt Johanna to acquiescence by the mere threat of repeating it.

At last he stopped speaking of himself and turned to Kirstina. He wanted her to talk, but it seemed she did not know how. She had been enthralled and drawn out of herself while she listened, but there was nothing in her own drear childhood she would willingly share with him—she would have preferred him not to know the little he did. She hesitated, and was shy, and finally obstinately silent.

Michael leaned on the wall and fingered some pieces of crumbling mortar and began to fling them one by one into the river. And so at length he arrived at the point they had both been skirting all that day.

"Shall I tell my uncle to marry us?"

When he looked round at her she shook her head, her eyes big and scared above her stubborn lips. The boldness and the naïveté of her amused him and he understood them very well.

"Then what are you doing here, Kirstina Brandt—alone here with me? I can also make bargains. I give nothing for nothing, and I do not want from you what I can get from another girl."

Kirstina flushed red with shame. Until that moment it had not occurred to her that he could guess her secret. The night before her misery had been acute. If she had been alone when she went to her cabin she would have taken out her dowry and played with the gold pieces as she used to do when she was still a child. That might have eased her, but with Helga present she was too shy to do it. She had climbed to her bed in a turmoil and lain there in the dark for hours, able to think of nothing but Michael Shea, and of how he had kissed her. She had felt his fingers hard on her wrist, the sun across her face, his mouth upon hers. And all she had wanted was to have it happen again. At last she had won release from her sleepless twisting and turning with a compromise, saying in her mind, Of course I will not do as he wants but I will go with him tomorrow and see what comes. Only now, from his words, it seemed that Michael knew what she had done, and as the blood rushed to her face she exclaimed unwisely, "But there is nothing I want!"

"Then why have you come away from the ship?"

"You asked me to come!"

"I am asking far more than that! Kirstina, you little fraud, why not say it outright? Say, 'I won't marry you, but I'll come with you to be kissed,' for that's about the sum of it. And indeed you would not be the first to say so. The trouble is that this time I'm playing another game. I want you, but if I can't have all of you, I'll do without anything else." He watched her face, from which all the blood had fled again, and her hands twisting in the folds of her gown; he went on slowly, talking his way against the barrier he had to break through.

20

"Of course there is something you want from me. You want me to hold you and make love to you. Didn't you say to me yesterday that no one had kissed you before? That makes me sorry for you, because once you are married to Nordrupp no one but he will ever kiss you again. You are choosing your life, but will it be as fine as you think —with everyone envying you and bowing to you and no one able to come near you but the one greedy old man? Will that content you? Will you grow like him so quickly that you will be old before you have had the time to be young? Or will you always remember today, and be sad that when the sun was shining and the birds rustling in the trees you did not take what was offered you and gladly pay its price?"

She had begun to cry, but more because she was the butt of his disapproval than because of his words themselves. She cried childishly, digging at her eyes with her knuckles.

He said gently, "Kirstina darling." He held out his arms and she fled to him, clinging and pressing up against him. He had no need to soothe her, for her tears were forgotten and the flesh of her came alive and dancing the very moment she was fed what she had desired.

They sat down on the grass bank and she drew up her knees and clasped them. Michael picked up the end of her gold braid and lay back smiling, bending it to and fro.

Kirstina said, "I won't marry you. All my life I have known that I had to make a good marriage. The money was given me for that. I asked to marry Herr Nordrupp. It is no good your trying to frighten me, because I know exactly what I want. I have talked about it with my mother. I want to have a house of my own and servants of my own and children of my own. I want to have money and be respected. I want people to be afraid to point fingers at me. I want them to visit me and to bow when they meet me on the street."

"Isn't that what I said they would do?"

"If I married you everyone would know how it happened. They all know about me. They would all say it was because of what I was born and that no one could expect anything else. And that is not true. . . . Also, I do not mind about Herr Nordrupp being old. He is not too old to give me children. . . . And if he should die I would not have to lose anything. I would still be rich."

At that, Michael was suddenly more angry with her than amused. He jerked sharply on the golden hair he held so that she cried out and put her hand to the nape of her neck. She turned to look down at him, aggrieved. Then she smiled guiltily and let him pull her down and gather her in comfortably until they lay together on the grass. "You arguing woman," he said, cupping her chin in his hand. She gave a muffled giggle and was still.

There was no wind where they lay. From time to time the light brightened or faded as the clouds changed. They could smell salt, and there was the sound of water lapping, always on the move.

His annoyance ebbed. He rubbed his cheek against her hair and he remembered how sure had been the instinct that had told him from the beginning that she was his to possess. There was no need to hurry; he felt warm and easy and content. His fingers gently explored the hollows of her throat and set to work on the fastenings of her bodice. She did not stir and her eyelids remained closed.

Until a moment of violent recollection made her start up and thrust him off. Her hands on his shoulders pushed him back on the ground and with the haste of panic she scrambled out of reach. He sat up furious and dethroned and saw the milk tone of her breast where she was struggling to pull the buttons together.

"Kirstina! I'll not hurt you! You don't know what you're afraid of!"

"You want to make me what my mother was!"

"It's not the same, girl! I want to marry you!"

"Whatever difference is there in that?" She was kneeling there in the grass, wary and contemptuous. "I would not let it make any difference. You are such a fool. You think if you could trap me I would have to marry you. But I am not simple like that. I can keep my mouth shut. I know you would never dare say what you had done. I would marry Nordrupp just the same."

Then she ran away from him out of the orchard, and he stayed and watched her go.

The day after that scene in the orchard the *Kronborg* set sail from Cork. Michael was not discouraged in his pursuit. Always he was inclined to want what was hard to get, and if Kirstina had been desirable before because she belonged to Nordrupp she was all the more so now because she was resisting himself. Again and again he went over the words she had used at the last. If he had believed them he would have been shocked, but he still would not have been turned aside.

For several days he left her alone, and noticed that she was carefully keeping herself out of his way. Then one evening he had occasion to go down to the saloon and went thinking that Kirstina might be there. She was not, but before he left again the door to her cabin suddenly swung open of itself and he saw her.

She was kneeling on the floor. Beside her stood a wooden, iron-bound box, and all around her were arranged neat little piles of gold coins. Momentarily he was bewildered. He stared and said, "What on earth—? What is this?"

Kirstina had very quickly closed the lid of her box and spread out her hands as a shield over the gold. Her memory flickered back through the years to Hans Brandt's surprising her and her mother in just this way and her face watching Michael was frightened— though of what she was afraid she could not have said, since she did not believe he would steal her treasure.

He said at last, harshly and with contempt, "My God! The money!" All his plan of procedure was swept aside by his fury at the insult of her hiding away here to count the gold for Nordrupp. What am I worth to her? he thought blindly. Or any man at all? And this was something like the indignation that he had felt years before on her account against Nordrupp, who had also believed that human flesh could be bought and sold.

He went in after her, stooped quickly to catch her arms and pulled her roughly to her feet. She struggled with him but he pushed her before him up against the wall and took her jaw in his hand as he bent her head back. He did not care how she was hurt and his own mouth was bruised and sore before he finished. He thought with satisfaction that this time at least he had given her no pleasure. Her face was white, and when he took his hand away the marks of his fingers grew red. He was aware that if he had not still been holding her she would have fallen; he himself had begun to tremble and he found that he was running with sweat. He turned back to the door and she followed after him until he let go of her. Then she dropped down upon the treasure on the floor, supporting herself weakly on one hand while the other crept to her throat. Michael leaned against the door frame and looked at her and at her money.

When at last he went Kirstina began to cry, and she cried bitterly all the while she gathered up the gold and wearily packed it away. She had been miserable before—how deeply disturbed was proved by his finding her handling the gold at all, a thing she had never expected to need to do again. Michael's indignation was something she could not understand. Her dowry, for which Aage Nordrupp had agreed to marry her, Michael did not care about. Her birth, for which everyone else scorned her, Michael was ready to accept. For this last she wanted to adore him, and yet she was convinced he was mistaken. It was utterly wrong of him to despise what others respected; wicked of him to condone what everyone else knew was disgraceful. If she had been at home again she knew she would have had no doubts; it was only here on the ship that she was in an alien world, where all her talismans broke in her hand.

It did not help her that the *Kronborg* ran into a second stretch of bad weather. She kept strictly to her cabin and the cabin boy brought food to her there. Helga became wretchedly ill again. Kirstina looked after her but otherwise had nothing to do. She was so unhappy and so confused that her troubles possessed her and prevented her from realizing how the fury of the storm outside mounted. All that bothered her at first was the noise, for the timbers of the ship never ceased creaking and groaning and even in the cabin the wind sounded abominably loud and clear, interspersed with the repeated boom and crash of the great seas over the decks.

With not a strip of sail on her, the *Kronborg* was being harried by the North Atlantic, buffeting the wind and the waves that tried to drive her back to Ireland. The great seas came in from due west at two-hundred-foot intervals over her bow, and as she slid into the troughs between them the shorter, steeper cross seas caught her at a forty-five-degree angle and sent her rolling to the side. On the second day of this treatment she sprang a leak; by the fifth she had three more and the first one had repeatedly spat out its plugs and had grown to a steady stream.

Kirstina that day took to sitting on her floor. There she felt safer than on her feet or in the upper bunk. The chairs by the table had been flung over, and after this had happened twice she let them lie. She took her blankets and settled herself with her back against the wall of the ship and her legs straight out before her, bracing them as the wall rose behind her and tipped her forward, relaxing when she was allowed to sink back. Sometimes she had to bite her lips to keep herself from screaming and she crawled over and unlatched her door to stave off the fear of drowning like an animal in a box. No one that day remembered to bring her food. She sat hour after hour in solitude, and her fear began to ride her as she wondered if Michael and all the others on the ship were already dead in this terrible storm. When she was tired out with her worrying she fell asleep.

She awoke to the sound of a tremendous crash and to water descending upon her. Not a torrent but an immense weight of water that fell, so that she was blinded and choking and dead. Only her body moved. The bunks were before her. She found the corner post and forced herself up. The water rolled back; for an instant she had air and she remembered the door. If she could not find it . . . if there was anything in the way . . . if she lost it now . . . Again the water covered her and her feet left the floor. She floated . . . drifting away. Then she walked and the door latch came into her hand. But the door opened inward and the weight of the water was against it. The water rose and rose while her ears roared and she held on because the trap was shut and there was nothing else to do. Then the *Kronborg* rolled back again and the door opened and the water flung her down on her knees and poured out into the saloon.

Even though it was spread out over a much greater area it was still waist-deep when she struggled up. She fought her way back to the bunk, where she had to grope to find Helga's head and drag it into view. Helga, who did indeed look dead. "Oh God," she sobbed. "Oh God, Helga . . ." The girl's eyes were shut and water trickled from her half-open mouth. Kirstina heaved at her and tried to shake her; then she knelt and twisted about till she grasped Helga's arms over her shoulders. The water dragged at her skirts and sent her staggering as she got to her feet; Helga's dead weight pulled her back; but she reached the door again and came through it into the saloon. Everywhere the water was rolling with the ship. She wondered if the holds were flooded; if, in a moment, the floor would settle and the deck above press her down. But as she reached the foot of the companionway the hatch above opened and two seamen came down to take Helga off her back.

"Cabin's stove in," said one. "Here, we'll take her up and below and come back for you."

Helga's limp body went up between the two of them while Kirstina said nothing. She steadied herself on a chair back that stood forlornly up out of the water. Suddenly the sea water she had swallowed made her sick. She retched and then pressed her hand to her shaking mouth. Into her mind came the recollection of what else she had to save.

Staggering with more and more weakness, she went back again

into the cabin. The box was up where she kept it, safely in her bunk. When she dragged it forward to the edge it shot off, one corner tearing a scratch in her cheek before it splashed and sank from sight. She went down after it, groping wearily and trying to hold her head above water. At last she had it and felt the ends for the handles. She glanced up before she tried to stand again, and so saw that it was Michael Shea who had come after her this time and who stood in the doorway looking in. Michael Shea with his face gray-white and with a dark stubble of beard.

Kirstina got up from her knees and brought the box into view. It seemed to her that he looked at it, that they both looked at it and saw nothing else. She struggled to get it to the table top and she hung there over it, panting, before she lifted her face and cried out to him in passionate justification, "But I did save Helga first! I did! I did!"

Then she saw that even if he heard her words above the storm they had no special meaning for him. His eyes took in the bleeding scratch on her cheek, her trembling arms, and the wide-open corner of the cabin where the sea had come in. He came and put his arm about her and caught up her box by one handle. He brought them both safely up out of the cabin and saloon, across a brief stretch of the open and storm-swept deck, and so down to where the emigrants were quartered. When she arrived there she had just wit enough left to understand that Helga was choking her way back into life before she herself was wrapped in a blanket and went to sleep.

Through the night that followed she awoke several times from a nightmare of falling water and each time she was grateful for the people around her. The scene was weird, with the lanterns hanging from the ceiling swinging with the ship and throwing wild shadows on the walls. Day brought only increased activity, for the hatches were battened down and no seam of light from outside penetrated this part of the ship. But the children woke and had to be fed. Small fires were lit in iron buckets and the women busied themselves over them in a silence that was a strange contrast to the bustling laughter they used to exchange on deck. The men were working in relays with the crew on the pumps, and when they came off duty they ate and slept.

Kirstina watched for Michael, and the first time he came he crossed over to her and kissed her as simply as if she had spoken

26

and told him what she wanted. "It's all right," he said. "I won't let you be drowned twice."

She believed him. And she was not alone in believing him, though every soul there knew that their plight was severe. It was strange how monotonous the routine became. A shift came off the pumps and slept. Another shift went down. The food was cooked and handed round. The children were put to sleep, or cried, or were hushed. A seaman fell on the deck above and broke his leg; once it had been set by the captain the man lay quiet in his corner and became part of the general scene. No one but the children asked questions; no one knew anything to answer what they asked.

When Michael appeared it was to get a plate of food from one of the women and come to sit beside Kirstina while he ate. His beard had grown and his eyes were sunk deep in their sockets. Sometimes he would stretch himself out with his head on her lap but he never seemed to fall wholly asleep. They were very silent together. He would kiss her, and smile at her, and take her hair in his hands, and she would almost hold her breath watching him rest. Then he would be gone and she would wait for him again. Once a day she loosened her hair and brushed it and braided it again, and she would have been astonished to know that not only Michael, but every man and woman there was grateful to her for doing so.

Gradually the emigrants forsook their stoicism for constant prayer. The relief they received from Michael vanished when the captain came among them, for his heavy face betrayed neither lightening nor faith. Methodically they divided themselves for work so that at all times there could be one group upon their knees, while always someone read aloud from one of their great, black-lettered Bibles. There was no escaping from the sound of their voices. It was quiet, but somber and insistent. They were more comfortable when they sang, for then the militancy of their hymns drowned out the noise of the storm and brought a wave of confidence through the gloom.

The fourteenth night after she had come between decks, Kirstina woke and found Michael beside her, watching her with red-rimmed, miserable eyes. She sat up and he spoke to her at once in a dry, tired-out whisper. "I want you to live!" he said. "I want you to live!"

She held out her arms to him and he hesitated and then sighed and gave in, and let her draw him down to cradle his head.

"Can you feel the ship?" he asked. "She used to ride so light but how can she rise now with all that water in her hold? She is drowning, and she will take you down with her."

He was speaking in one breath of his two loves and mourning them jointly. Kirstina murmured softly above him. She was pitiful and she wanted him to stay and sleep where she could hold him. But he shivered and lifted himself again and looked around. So many people in the fitful light were praying or lying asleep.

"The ship is a coffin," he said. "We have all been dead and buried in her for days."

When he had gone again she lay thinking, and wondering if it were true that she was going to die. She could not picture a world from which she had disappeared—though neither, when she tried, could she picture clearly what was going to happen to her if she did not die. She began to tell herself that if there had been no storm she would by now be in Boston and already married to Aage Nordrupp, but since that was not what had happened it also had no reality for her and kept slipping away from her mind. Try as she would she could see nothing beyond an eternal prolongation of the present moment, wherein she waited for Michael to come to her, and the violence of the storm held them both prisoners together.

Morning came without her going back to sleep and so she got up and made herself busier than usual with the children and with poor Helga. It was much easier to think of Helga dying, who was already so thin and so pale and so weak. The men who came up from the hold did not say that the water was rising, but perhaps they did not know. A half inch at a time would be hard to tell when there was not much light and the water spilled about with the moving of the ship. She thought of Michael's saying, "How can she rise with so much water in her hold?" Did that mean that at last the ship would dive under some great wave and go down and the sea would break in through all the walls? While she could not imagine herself dead, the terror of the water was a thing she knew and it pursued her. She began to know how frightened she was and she hid from the knowledge and wanted Michael again.

When he came it was hours later and the captain was with him. They stopped by the companion, neither of them advancing farther into the light, but Michael's look reached and held her across the intervening space.

The captain spoke in German and Kirstina neither listened nor understood. Only something in the solemn tone of his voice touched her consciousness and she saw the face of one woman and saw another drop down on her knees. She saw the ripple that passed through the rest as one by one they followed suit. She felt it was as she had known it would be, and she was sure he was telling them what Michael had already told her.

Then they began to sing, and the hymn was one of thanksgiving.

Some were weeping, but no one cried out, and they were singing "*Nun danket alle Gott.*" She looked down at them in bewilderment. Then panic came over her and she broke from where she stood and came running to the captain.

"What is it?" she demanded. "Are you saying that we are safe?"

Erik Warre smiled at her. "I believe so. The wind has changed. By tomorrow the seas must be less."

"And then?"

"We should be in Boston in a week."

Her mouth was dry and open. He thought she was overcome by her reprieve from death and patted her shoulder before he moved on.

Kirstina clapped her hands to her face. She had never known such terror in her life. It was a black darkness that swept up on her and enwrapped her. She could feel herself shrinking within it, shriveling up while somewhere on the outside Michael Shea stood and watched her fear.

But this was no longer the world of the *Kronborg* that she was in —this was the other world, the world that existed on either side of the ocean, that she had left in Denmark and would find again in Boston. This was the world she knew. She needed her old anchors and she groped for them in her mind.

Michael came and pulled her hands away.

He said, "My God, I believe you have already—"

"Yes, yes!" she repeated impatiently, for since she was not going to die she had very little time. She shut him out and went on searching frantically in her mind until she found what she was looking for and had made herself safe. The shock of terror began to recede. Nothing had been lost. It was all there waiting for her just as she had left it.

Michael shook her and she said, "Leave me alone."

"What are you going to do?" He shook her again. "Are you going to marry him?"

"Leave me alone! Of course I am. I am not going to die."

He let her go. She met his eyes and hated him. Very slowly, as if it were something he could not believe, he said to her, "But I loved you. . . . You little, mean slut."

They were longer than a week. It was ten days more before the *Kronborg* reeled into Boston Harbor and in those ten days the pumps were never left, nor was there ever an hour when the ship was at ease. After such a battering even a following wind was a menace and any large sea might have plowed them under. They could feel no overflowing relief and it was strange to come out into the air and see the sky turned blue and the ship moving steadily through the moderating waters.

Kirstina sat on deck every day and was lonelier than she had ever thought to be again. She shrank from the German women's wordless condemnation and she could not endure Helga's convalescent miseries. Even the children understood that she had become outcast and left her alone. Captain Warre sometimes came and talked to her approvingly but that was because he was glad his nephew was rid of her.

They came into Boston one afternoon. They tied up at the wharf and a crowd gathered and shouted questions in English. She wondered how soon Herr Nordrupp would come. With everything made ready she waited for him in the saloon—which was tidied up now, though it still bore signs of grief.

Nordrupp came down with the captain. Kirstina rose and gave him her hand. He kissed her forehead and said he was sorry to hear of so much ill luck. She told him all her linen and trousseau had been ruined and he said: Yes, so he had heard.

Helga was watching him open-mouthed, for she knew he was a great man. Then they all went up on deck. Nordrupp nodded to Michael Shea. A seaman came carrying Kirstina's iron-bound box and it was taken ashore with her other belongings and set in the carriage Herr Nordrupp had brought. She shook hands with the captain and he handed her into the carriage. She saw the *Kronborg* again from end to end, as she had seen it from the quay at Aarhus, and yet no longer as it had been then. They drove off, she and Aage Nordrupp, with Helga facing them.

The inn was a trim, neat building in a respectable street. It was larger, but not otherwise so very different from what it would have been in Denmark. The floors inside shone with a preternatural cleanliness; so did the brass fixtures and the windowpanes, and the window curtains were severely tied in place.

Aage Nordrupp had waited years to show off his achievement to someone from his own village—specifically, he had waited two years to show it off to Kirstina, and a further three weeks because of delays that were no fault of his. He was not moved to make any allowance for her probable fatigue and took her at once on a tour of inspection that comprised all there was to see.

He opened cupboards and showed the neatly stacked linen; he exhibited the rows of warming pans and the shelves of lamps and candlesticks. All the rooms had white painted doors with shiny brass numbers; there were keys with numbers to match, one set of them on a board in Nordrupp's office and one on another board in the linen room. There was a dining room laid out for the evening meal in a fashion that was new to Kirstina, and a bar at which a few men stood drinking. She noticed the beer steins among the glasses. They went down into the kitchens. The big stoves were lit but the rooms, being half below ground, were not hot. A Swedish woman was the cook; she smiled a greeting at Kirstina and went on kneading with her firm red arms at the paste on the table before her. A dark, grayish paste, very solid: the rye bread for the household. Kirstina looked for the bread oven. At home it had always stood out of doors. How often she had raked the ashes from it and seen the long loaves slide in! But here the oven was beside the stove, in the wall. The bread would have a slightly different flavor, would lack the wood smoke, but the sour, hard crust would be the same.

In the storeroom the groceries were stacked in scrupulous order. There were the tea chest, the coffee grinder, the various sugars, the wheat and rye flours, preserved fruits in white stone jars. The larder next door held hams and sausages hanging from the ceiling on hooks, strings of onions and bunches of herbs; on the cold soapstone slabs were fresh meat and fish, cheese and milk, new butter and eggs, cake, bowls of fruit; on the floor bins of vegetables—potatoes, carrots and yellow turnips—all smelling of dry earth and all ready for winter; in one corner pumpkins, in another a barrel of new red apples. Kirstina wrinkled her nose at the familiar smells and found them very good after so many weeks of salt.

One part of the building was set aside for the owner and his family. It had a separate entrance. There was a parlor there and a dining room, and Nordrupp's office, which led on into the hotel. Upstairs there were two bedrooms, one of which Kirstina would share that night with Helga. This evening the pastor and his wife would come, and in the morning she would be married in the German church.

After being asked to admire so much she was thankful at last to be left alone. A girl brought water to her room and she washed her hands and face. Helga sat and watched her, her eyes very large and round. Kirstina said suddenly, "I suppose you think I am very lucky."

"You have always been lucky," answered Helga simply. "It is a very fine inn."

"And Herr Nordrupp is a fine man?"

"But yes."

Kirstina rubbed her face dry. And why did I ask that? she wondered. There is nothing the matter with the man. He is no worse than any of the others.

"Come," she told Helga. "Wash yourself also. We shall have to go down and eat."

The pastor and his wife had arrived for the evening meal. He was a German, a stocky, square-headed man with alert, sharp eyes. He took Kirstina's hand into one that was too soft and too warm and he congratulated her and Nordrupp upon her safe arrival. Frau Winegar, his wife, was taller than he and fat. She wrapped each girl in an identical embrace and said, "*Ach*, the terrible ocean! What you must have suffered!" Like her husband, she spoke Danish indifferently, with a strong accent.

They sat round the table, the three middle-aged people and the two young girls. Kirstina found that she was hungry and the food was good; they were all settling to it with relish, and while eating Nordrupp showed the same animation that he had when telling over the excellencies of his inn. She broke her rye bread into the sour-cream soup. She was not called upon to talk. Herr Nordrupp watched her and the two strangers eyed her covertly, but they addressed themselves to each other. When Frau Winegar asked her if it were true that her trunks had been washed overboard, Nordrupp answered promptly for her that it was not. He went on to tell of all that had happened to the *Kronborg*, appropriating Kirstina's experiences as his own, just as he was in the process of appropriating her person. His voice implied clearly that if it had been he, Herr Aage Nordrupp, who had been making the voyage, not so much would have gone wrong.

32

At last the Herr Pastor interposed benignly, "Well, the *Fräulein* cannot be held responsible for the storm. And after the disaster we feared, these misfortunes are but slight."

"Ah, yes," agreed his wife, straightening in her chair. "What if the dowry had been lost!"

Kirstina accepted the fact that their concern had been for the gold rather than for her and she saw how the mere mention of the dowry restored Aage to equanimity; his expression became serenely complacent. The other two looked at her with an intense and curious expectancy, as if the golden symbol of her desirability were written on her face. She cast her gaze down to her plate, knowing she would be esteemed for her modesty. The Herr Pastor sniggered.

She did not like Herr Winegar. She eyed him with aversion and with the uneasy suspicion that he was aware of her dislike. He was polite to her and more than polite to Herr Nordrupp, but he had a way of glancing from one to the other of them as if in his inner mind he were smirking at something he imagined he saw.

"The *Fräulein* looks older than I expected," he said all at once. "I forget that the betrothal was two years ago."

"I am sixteen," said Kirstina curtly. "A girl in Denmark is no longer a child at sixteen."

At the end of the meal the pastor was still helping himself with a liberality that evidenced greed rather than hunger, his wife and host still keeping pace with him. Helga was yawning helplessly. At last they had coffee and moved to the parlor.

Kirstina foresaw by then what would be the entertainment of the evening. She was not surprised when Nordrupp disappeared into his office and came back with her locked box. He asked for the key and with a curious sense of abdication she took it from the chain round her neck. The lid swung back and the lamp beside it on the table showed her the three avid faces converging to peer in.

"Ten thousand kroner," said the pastor, with a reverence that his voice would rarely show at the altar. "Friend Nordrupp, it is a rich gift from God. Have you thought how you can best give thanks?"

Nordrupp chuckled as if he had heard a joke.

The Herr Pastor's wife did not speak. She had taken up a handful of coins and was fondling them under the lamp.

To Kirstina it was like the moment on the *Kronborg* when the great wave broke over her head. She saw Frau Winegar's greedy, avaricious face as if it were her own, and she looked on it as Michael

33

Shea had looked on her that day in her cabin. God in Heaven, she thought, that in thirty years' time will be I.

She began to shake where she stood and she leaned on the table for support. Nordrupp looked up and asked if she were not tired, adding, "The little Helga is half asleep on her chair."

Kirstina collected Helga and made excuses for them both. She went up to their room and sat there on the edge of the bed, feeling as if she were being stunned by wave after wave.

This was the inn, this the house where she was to spend her days, and it was a very fair copy of many she had seen before. She had seen gross feeding before, and avarice. Nordrupp's cupidity was not greater than that of the Winegars—perhaps it was less—and she had been prepared to see it. There was nothing anywhere to surprise her.

Already she could trace what she would be doing a year, two years, ten years from now. She could see that Nordrupp had thought out the problem of her youth and decided upon how to treat her. Not as the partner in business whom he had once set out to obtain, but like a good child who must be occupied, and kept out of the way, and sometimes rewarded. By making much of his wife, Nordrupp could persuade everyone that he had married very satisfactorily, and so he would be conventionally kind to her. She would live in this part of a house and be visited and talked about and envied. In a year or so she would have a child of her own, and perhaps one more later, but never a large family because an aging man might find that tiresome. Two children would be enough to keep her from moping (so he would reason) and once she had them there would be no longer any need for Helga, who would doubtless also marry. Kirstina would have her babies, and whatever clothes and luxuries she asked for if she took care of them. She would become lazy, and probably fat because of her laziness. She would hoard what she had because she would have nothing else to do. Sooner than she expected she would be too old to care that she had never had anything else.

Suddenly she slid from the bed onto her knees, and hid her face, pleading frantically and silently, "I didn't understand! I didn't know how it would be!"

Yet she had said she knew. She had said it over and over again. It was what she had asked for, what she had planned to have. She had chosen it twice, and the second time was after she had met Michael Shea.

She thought of tomorrow, how she would wake and there would be Helga to help her dress. There would be less time then even than now—and how much time there had been a week ago! There would be the church and the feast. There would be Herr Winegar's flushed, gloating face. She thought of the room next door and of the bed she had seen there, on which she would lie and wait.

With that, calm descended upon her. She stayed kneeling and very still. She saw that she did not need to torment herself. She saw what she must do, what she was going to do at once.

She got up and went to take her shawl from the chair where it had lain these last few hours, and put it about her shoulders. Helga, who had been brushing her hair, said, "Are you cold? Why do you want that?"

"I am going downstairs. I am not going to marry Herr Nordrupp, Helga."

Her friend stared uncomprehendingly and Kirstina laughed and said, "Do you think it is a joke?"

"Kirstina—"

"I have quite made up my mind. I never wanted to marry him and now I shall not."

"But Kirstina, you are promised!"

"Only not married, Helga."

Fright parted Helga's lips. Kirstina was swept with affection for her, as she had not been since they left Denmark. She went and kissed her and passed a caressing hand over her cheek. "I am truly sorry," she said, "I am leaving you alone. But you should have been in my place—then Herr Nordrupp would still have a bride. Aren't you going to say good-by?"

"But where are you going?"

It was Kirstina's turn to stare. "Don't you know? Surely you must know! Come, kiss me quickly."

She had no time to grow apprehensive. She hurried down the stairs and pushed the door into the parlor wide. The three figures seated before the empty grate turned their heads. She looked so expectant that Nordrupp asked at once, "What is it?"

She came on into the room until she was quite close and she addressed herself to him alone. "Herr Nordrupp, I am not going to marry you tomorrow. I am sorry, but I do not want to be your wife."

She saw him glance to left and right before he asked, "What—? I don't understand."

"I said I do not want to marry you tomorrow."

A look of annoyance and of real distaste came into his face. The Herr Pastor smirked. At Kirstina's side his wife said comfortably, "*Ach*, this is nothing! Every young girl feels the same."

Understanding them all three, Kirstina started to protest. "But I am not being coy. I am in earnest. I thought I could marry Herr Nordrupp and I find I cannot. I love someone else."

"But since you have left him in Denmark—?"

"He is here. I am going to him tonight."

In the little silence the Herr Pastor leaned back and crossed his legs. She met his bright, malicious eyes. "You came on the *Kronborg*," he said reflectively. "You are not the first girl, my dear, to fancy yourself in love with Captain Warre's Irish nephew."

Nordrupp, listening to his friend, looked back in time to see her flush. With dawning comprehension he said, "Shea!" His face mottled with dark color; he pushed himself from his chair and came to seize her shoulders. "What are you telling me? Shea? Has he . . . How far is this gone?"

Sudden fury invaded her and she flamed out, "No, he has not! If he had I might still have been ready to marry you!" She felt his right hand leave her, and the next moment she reeled back from his heavy slap.

He was not a young man, and more than anything else he valued his dignity. He would sooner kill her than be exposed to ridicule if she went. The sullen vengefulness in him was shocking and she stood quivering with her eyes on his face.

But the Herr Pastor had no use for violence. "Where is the need for this?" he asked, his smooth voice unhurried. "Aage, my friend, sit down again. And perhaps the *Fräulein* will also sit while she considers."

"I have nothing to consider."

"Then you will listen. *Fräulein*, you are frank, but you are not wise. If you were you would know that you have been talking nonsense. You have been betrothed for two years and those vows are not made to be broken. Herr Nordrupp has paid to have you brought here. It is the very eve of your wedding. This young man you have known only in the past few weeks and at sea. He was baptized a Papist. It would be difficult to find anyone to marry you in either

36

your faith or his. You are very young. Childishness may excuse your errors and the good man who is to be your husband will no doubt forgive your words, but he and I would fail in our duty towards you if we did not prevent you from foolish action."

"But I love Michael Shea!"

"Love between a man and a woman is not known to a maiden before her marriage."

The formula of the last phrase woke her reason and a measure of control returned to her. She had not sat down and, from where she stood in the room's center, she looked at Nordrupp, at Frau Winegar's face of gloating attention, at the Herr Pastor. Her direct gaze returned to her would-be husband.

"It is the money," she said slowly, "that is it. The money, and because you do not know how you will explain if now there is no wedding. You do not want me, but you do want the money, and without me you cannot see how you will get it."

Nordrupp muttered below his breath but she did not listen to him and she went on deliberately.

"Well, it is my money. It was given to me to buy me what I want, and that is what it is going to do. You brought two girls out from Denmark, Herr Nordrupp: you can have the other one. Helga Brunker is a good girl. She thinks I am mad. The Herr Pastor will tell you how much wiser it is to take a bride who is willing. Helga has no dowry, but that does not matter, since I will give her mine. . . . You see, I am showing you how you can have both the wedding and the money, if you let me go. . . . And you need not be disgraced. The Herr Pastor is your friend. You will give a rich gift to his church, and he will help you."

From his chair, Winegar chuckled.

Kirstina kept her eyes for Nordrupp. When he came at her she flung up her arms, but he was too strong for her and his big hands settled about her throat. She clutched and kicked uselessly while her ears began to roar.

The Winegars had to come and pull him off. Kirstina staggered back against the table, gasping for breath, while they soothed him and held him still. Her hands went to her throat; she tried to swallow and the room spun round her, but while Nordrupp was being held she turned to the door and swiftly went out.

She was lucky in that, though the inn was some distance from the water, the way they had taken in the afternoon had been direct.

She knew where she had to go; she had only to hurry over the ground. The street was dark and none too smooth, but she ran until she had to walk and then in a little while she ran again.

It did not occur to her that Michael Shea might turn her away. Certainly he had walked away from her on the deck when she left that afternoon, and there had been these last ten days at sea, but they would not be what he would remember, any more than she herself did now.

At last she came out where she saw masts against the clouds and the bows of the ocean ships stretched high over the wharf. Among so many it was harder than she had expected to find the *Kronborg*, and when she did reach her the man on watch stared in alarm and ran to fetch the captain before he would let her on board.

Erik Warre was there still only because the harbor authorities had left late. He came out from his cabin and gazed at her as if she had been a wraith.

"Froeken Brandt, what is this?"

She said, "I want Michael Shea."

He took her into the saloon and made her sit down. As he lit the lamp he kept saying, "But you should not be here! You should not be here!"

"Please, Captain Warre, I have to see Michael. Where is he?"

Warre finished lighting his lamp. He turned it up. Her face was bathed in golden light and he saw her anxious eyes and the quivering mouth that she was trying to keep still. He sat on the edge of the table beside her and took her hands in his. "Froeken Brandt, why must you see my nephew?"

"I—" What she had been going to say she could not. A moment longer she stared up at him, then she broke into tears. "Oh, Captain Warre!" She cried helplessly, and her head went down upon his sleeve.

"But you are to be married in the morning to Herr Nordrupp?"

"No. I have told him not. I cannot do it."

"You have run away?"

"Yes."

"And you want Michael." His usually kindly expression had become grim. He had not wanted this. He had been thankful when it had seemed to be averted. He wondered now just how far she had gone—what she had said. What, in fact, had there been to tell? If

Nordrupp had let her get away like this, alone, then in all likelihood he had finished with her.

"Where is Michael?" she asked him again. She had lifted her face and the tears lay on her cheeks.

"I have no idea. The men are all on shore and Michael with them. They have been gone for hours."

"Will you find him for me?"

"I will try."

He went not so much because he wanted to help her, as because there seemed to be nothing else for him to do.

Michael was sitting in a waterfront bar. He had been drinking, but he was not yet drunk. He understood at once what his uncle was telling him, and he heard him out in silence. For a measurable time he sat looking straight in front of him. Then he left the rest of his drink standing on the table and stood up.

Once he was outside he traveled fast. He began to whistle as he went and he was still whistling as he came on board the *Kronborg* and down the steps of the companion into the saloon.

Then he stopped, and the corners of his mouth lifted as if he were ready to laugh. He saw her standing alone, her eyes wide with the sudden and deadly fear that he might not want her after all, and he came across and held her without a word. Her arms came up and she buried her face against his neck and he went on holding her and rubbing his cheek on her hair.

II   CAPTAIN Warre's house was not in Boston proper but in Charlestown, across the harbor. This was not where most of the German and Scandinavian colony was settled, but when Warre had first arrived he had had his parents with him and since they had always been used to living in the country he had bought what at the time amounted to a small farm on the very edge of the city. Later the town had grown out and engulfed it and Warre had gradually sold most of the land. What remained was a square front lawn ending at a white picket fence along the street, and an acre of garden and orchard behind the house. These were just sufficient to preserve a little of the property's countrified air, and Warre liked it and never minded the length of the trip he had to make into town. It was in this house that Michael Shea had grown up, and to it he brought home his bride.

Aage Nordrupp kept the dowry and married Helga, but, after he had seen Kirstina safely installed in Charlestown, he sent back her linen and trousseau. When these came she eyed the stained trunks with distaste and said she did not want them opened. It was Michael who insisted she was foolish and got his aunt to do the unpacking. Then Kirstina was glad because so much had been ruined with sea water and could only be thrown away. "I did not make it for us to use," she kept repeating, and there was more than a little superstition in her anxiety to sever herself from all she had known before.

The Charlestown house pleased her. It was built of wood and painted white. In its center rose a solid red-brick chimney. The front door was so wide as to be almost square. To Kirstina the town houses in Boston were more familiar, for at Aarhus she had at least seen houses built in rows and standing directly on the street; all she knew otherwise from experience was the traditional farmstead of Jutland, with its stone walls and floors and thatched roof, and with its rooms always dark from having too-small windows. The Warre's house resembled that but little, and in nothing so little as in the lightness of the rooms, which because of their square windows and the shiny white paint on the doors and cupboards and shutters were as bright as outdoors.

In the room Kirstina was given upstairs there was a flowered paper on the walls and a bed with four slender posts; the rugs were in bright colors and the white muslin curtains were starched stiff and tied with flat, symmetrical bows. "It was my mother's room," Michael told her, and his voice was full and satisfied.

Downstairs in the parlor the ceiling was low; the polished floor was again ornamented with bright mats. The windows, with their white inside shutters folded back, looked upon the lawn and the street beyond. The clock standing against the end wall had come from Denmark and the date woven into the fruit and flower design of its painted case was 1763—or perhaps '68, for the last figure was half worn away.

To the left of the door as you entered was the fireplace, surrounded with white-painted brick, and on the mantelshelf a boat, neatly stored away in a bottle. Above was a mirror with a rounded surface that showed everyone and every corner of the room, but all awry as in the back of a silver spoon. There was a gilt eagle on its frame. And between the fireplace and the window wall was a glass-fronted cabinet with just such a collection of oddments as belonged properly in a sea captain's home. Kirstina sat on the floor and took them out one by one. Lumps of quartz; shells—one of them an oyster shell with a half-formed pearl embedded in the nacre; dried sea-weed; coins with holes through them, stamped in unreadable tongues; a flintlock pistol with a broken ivory butt; a dagger from the East with a strange, corkscrew blade, and another thin, sharp dagger from Spain; a bird's egg bigger than the egg of a stork; a peacock's feather; a flat piece of milk-white stone most beautifully carved that was a luck charm from China, and a square of embroidered silk that the captain had had with it from the same trader; a sandalwood box and an ivory elephant.

Michael laughed at her handling these objects with such care but he told her what they were and promised to bring her more curiosities to add to the store.

He was happy and amused with her all the time. It was obvious that she had not a thought in her head beyond what he was and what he wanted. She followed him about the house, watching him, listening to him, not attempting to do anything on her own. They went and sat on the grass in the little orchard—so trim and cared-for and unlike that other orchard in Cork—and he started to teach her English and teased her because the only words she already knew were the orders he used to shout on the *Kronborg*. He took her with him into Boston to see where the *Kronborg* was being refitted, and they walked on the Common and saw the fine new State House with its great dome. They went to the Market on Fridays and continued the English lessons while they bought fish and vegetables and cheese. They went by ferry to East Boston and admired the great Cunard wharf and the shipyards growing in size every year. One day he borrowed a pony and trap and drove her out of Charlestown into the country beyond, where the sight of the late October maples flaming on every hill sent her wild.

"What is it? What does it?" she cried to him. He drove to the edge of a wood and let her down where she ran about exclaiming and picking up the scarlet leaves, the ones that were streaked with crimson, the ones like gold. With her arms full she raced back breathless and dropped the leaves about his feet as she flung herself at him.

"It is heaven!" she cried.

Michael hugged her and laughed and said, "It is America."

They had never been more excited with one another, never so pleased with their world. Later, when they were lying together on the gold and brown bed of leaves, the wood was not quiet, but full of the little rustlings of companionship. The sunlight fell dappled through the half-clothed branches and every now and then a solitary leaf fell, like a star. It was late in the evening when they drove home —very late, with the nip of winter in the air and the true stars coming out icily in the clear sky above. Erik Warre met them at the door and asked them dryly if they meant in the future to use his house only for eating and sleeping. His wife was already upstairs and he did not mention that it was she who had first raised the question.

Very early Michael took his bride to visit his Irish relations. They went together to the narrow brick house in North Boston's crowded area and Patrick and Martha Shea gave them a royal welcome. Martha was Patrick's second wife and he and she and their six younger children occupied the ground floor of their house. Martha's two eldest and Patrick's children by his first marriage were all grown and married themselves and living elsewhere in the same neighborhood. On the upper two floors of the house lived Patrick's brother Dan, and three of Dan's daughters, and a dozen or so other cousins and friends who were Patrick's boarders and might just as well have been also part of his immediate family.

All of these people crowded into the parlor in the course of the evening when Michael visited there, for Michael was their hero and they were exuberantly pleased with his marriage and his bride and the swipe in the eye he had given Nordrupp in acquiring her. "Eh, he's a great boy, is Michael," they said one to another and they clapped him on the shoulder and dragged him away from Kirstina and bellowed ribald advice into his ear. Gales of laughter swept the room which was as overcrowded with furnishings as it was with people, and smelled of humanity and dust and food and tobacco. The food and the drink were both good and plentiful; pipes were lit and healths drunk and as the evening wore on the gathering broke in and out of song. In the middle of it all arrived the priest who had performed the marriage ceremony on the *Kronborg*, who was as merry as the rest of them and told the best stories, to judge by the shouts whenever he finished speaking. When at last Michael came and took Kirstina away in a cab she was strangely subdued. Her head ached with noise and bewilderment and she let Michael pet her and leaned against him without speaking.

"And did you understand a word?" he asked her.

She shook her head.

"My poor sweet girl! They're all as Irish as the day they left Cork —yes, and some of the most Irish are the ones that were born here, like myself. But did you like Martha?"

Martha was his aunt, she recalled: the big woman, blowzy in a streaky green silk dress with a mass of red hair piled like a cushion on her head. She had a hoarse voice—unexpectedly pleasant when she sang—and she could make herself heard with ease from one end to the other of her crowded, uproarious house.

"She was very kind," Kirstina said.

"And why should she not be? Didn't she take one look at you and shout at me how I was in luck? Which is no more than the truth, as I know well. And Father Callaghan too told me I was doing finely. He said you were prettier now than on your wedding day."

"He was more serious that day," she said.

"Sure, then he was on duty! It's a sad life to be a priest—though not so hard on an evening like this! Well, they were all strange to you today but soon you'll know them and indeed there are no better people on this earth."

She thought: When he has been with them he does not even talk the same as usual. And I shall never like them. I do not want to. They are wild people.

It was dark inside the cab. He could not see her face, which was as set and uncommunicative as it had been sometimes in the days when he first knew her.

Six weeks was all the time it took to refit the *Kronborg*, and six weeks was the time they had for their halcyon period. Michael, if he had ever given it a thought before, which he had not, would never have expected so long a honeymoon. As a rule, two or three weeks was what he had between voyages, and he now blessed the storm that had granted him this one much longer delay.

Although the marriage had been hasty, ill-considered, and unadvised, the Warres were in a position to give Kirstina the security she craved. She stood to them in the relationship of a daughter-rather than a niece-in-law, for Michael was far more their son than their nephew. She had never known before such happiness as she had so far enjoyed in the Charlestown house. If everything there had been as it seemed when Michael left, all might still have gone very well.

But Johanna Warre, Michael's aunt, would have disliked his wife no matter whom he had married, and in her worst imaginings she had never pictured his choosing such a girl as he had. It was of Johanna that Erik Warre had been thinking most the night Kirstina had fled to him from Nordrupp's inn. Over a period of years he had learned to know well his wife's unhappy nature and jealousies and misgivings. Johanna had disliked his old parents, who fortunately had died soon after his marriage. She had viciously disliked his pretty sister who had married Brian Shea. It was a part of her tragedy that she had lost two children of her own while they were still infants, but after that she had found compensation in taking possession of Michael wholly and lavishing affection upon him, quite openly relieved that his mother was dead.

Johanna was an energetic housekeeper and an inspired cook, a devoted member of her church, always ready with practical help and advice. When life was treating her well she had a bustling, cheerful manner and would go to any lengths to please those about her. Michael had been a spoiled and happy child.

But as he grew older Johanna had grown more and more demanding. She had wanted protestations of devotion that he was too shy to give. She had wanted assurances that he was happy only when he was with her. When she did not get what she wanted, she sulked. Michael ran away from her and was returned to her and thereafter made repeated efforts to assert his independence. Johanna clung all the harder. She became idiotically strict, forbidding whatever he asked, so that he was literally forced into rebellion, whereupon she created scenes in which she wailed at him that he did not love her and begged him to be kind to her. Michael had no brothers or sisters to share the brunt of this with him. He was vividly affected by it and though he longed for Johanna to be comfortable and undemanding like his Aunt Martha, yet he was so fond of her that he suffered emotional storms of remorse whenever he had upset her. It was a bad situation which would have grown progressively worse, had not the captain removed him to sea.

Once he was out of reach of his aunt's complexities he quickly forgot them, and he loved the fuss she made over his every return. He grew up and learned to tease and flatter her when he was on leave and she was happy because while her menfolk were with her she had their undivided attention; also, these periods were never long enough to exhaust her welcome, or their patience with her ministrations. This was the woman who stood by when Kirstina came into the household; who brooded over what she made sure was Michael's callous neglect of herself since his marriage; who looked ahead to a lifetime of shared authority and shared affections with a girl for whom she had no sympathy.

There was already plenty of rumor concerning Kirstina. There was Nordrupp's repudiation of her and his marriage to the other girl. There was the transference of the money. There was Kirstina and Michael's hasty marriage by a Popish priest. There was Michael's reputation among the Danish colony for wildness and irresponsibility. No one saw good reason to doubt that the pair had been lovers on board ship, and the flavor of scandal was appetizing, but still Johanna Warre's sponsorship could have ensured that Kirstina would be received with respect.

Instead, as soon as Michael was gone, Johanna allowed Kirstina to follow her to the church groups made up of the middle-aged, cold-eyed matrons whose elder sons and daughters would have been the girl's contemporaries, but she rejected any further obligation. She stood by with the air of a martyr while her nephew's wife was examined and condemned. Her friends lapped her in sympathy and then turned their hostile looks upon the intruder and said, in effect, "We know you for what you are. We will not lower our standards, and we do not welcome you."

It would have been of no use for Kirstina to protest that she did not deserve censure, that she had not behaved loosely nor injured anyone, that she was now a married woman and so her illegitimacy could no longer be so important. Because she spoke no English she was restricted to the society of the Danish colony, in which she could go nowhere save under Johanna's patronage, could meet no one unless Johanna allowed her to, could enjoy no shred of reputation that Johanna did not choose to leave her. She saw at once that she was being caught again in the trap from which she had never truly escaped, for these were people of exactly the same sort as those she had left behind her in Jutland—narrow-minded, righteous-thinking people—before whose contempt she was paralyzed and helpless.

When Michael arrived in the second week of January she flung herself at him as if he were her deliverance personified. He was so handsome and strong and he had promised her that she should be happy. She stood within the circle of his arms and looked sideways at Johanna, while a little paean of anticipated triumph piped in her heart. Through all his first evening she could not bear to have him out of her sight, and she sat pressed close beside him, her hand in his, drinking in the comfort and the support of him. He was tenderly delighted with her, and they spent a night of blissful excitement and rediscovery. Sometime the next day she said to him, "Your Aunt Johanna hates me. She is doing everything to hurt me. You must make her stop."

Michael did not believe her. He first laughed at her and then indifferently questioned her. Nervousness and anxiety made Kirstina loose floods of words at him until he could think only that her complaints sounded as childish as they were unbecoming. He would have been angry with her if he had not still been touched by the warmth of her welcome. As it was, he made a forbearing attempt to soothe her immediate distress, and at the first opportunity afterwards he went to talk the thing over with his aunt.

This was an irony there was no one to appreciate.

Any faint apprehension that Johanna had felt vanished, and she became smug. She denied little of what Kirstina had said, but she belittled the scandal and laid the blame for most of it upon

Nordrupp's resentment and the Winegars' unbridled tongues. People were so uncharitable, she lamented. They were only too ready to believe the worst of young ones who took the bit in their teeth, and Kirstina was bound to suffer for having gone her own way. "You, Michael, are so much luckier—you are always away at sea." She went on to say that Kirstina had certainly not received the welcome she should have, while by contrast that accorded Helga Nordrupp had been out of all reason. Helga had been feted and praised as if she, and not Kirstina, had been the original heiress. Johanna reproached herself for having let Kirstina become so unhappy but there was little anyone could do but have patience; all gossip blew over in the end, and Kirstina was a pretty girl, who would make friends easily if she were not sometimes so unsmiling and sullen.

In essence Michael heard exactly what he would have chosen to hear: that there was nothing to worry about, that Kirstina was exaggerating and was possibly jealous of Helga. Johanna managed, besides, to impress on him that it was she who was called upon to deal with the unpleasant effects of the gossip caused partly by his own thoughtlessness and augmented by Kirstina's unamiability. He wasted a lot of time and breath in the next few days trying to explain this to Kirstina. Between the two of them, his wife and his aunt, Johanna held a distinct advantage because of the guilt she could always manage to inspire in him, and Kirstina was stunned at his rejection of her appeal.

At the same time, she had missed him so cruelly that she craved his affection and could not afford to anger him. He had brought her a number of presents; he made violent love to her each night; he wanted her to be again the gay companion of their honeymoon. Under his compulsion she thrust her distress aside. They went sleighriding together, and skating on the harbor, and dancing at parties with his Irish cousins. They were very seldom quietly at home, and in the three weeks he was with her, Kirstina was never alone with Johanna.

But then he was gone again, and she was given over to the pattern that she already knew so hideously well, wherein she went everywhere in Johanna's wake. Sometimes the older women ignored her entirely, sometimes they dropped her a few grudging, disapproving words. The young matrons looked at her with curiosity and avoided being seen at her side; if she met them in the street one or two of them bowed to her, but none ever stopped to chat. When she went to church the young men standing in the porch stared and nudged each other; older men—the husbands of Johanna's acquaintances—made excuses to waylay her when she went to market, and to talk to her unless she walked quickly and unseeingly along. If anything, she disliked the men more than the women, and Pastor Winegar in particular she detested. She was a godsend to him in providing his flock with an example of the evils against which he preached, and yet he and his wife pursued her and even came to the Charlestown house on a pastoral visit.

At least when she was on her stepfather's farm she had always been occupied indoors and out, but here Johanna rebuffed every attempt Kirstina made to assist in household tasks. Idleness as well as loneliness combined to depress her; she had far too much time to sit and brood, and bitterness and rebellion grew within her.

On Michael's second return she did not need to assail him with complaints, for he was shocked by her evident misery. Under his belated sympathy she broke down and sobbed through most of one night: "She hates me so! They all hate me so! No one will even talk to me! Michael, what am I going to do? I'm so alone!"

He held her and rocked her and for the first time was afflicted with a sense of his own responsibility. Though he could not feel that even this was Johanna's fault, he did feel that Johanna had failed him. After thinking the matter over from every angle he went across to North Boston to talk to his aunt, Martha Shea.

There was nothing he himself wanted less than to see Kirstina installed in the Sheas' household; such an idea had never occurred to him before and would not have now if it had not been the only alternative to having her stay in Charlestown. He had no doubt Martha and Patrick would do anything he asked of them, and he was right. They offered him two rooms, above the parlor. Martha promised to turn her Cathleen and Sadie out of one, and Mrs. Daniel O'Brien, the sister of Patrick's first wife, would move from the other up to the third floor. Michael thanked them soberly and said he would bring Kirstina to see the rooms, which he did the next day.

Surprise and overmastering relief at the mere possibility of a change robbed Kirstina of other considerations; she sat listening to Michael and Martha talk, still understanding less than a tenth of what was being said, but not as conscious as she used to be of the odors of dust and stale food and drink. Only to get away from Johanna was her thought—to be somewhere out of reach of that watching, malicious intent—and she would have adored Michael if he had taken a high hand and installed her at once in the new place.

Instead, Michael was careful to hurt the Warres' feelings as little as possible. He arranged with Martha that he would bring Kirstina over the day before he sailed. Then he took his wife home again and proceeded to spend his time in persuasively explaining the move to Johanna, and in being particularly considerate and affectionate toward her. Kirstina received less attention from him than at any time before, and it was borne in upon her that he had no intention of quarreling with his people on her account. She watched him and was frightened. Her fears increased when she began at last to reason her position out.

Michael had planned the change himself and no doubt he would abide by it; when next he was ashore he would make her apartment with the Sheas his headquarters. But that did not mean that he would refrain from going to Charlestown. And though he would not insist upon Kirstina's accompanying him, unless she did so he would be there every time with Johanna alone.

At present Johanna was spoiling Michael and fussing over him, and displaying silent sympathy for his troubles with his foolish young wife. Johanna was being clever. Eventually Kirstina had to ask herself how much she would really gain by going to live in that tall, ugly house with the Sheas? She would not please Michael. She would hardly even please herself. How could she be happy with people whose speech she did not understand, in a household where, even if she had rooms of her own for which rent was being paid, some friendly, importunate creature would always be bursting in upon her?

She would be giving up the house in Charlestown—the house that was finer than any she had ever lived in before, finer than any she had once ever hoped to live in. Sitting in the parlor by the window, she appraised its treasures: the bright mats Johanna had made, the painted clock case, the convex mirror and the cabinet of curios. Even when she was most miserable she had still the warm assurance that one day all this would belong to her. If she were to run away from it, what guarantee was there that she would ever be able to come back?

She was making herself struggle against all her inclinations, and there were times when she yearned towards the Sheas' untidy domain as once, in Denmark, she had yearned towards America. It took her nearly the whole of Michael's stay to admit that leaving Johanna would only defeat her ends. But once her decision was reached, there grew in her a certain contempt for the single, unsatisfactory effort that was all her husband had made to help her.

On the day on which she was supposed to move to North Boston, she got up early and dressed herself and was sitting brushing her hair when Michael woke. She looked at him with the challenging light of battle in her eyes and said, while he was still sleepily stretching, "I have changed my mind. I am going to stay in this house after all."

His first reaction, as he took this in, was "Be damned to you, my girl! It would serve you right if I made you go!" He did not voice it, and after a moment he began to laugh. He lay in bed roaring with mirth, and Kirstina was in a rage at once because she wanted him to take her seriously. He did not remonstrate with her. He cheerfully reversed all the plans he had made, did not notice that Johanna was thwarted, and in his remaining twenty-four hours he was touched again with amusement whenever he caught sight of Kirstina's reproachful, indignant expression. As he saw it, they were back where they had started, and he was glad to have it so. It never occurred to him that Kirstina's decision now could possibly be as important as her earlier decision to offer herself to be Nordrupp's bride.

She wasted no time after he had gone. The first afternoon when Johanna went visiting, she put on the bonnet with blue ostrich feather tips that Michael had bought her for the New Year, and set out to call on Helga Nordrupp.

She had seen but not spoken to Helga since that initial, fateful evening at the inn. Every instinct of propriety argued that Nordrupp's was the last house in the world that she should visit, and Kirstina would have preferred, always, to be conventional. But necessity drove her. She had always liked Helga and she believed that she could still rely upon her friendship. She was not mistaken. Helga greeted her with affection and a few sentimental tears; she was contented and happy and consequently as wholeheartedly grateful to Kirstina as she had been when her bewildering good fortune first came to her. Kirstina sat and listened to the accounts of Aage Nordrupp's goodness, of her friend's clothes and pin money and general well-being, until it was strongly borne in upon her that Aage was more generous to the substitute bride than he would ever have been to the original.

While they were still in the midst of their talk the door opened and Aage himself strode in upon them. Helga broke off in confusion and half alarm. Kirstina rose and looked the man over calmly, with no outward embarrassment or antagonism. Nordrupp, who had not been pleased when he had heard who was his wife's visitor, found himself hesitating and taking her hand. He did not bid her welcome and he hovered suspiciously during the remaining minutes of her stay; when she left he came to the door and stood listening while Helga pressed her to come again.

Even so meager a reception was good when she had half expected to be denied the merest foothold. After a few days she went again, and met Nordrupp again. He was patronizing, but more cordial. There was no doubt that he was glad he had married the quieter and more decorous of the two girls. Helga suited him excellently, and Kirstina would not have. He was not averse to showing magnanimity and letting her come to enjoy his wife's protection. Kirstina was quite able to eat a modest portion of humble pie, so long as it helped further her ends.

And once she and Helga had joined forces, the good women of the Danish community had either to accept both, or ignore both. Because Helga was a young matron of standing, whose husband no one could afford to offend, they yielded with as good a grace as possible. Kirstina accepted their capitulation, and made sure that she would retain what she had won. As soon as there was no longer a social ban on her, the younger women seized the chance to gratify their curiosity and made every excuse to visit the inn. Nordrupp's parlor became a general meeting place, where several afternoons a week a group of girls would gather and sew and chat in delicious freedom from the surveillance of their elders. A month after Michael's departure Kirstina had so effectually broken out of Johanna's prison that when she went to church on Sundays it was she who made a smiling progression up the aisle and Johanna who followed.

Less apparent but more revolutionary still was her resolve that she was not all her life going to be restricted to the society of these people. She saw that, to escape them, she had to learn English, and so she started to go regularly to Martha Shea. Usually she went in the morning, when she would have a chance of talking to only one or two people at a time, and gradually her ears began to pick out sense from the maze of words that assailed them.

Michael was home in June and again late in the summer, and

found her blooming, busy, and apparently recovered from her earlier distress. He was not pleased to have her become intimate with the Nordrupps, but when he remonstrated she listened with polite amiability and said, "Yes, only I was friends with Helga years before I knew you." This he was too just not to accept.

Now that Kirstina's and Johanna's positions were reversed he was able to see that his aunt had violently resented the younger woman's intrusion, but he was embarrassed to have to admit it. He glossed it over by repeating to himself that Johanna loved him too well to be willing to share him with anyone. Johanna had begun to look pinched and tired. He did not think it would have hurt Kirstina to forget her resentment and do a little to help about the house. He spoke to her about it. Again she listened and then said blandly, "Fru Warre does not like to have me in the kitchen," and "Fru Warre would rather I did not meddle with the linen." Only when he asked some service that was specifically for him did she do it at once, and very willingly. It was Johanna's own weapons that were backfiring, but in the sticky heat, with four people at home, it was difficult to allocate the blame. Michael offered to pay for a servant girl but Johanna so much preferred to struggle unaided and have matter for complaint that she refused to have one, and when he recognized this mood in her he found her as un-co-operative as Kirstina. He appealed to his uncle, who shrugged his shoulders and said no one could ever do anything with two women under one roof.

By September Helga was expecting a baby and Kirstina was spending more time than ever at the inn and occasionally stayed the night there. Nordrupp had learned to like having her about, and so had his friends—older men, who dropped by in the evenings and found Kirstina Shea cozily ensconced with Helga in the private parlor, and who enjoyed talking and joking with two such very young wives. Pastor Winegar was not one of this group—he was no longer in favor with Nordrupp and wished he were. When he met Kirstina on the street now he bowed and complimented her, and she was polite and cool and a little gracious in her response.

The men whom she met at the inn commanded her respect for their prominence and solid achievements. They owned businesses; they made money; they invested in industry. She was quick to see their difference from Erik Warre. These were the men who employed ships to carry their goods for them, and in their eyes the sea was not a serious profession. They talked a great deal about ships and shipping (for all of Boston was ocean-minded) but they talked in terms of trade and cargo and freight charges. One of them, Nils Jorgensen, a shipbuilder, had sent his son to sea to keep him out of mischief while he was growing, but next year, when the boy was twenty, he was to be put to work on shore to learn his father's business. "If I wait too long," said Jorgensen, "he'll get a taste for wandering and won't settle down. But it's a good training for him—none better. You learn to obey orders on a ship, and later you learn to handle men." No one questioned Erik Warre's choice of a career, because he had gone into the service in the old days, when a ship's captain was always her part owner and a man of considerable standing in a community. In the new concerns, the vast shipping empires such as Cunard was building up, there was no room for a flock of independent captains. The shipbuilders were now going to be the shipowners, they and the big trading companies ashore. Ships' captains were going to be hired hands and learn to toe the mark—yes, and to be mechanicians as well, if steam and engines had come to stay.

Kirstina's ears were astonished and she learned fast. She had realized before that no one ashore could regard Michael with quite the same reverence as he inspired on the *Kronborg*. He was a good sailor who, if he chose to leave his uncle, could command a berth on any ship he wanted, but there were other good sailors in Boston and his prowess excited no special comment. Always at the back of her mind she had anticipated that one day, with Michael, she was going to enjoy fully all the importance and consequence that she could ever have had with Nordrupp. Now suddenly she was made to doubt this. Michael was a sailor on a little, old ship that was already thought to be a poor risk; even the captain's half share in her could not amount to much. And after the *Kronborg* had been broken up what did Michael intend to do?

She talked to him about it that autumn and at first he welcomed her interest. When he was still quite small, it had been a dream of his that one day he would build ships. He had made models that were perhaps a little better than most boys'. He had haunted shipyards and made a nuisance of himself watching and prying and asking questions, and had been overjoyed when any of the men there found a use for him and let him run their errands. His favorite expedition had been across the harbor to East Boston, where the now enormous Cunard yard had then just started building. He had stood amid the fury of hammering and sawing and stone-crushing, looking back at

Boston, digging with his toes at the loose earth and dreaming of his own white-sailed ships putting out to sea in the sun. But, instead of apprenticing him in due course to Samuel Cunard or Donald Mc-Kay, his uncle had taken him away to sea.

The interest in the making of ships had persisted and had inspired the drawings and sketches of ships which it was his hobby to make and which were pinned up on the walls of his small cabin. Whenever he was in port abroad, he would be off sometime or other to the local shipyards to see what was in the slips and to join in the talk of the men working there. But long ago he had ceased to envy those of his friends who had gone into the shipyards at home. Movement and excitement were what he needed, and on his ship—sailing his ship—he had both. He had also authority such as he would never have enjoyed elsewhere, and the magnificent independence which he wore with such arrogance and unconcern.

Before he met Kirstina he had thought sometimes that he would like to take ship on a clipper, to go to China and Malay to see the wonders of the East. He had put it off from year to year, promising himself that he would go one day, but not while his uncle still needed and depended upon him. As soon as he had married he had put away the idea for good, for year-long voyages were not for a man with family responsibilities. Now, when the *Kronborg's* days were ended, he would look for another berth in another ship plying the Atlantic route. When in due course he would get his first command and a ship of his own, he knew he would have reached a satisfying goal. He thought he would take Kirstina with him on the first voyage he made as captain, to England, perhaps, or even home to Denmark. Later they might make many voyages together, in his fine new ships, in smiling, sunny weather devoid of the terrors that now she inevitably associated with the sea. This was a good, stimulating life; he talked about it with confidence and he could honestly declare that he had never seen another he would wish in exchange.

Kirstina listened to him with deepening dismay. She was sure she would never enjoy going to sea—she, who never wished to travel anywhere that was not strictly necessary. Certainly she wanted to be more with Michael—that was one of the points she had in mind —but she wanted him to stay with her and not expect her to go off with him.

"Very well, then, I won't make you come," said Michael easily. He did not give a fig for the rigmarole she repeated about Nordrupp

54

and Nordrupp's land-loving friends. What the hell did they know about it? So long as men had goods to trade and seas to send them across, so long would they need ships and other men to sail them. He asked her, "What exactly do you imagine I could do, if I left the sea?"

"Build ships as you said you wanted to."

"The time for that—even if I still wanted it—would have been when I was young enough to learn the trade. Now I am twenty-three, and I'm a sailor. I have my place on a ship, but I would have none on shore."

"I don't believe you. Anyone would find a place for you. And what about all the drawings you make, on every voyage? Why do you bother with them if they are no good to use?"

"Because I like to make them. I always have. Every time a ship takes my fancy I make a sketch of her. I make more detailed drawings too—cross-sections showing deck spacing and cargo storage. You would find those very dull and they don't mean a thing, except that in his spare time a man has to have something to do. Other men make model ships to put in bottles—like the one on the mantel there. I like to make drawings. If I ever hit on a good innovation I would make a present of it to Mr. Cunard, but that isn't because I want to work for him."

No explanation could have been less likely to convince Kirstina, because she did not understand purposeless activity. Until the time came for him to leave her she was still urging him to go to see Jorgensen, the shipbuilder, him whose son had been sent to sea but was not to be allowed to stay there. "It is all nonsense to talk about apprenticeship," she said. "Sven Jorgensen will be twenty next year and that is not so much younger than you. You don't understand my ideas and Herr Jorgensen would be able to explain."

"Not to me, he wouldn't! You have never spoken to him?"

"No. I wanted first to talk with you."

"Well, be careful that you don't talk to anyone else. I won't have you discussing me all over town. And rest easy, Kirstina, my love. I know my business, and I'll never let you starve."

Then he was at sea again and the tough Atlantic gales harried him all the way across the ocean and all the way back. It was the worst crossing since September the year before. The *Kronborg* was gone twelve weeks in all and, when she did cast anchor next in Boston, Michael was as exhausted as his uncle, fit only to be put to bed and left to sleep. Kirstina watched over him with a very white face, feeling thanksgiving because he was safe and her fears had been harrowing her, but also very angry because such risks belonged only to the profession he clung to, and it was her safety as well as his own with which he gambled. Michael woke after fourteen hours and was hungry. He sat about the house joking and smiling at Kirstina, stretching his long legs before the fire and eating the food which Johanna brought him from time to time. Then he took his wife off to bed with him and charmed her disapproval away, and slept dreamlessly beside her the whole of the second night, and awoke refreshed.

The unloading of the battered cargo had to be completed soon and so he went over to the *Kronborg* and watched operations on the deck. It was a cold, quiet day, with the snowflakes of a late January flurry feathering down. In mid-afternoon a man came up the gangway, a businessman by the look of him, and when he came closer Michael saw that it was Nils Jorgensen. He knew him slightly and greeted him and asked if it was the captain he wanted to see. Jorgensen shook his head and said, "No, Mr. Shea, I came hoping to find you alone."

At the very words a shrill whisper of foreboding came to Michael, but he looked the man over calmly and invited him into the saloon. There they sat down and drew out their pipes. Jorgensen also took from an inner pocket a roll of papers which he laid on the table between them. Michael was frowning and very much alert, and the only question in his mind was just how far Kirstina had dared to go.

Jorgensen took his time with his pipe but between puffs he said, "Those—are your property," and he jerked his elbow and pushed the roll of papers in Michael's direction.

Michael picked them up, unrolled them a little. It was a drawing of his own that he glanced down at: the cross-section of a steamer hull, made at Bremen six or seven months ago. He realized he held three sheets in all and he leafed over the other two; details of clipper rigging, and a plan for cargo disposal, for a brig of two thousand tons' displacement. Kirstina could hardly have chosen better. There was nothing sketchy or artistic about these; they were workmanlike, informational drawings, and in the third were several innovations of his own, which he remembered having explained to her.

"You were wise to send them to me," Jorgensen was saying. "I am a man who knows how to judge of such things." He waited, but in the face of Michael's silence, resumed, "Yes. Your wife says that you want to work with me. I should have expected you would have come to me yourself, but I understand there is a difficulty in the matter of leaving your uncle."

If Kirstina had been there, Michael thought, he would have wanted to choke her. He tried not to show any feeling when he answered, "I have been shipping with my uncle for the past nine years."

"Yes, as I thought: a matter of sentiment and habit. And naturally you do not wish to leave until you have had a definite proposition. You are very lucky in your wife, Mr. Shea. She is a practical young woman, as well as a handsome one. She did your business well for you. I should be glad to hear just exactly what you had in mind?"

"What I had in mind?" repeated Michael. "I am listening with much interest, sir. I think I would prefer to hear your opinion first."

"Quite right, though there is nothing for you to be afraid of. Your wife told me that you wanted a job ashore. Frankly, when she first spoke to me, I told her you must be a fool. You are a sailor, and by and large a man should stick to his own trade. However, you also have eyes in your head and when I thought things over I saw that you could be very useful to me in my firm. I do not need a draftsman; I need a man who understands drawings, and who knows ships and ports and men. You seem to be such a man. When my son comes home I plan to take him into the firm with me. At the same time it would be possible for me to make another opening available to you. You would have to buy an interest, but I assure you I mean to make my price moderate. Talk to Captain Warre about it. He is a generous man, and he has no son of his own. Once he understood this was to your advantage you could persuade him to help you."

Michael said, slowly, "I don't understand why you should want me," and saw Jorgensen bridle with satisfaction as he replied, "I always know what I want. Don't think I am doing you a favor. I could use you, and I intend to do so."

"Has . . . my wife . . . heard your proposition?"

"Far from it. She talked to me of you; I listened. You will have the pleasure of telling her yourself what is arranged."

"Only, unfortunately, I am not going to accept."

The man goggled at him. "You are not—? But—?"

"My wife said rather more than I expected, Herr Jorgensen. I am afraid she unwittingly misled you. I wanted an expert's opinion on the drawings, but no more than that. I have never made up my mind to leave the sea and, if I were to leave it, it would not be soon."

"But I have made you a very good offer! No one else would offer more! Who else were you thinking of going to?"

"No one, Herr Jorgensen. I shall remain at sea."

"You understand, don't you, that the drawings are nothing in themselves? It was not they that interested me. It is only that I need a man with your experience. If you ever mean to leave the sea, now is your opportunity to do so."

"I am sorry."

"Your wife will be disappointed. She is counting on this. The poor girl, what kind of a life is that for a woman, to have her man always away?"

Without answering him again, Michael stood up. After a moment Jorgensen followed suit, scraping his chair back angrily and thrusting his pipe into his pocket. They went up again on deck without speaking further. But standing there in the open, Jorgensen glanced up at him and said suddenly, "You're a fool, and obstinate. However, if you change your mind, come and tell me." He went down the gangway and walked away.

In the gray dusk the men were still working; Michael buttoned his coat and hurried them to finish and be off. Then he set out to walk to Charlestown, his long strides carrying him rapidly over the ground, his fury riding blackly within him. Kirstina was in the hallway when he arrived. "Go upstairs," he told her and she went, probably expecting anything but what was in store. He came into their room after her and shut the door and looked her up and down. She frowned in surprise. He reached into his coat and drew out the roll of drawings and saw enlightenment dawn. Still watching her face he lifted the roll and slapped her with it, twice, as hard as he could. Then he took the drawings in both hands and tore them across and dropped the pieces on the floor.

Her hands to her cheeks, Kirstina cried, "Don't do that! Oh! Now you will have to draw them again!"

"I shall not. I have no intention of drawing them again."

"But Herr Jorgensen liked them!"

"Did he?"

She stared at him, recollecting herself, and at last she said, "You hit me."

"I did. As I shall again if you meddle again in what does not concern you."

She was too impatient to pay attention to this and rushed on. "Tell me what happened. What did Herr Jorgensen say?"

"Your friend Jorgensen made me an offer. There will be an opening in his firm that would cost no more than my uncle and I could manage to pay."

"Oh-h!" She was still fingering her cheeks, but a sigh of pure gratification left her lips. Michael's tone became flat and brutally final. "I told him his offer held no possible interest for me. If he wishes, he can take it elsewhere."

"What do you mean? How could you say such a thing?"

"I have told you before that I do not mean to leave the sea."

"You told me no one would hire you! Now it is different—you have a good offer!"

"I told you not to go to Jorgensen."

"I never said I wouldn't!"

"How did you steal my drawings?"

"I went to the *Kronborg* alone. Before you left. I knew which ones to take, which would be most interesting. You weren't going to do anything with them! You didn't know what to do with them! They were just wasted, and I knew they could be useful!"

"They didn't belong to you. I trusted you to do as I wished while I was away. I shall always have to trust you while I am away."

"Unless you stop going away."

Her stubbornness was a slippery, blank wall. Michael was very white and he had never felt so helpless. He exclaimed, "What's the use of talking to you? You don't even understand what you have done!" and he had his hand on the door handle when she said, "Michael!" and he stopped and half turned.

"You didn't make Herr Jorgensen angry, did you? You didn't offend him? He is a very kind man. I am sure if you wanted to you could change your mind."

He swore and wrenched the door open. At the bottom of the stairs was standing his aunt to tell him supper was ready, but he pushed past her with a brief apology and flung out of the house.

The snow was still falling slowly, the air only just freezing—warmer than it had been in the afternoon. Both the snow and the dark were soothing, and as he walked it became easier to think. He tried to understand how it could be Kirstina who had done this.

Kirstina, whom he had wanted for his dear love and other self. How could she have gone behind his back and made a fool of him? How could she now be unrepentant?

For the first time he let himself remember the scenes on board the *Kronborg* in which she had done and said other things which he had neither liked nor understood. In spite of that he had married her. He had obstinately overlooked the difficulties that were bound to come, and so had allowed an alarming situation to develop. Years before Michael had suffered under Johanna's domination and with much trouble escaped from it; if there was one thing certain it was that he would never again submit to the same sort of tyranny. He could see now that there were several courses open to him and he hesitated over which one he should follow, but he did not hesitate at all over the main issue, which was his determination to end up master in his own house.

At this stage in his thinking he had walked nearly into town, so he went on farther and turned into a saloon where he met with two of his cousins. The rest of the evening passed pleasantly and finished with his going home with them instead of returning to Charlestown. If Kirstina waited for him or worried over him, he thought that would be good for her, and he was not surprised that when he saw her next day she tightened her lips and refused to give him the satisfaction of knowing whether she had been distressed or not.

He went out of his way to discover the reasons behind Jorgensen's offer, and he was amused to find they were as selfish as he had expected. Competition in Boston was growing harsher year by year, with the bulk of the shipping contracts going to the big new firms which had unlimited capital behind them. Jorgensen's yard was not equipped to build big ships; he turned out trawlers and fishing smacks, small barks; he kept his old customers satisfied and he was holding his own, but his time of expansion seemed to be past and he would no doubt be very glad to get his hands on the few thousand dollars in cash which he might hope the Warres could put up. In the past he had always managed his business alone, jealously refusing to give any of his men responsibility or authority, and he was not popular with them. Now, this year, his son was due to come into the firm and the younger Jorgensen (in spite of the apprenticeship at sea) was a creature of the same kidney, conscientious, uninspired and self-important, who was to be thrust into a position for which he had neither the personality nor the experience. It was easy to see how Michael had been designated as henchman to both father and son. Naturally it did not matter if he were a draftsman or not, if he were trained or not; all they wanted was an overseer with the magical, dual talent of getting on with the men and getting work out of them.

Michael was grimly satisfied because the joke was on Kirstina. He told her what he had learned, and saw that she did not believe him. He had the impression that she was waiting only until he had left in order to begin her scheming again, and he wondered what more she thought she could do. He had demonstrated that he had no intention of changing his ways.

It was a curious interval in their relationship. They were both underestimating each other's strength, and overestimating their own. They had no further open disagreement and yet made no attempt at reconciliation. They were both blind to the interest Johanna Warre was taking in the quarrel.

Before he left, Michael asked Kirstina point-blank, "What is it you have up your sleeve this time?"

She closed her lips and looked at him with sulky obstinacy, and he laughed and went on: "So long as you understand that you are not going to make me change my mind, and learn to leave me to manage my own affairs. I won't put up with anything else."

There was a note of warning in his voice, to which he was sure she paid no attention. Later that night, even while she lay comfortably within his arms, she said suddenly, "I don't know why you should want to make love to me when you will never do as I wish!"

All the same, Michael went away hoping, and half expecting, that by the time he returned she would have come around. He had decided that leaving her alone was probably the best way of making her remember how much she needed him, and he was prepared to wait a little while to have that happen.

Where he made his mistake was in not realizing that his influence with Kirstina was strongest when he was with her. If he had been there all the time she could never have remained proof against her own hunger for his affectionate approval, and if she had once admitted that, she might have discovered how much easier it was to coax him into the path she wanted than to drive him.

But Michael could not stay with her, and she was left to her own devices, and to the conviction that it was necessary to force her own way. By the time he returned in April she had seen to it that there was not anyone he knew, or whom she could reach, who had not heard how on his last leave he had been offered a partnership at Jorgensen's and had refused it for no understandable reason.

Captain Erik heard the tale from the harbor master, and was at first touchingly gratified because he was sure his nephew had refused the offer on his account, and then deeply disturbed because he might unwittingly have been standing in Michael's way. The first time Michael went back into town some of his own crew met him and wished him luck, and shook their heads over changing times. His Aunt Johanna was tearfully thankful because of the chance that from now on he was going to stay ashore, and she would have his company in her declining years. His Aunt Martha and his Uncle Patrick were quite frankly overawed: one of their sons worked in Jorgensen's yard, and they saw Michael achieving overnight a position of substance and wealth.

This time he did not risk scolding Kirstina at home but took her out of doors and walked her along the shore. There was smug complacency in every line of her, and she successfully hid whatever alarms she felt.

"You were so wrong, Michael!" she told him. "You must see now how wrong you were. Everyone agrees with me. They think it is a wonderful chance. Even the captain is pleased. Even your Uncle and Aunt Shea."

"And what difference should that make to me?"

"It must make a difference. You told me I didn't know what I was talking about. But now you will see that I did know, and I was right. I had to talk to Herr Jorgensen and tell him to wait—that you were only hesitating because of the captain. He understood. You will see; if you don't do as I want now, they will all think you are a fool."

The waves were pounding on the stony beach, a rushing, incessant background for their voices. Michael began to tell her, softly and virulently, the extent of her insignificance and unwisdom. She was somebody's bastard brat from Denmark, who had no claim on anyone's especial consideration. She had schemed to betroth herself to a well-to-do man, who had later repented of his bargain. He, Michael Shea, had been unlucky enough to find her upon his ship and to take notice of her and be deceived in her and fancy himself in love with her. He had married her and brought her into his home and given her everything he had, all of which was too good for her and none of which she had the grace to appreciate. She had repaid him by waiting until his back was turned, to steal his work, and plot, and make him ridiculous. If she thought he was in love with her now she was wrong. He wished he had never laid eyes on her. He would teach her to keep her place if it cost him a year's pay, but so help him he would never give in to her and never let her tell him what he should do.

He did not let her interrupt him. His voice rose and battered hers into silence and, when the tears of rage started to pour down her face, he took hold of her and shook her.

Kirstina's own fists came up and hammered at him. When he let her go she screamed furiously, "I hate you too! You made me marry you! You promised me I should be happy! You won't do anything for me! If I had married Nordrupp I would have all I want!"

Her face was white, with every muscle quivering and deep purplish smudges below her eyes. Even at that moment Michael was conscious of the difference in quality between her fury and his own, knew that his had been unprojected and would pass, but that hers was the explosion of months of discontent and suppression and that what she said now was what she must for long have been secretly thinking. He said, "Yes, I know that. But Nordrupp has another wife, and you must put up with me."

Kirstina recovered her breath and her self-command. Her face began to look more normal. She seemed to have nothing further to say and he took her elbow in his hand and started her home.

He had already decided on the course he would follow if he found her still defiant. Now he thought he had perhaps been foolish to wait so long.

That same evening he followed Kirstina up to bed and told her very deliberately that he intended to leave the *Kronborg* and take ship to the Orient. She listened to him in silence, and he saw astonishment at least come into her face.

"But Michael—why?"

"To teach you the lesson you need. Because I won't come home every eight weeks or so to find you have been doing your best to make a fool of me while I was gone, and to be hounded and badgered into doing what I've no wish to do. I want a quiet house, Kirstina Shea, and a quiet house I mean to have."

"How long would it be?"

"A year," he said. "It would be at least a year."

Their eyes met. She was sitting up in bed, her gold hair in two long plaits, her expression still childish and surprised. Then, slowly, a little narrow smile curved her lips, and she said: "You are running away. You are afraid to stay and do as I want. I might have known that you would run away."

At that moment her contempt was naked and ugly. Disappointment made him hate her. He had not realized until then that he had been gambling on the chance that she would beg him to stay. If she had been frightened, if she had cried, if there had been even a hint of weakness, he might have given in to her and tried what loving could do.

He had no trouble in finding the berth he wanted, but he was beset by the incomprehension of his friends. Captain Erik, who had been willing to give up his ship and retire in order to help establish him on shore, was deeply wounded by his decision to sail under another master. Johanna wept that it broke her heart to have him go for so long—he was her son, the child she had taken to herself instead of her own, and he owed her more tenderness than this. Martha and Pat shook their heads over him, and he felt like some sort of traitor with the members of his old crew. All their entreating made him the more determined to get away and to prove that he would follow no road but his own.

The *Kronborg* left first. He had not meant to be on the wharf when she pulled out, but when the time came his tugging, possessive affection would not let him stay away. He went down, and there lay the beloved ship. The captain kissed Johanna and Kirstina good-by, and looked at his nephew with eyes from which he could not quite keep out the reproach. At the last he exclaimed, "*Ach!* Good luck, then! . . . Good luck, my dear boy," and clapped him on the shoulders and shook him a little, from side to side.

A week later the *Canton Queen* was loaded and ready. Michael spent his last evening in town with his cousins, drinking more than he needed; he was so alert and suspicious of disapproval that he was on the verge of a half-dozen fights before he left for home.

He woke Kirstina by shaking the bed, leaning over its foot.

"I've come for my good-by," he said. "You may be able to do without me, Kirstina Shea, and after I'm gone you're at liberty to try. . . . Only, before I go, I'll make damned sure you don't forget me."

He stood up and swung to the door. He locked it and brought the key away in his hand. Kirstina had gathered herself up rigid. She was furious and also, he thanked the blessed Virgin, she was frightened.

64

She whispered sharply, "Keep away from me! You're drunk!" and after that he left her no breath even to whisper. She fought him fiercely and long; he hurt her and was glad that he did, and he took from her all that he could enforce. He would have given his soul to be sure that, after he was gone, it was going to be she who would suffer most.

III   AT first, after Michael left her, Kirstina found it easy to maintain her indifference and contempt. She was very angry, very self-righteous, very proud of her own strength of will.

Then she discovered she was to have a child.

Nothing else could have so shaken her complacency nor reasserted Michael's domination. She was frightened and ashamed. Michael was gone; it was hardly respectable to carry and give birth to his son while he knew nothing about it, and by the time he came back the baby would be a heavy, growing boy. In driving him away she felt she had done something indefensible and had robbed both him and his son. Yet she blamed him for going. He should never have left her alone, and, if he had done as she wished, she would not now be placed in the wrong.

She did not tell Johanna about the baby, and feeling no particular discomfort went on every day as usual. Most of her time she spent with Helga, whose child, a girl, was born in May and turned Nordrupp into a besotted father. Helga was homesick for Denmark. She sat knitting and sewing with Kirstina and talked and talked of her home, her brothers and sisters, her mother, places and people she and Kirstina both remembered, customs they had never recognized as such before they came away. She recalled the Sunday feasts, the dances, the beech forests, the shallow, reed-grown lakes. In her home they had used tallow dips instead of candles. There had been a stork's nest on the thatched roof of the house—"and the year my father died, that spring the storks did not come back."

Kirstina listened and took her share in reminiscing and learned the queer perversity of memory, for, though she knew how unhappy her own childhood had been, she could still share Helga's nostalgia.

She went rather shyly to visit the Sheas and was not offended when almost at once Martha guessed there was to be a baby. It

66

pleased her that they were as convinced as she was that the child would be a boy.

Her best support came from Captain Erik, who when he heard the news was delighted and kind, and disgusted with Michael for being away. He brought her presents every time he came home and busily tried to placate Johanna's resentment over having been the last person to be told. When the time came in January he was at home and he put off sailing from day to day, waiting far more anxiously than Kirstina. The boy was born on the sixteenth of the month and was named Rudolf, which his mother shortened at once to Rudi. He was a fine, strong baby, and she was evidently built for motherhood, for he made her suffer very little.

The captain sailed again. Patrick and Martha Shea came to see Michael's son, and so did Helga. Kirstina's strength returned quickly and she was not long in bed. Once she was up she bustled about the house, busy and self-important as she had never been before. But much of her belligerence left her, for she felt now that she had a right to what she enjoyed: it was vested in her son, and through him in herself. For giving her Rudi, under no matter what circumstances, she was pleased with Michael again as she had not been since the start of her marriage, and she was sure that when he came home everything would change as much for him as it had for her. What he had not been willing to do for his wife alone he would surely do for his son, and she resolved earnestly that from now on she would manage him with patience and care, so that he would never go away again.

Captain Erik reappeared in April with a feather-soft shawl for the baby and a silver-backed mirror from France for Kirstina. He kissed her and pinched her cheek and guessed the next month would see the end of her waiting. Kirstina took to sitting on the parlor window seat in the sun, holding her baby close while she nibbled his tiny ears and all over his downy head, telling him how soon he would see his father.

But May wore away slowly into June. The weather grew suddenly warm. On the wharves they began to say that the *Canton Queen* was overdue; there was no word either from Captain Erik. And so, in due course, it was two strangers who came to tell Kirstina that her husband's ship had gone down. The second officer and ship's doctor off a China clipper, they were as circumstantial as they were kind. The *Canton Queen* had been wrecked off Valparaiso in a storm.

She had been held up some time off the coast of Southern California by the embargo on shipping in Mexican waters during the war. When she sailed again she had made good time until she ran into this January storm. She had broken up within sight of the shore, hammered by terrific seas. Not a soul had escaped from her alive.

They told this to Kirstina Shea, who listened as if she did not understand at all. Her pale face was still, and her hands quiet in her lap. The ship's doctor's eyes wandered pitifully from her to the cradle beside, where he could just see the brown head of her sleeping child.

Johanna Warre showed the two men to the door. When she came back she stood looking at Kirstina, and after a while turned and went upstairs to her own room.

Kirstina rose stiffly. She went to find her shawl and she went out of the house. She began to walk, and walked street after street, and mile after mile. She tried to tell herself that Michael had been drowned in January; she told herself over and over again, and it made no sense. Instead, all she kept remembering was that in January his son had been born. When her steps led her home again, she had been walking nearly four hours.

She came up the path to the Charlestown house, went in through the door and leaned back on it as it closed, the palms of her hands on either side of her against the wood. As she lifted her eyes to the stairs, Johanna Warre was coming down.

Johanna asked, "Do you see now what you have done?"

Kirstina's mouth fluttered open, and closed.

"You wanted him changed. You couldn't leave him alone. He was a sailor, but that wasn't good enough for you. He was a man, but you wanted him to follow you and obey and beg. You didn't want him as he was. You drove him away, and so he is dead. Do you see now that you killed him?"

"I . . . didn't."

"Did he ever go before? Would he have gone if you hadn't driven him off? What did you want of him? He was beautiful, and big and strong. Wasn't that enough? He was my son. . . . He was my only son. . . . You killed him."

"No . . . no . . ."

"He was my son . . . my dead son."

Terror choked Kirstina's throat. She broke away and ran to where the cradle stood in the parlor. She caught up her own baby and held him to her, breathing and alive.

Johanna followed her. "How will you save your child?" she asked. "Will you watch over him and hold him? Will you pray for him? . . . Michael was mine. I held him. Whatever he asked for I tried to give him. But I could not save him from you."

"No . . . no . . ."

"My son is dead. . . . I shall pray God you live to see your child die."

Kirstina's knees buckled under her. She went down on the floor by the cradle, Rudi clutched to her. He struggled and began to cry as he woke.

It was then they heard the door knocker. When Johanna recollected herself and opened the door, Helga came in.

After Kirstina had left the house, after Helga had taken her and Rudi back to the inn, she could talk only of how she must get away. She said it over and over. "I must get away, Helga. Please help me. I must get away. Don't make me stay here. Help me to get away."

Helga pursed her lips and fussed and tried to pay no attention. She was enjoying being for once in command. Next day Kirstina was white after a night of no sleep, and was too nervous to let Rudi out of her arms. She did not improve in the week that followed. Helga watched her and worried, and at last said slowly, "I am not sure I should tell you. You are in such a hurry. But I believe I know of a way in which you could go."

"Helga, I must get away."

"You can stay here with us."

"No."

"There is a young couple here now—an Englishman and his wife. They are on their way to Canada. They have a baby girl and they have lost their nursemaid. Yesterday the mother asked me if I could find her someone else."

"Helga—"

"But you can't be so foolish, Kirstina! Your home is here. This is where you ought to stay. You have Rudi to look after. And soon the captain will be home."

Kirstina shuddered. Captain Erik, Oh God, Captain Erik! And Patrick and Martha Shea. . . . She had not seen them—would not see anyone—and long, long before Captain Erik came home she must be gone.

"I will go."

"The captain will fetch you back."

Not from Canada, she thought. Not from another country, even if he wished. "I will go. And I will tell them my name is Kirstina Brandt."

"But that is absurd! You are Mr. Shea's wife."

"Not any more."

"Rudi is his son."

"Michael never knew it."

Helga shrugged her plump shoulders. She was kind, and so she was doing as she had been asked. She was also afraid that unless she helped, Kirstina would manage to disappear entirely on her own. She resolved privately that when Captain Warre returned she would disregard any vows of secrecy that Kirstina managed to exact from her.

So Kirstina left, and only a week later Captain Erik came home. He had had two difficult crossings, more exhausting than any he remembered for years, although it seemed to him that each one since Michael had left him had become more trying. Now he arrived to hear from Johanna that Michael was dead, and Kirstina and the baby gone away. By the time Helga saw him, he seemed to her to have grown old overnight. He was so anxious, so relieved to hear that Kirstina was probably in no immediate want, and so unable to decide whether he should fetch her back. Talking to him, Helga suddenly realized that he knew his wife's nature only too well, and that he was afraid of her vindictiveness.

"They could go to Patrick Shea," he said, speaking of Kirstina and his great-nephew. "Yes, that would be the best."

In the end he did nothing but leave a letter with Helga, to be forwarded as soon as Kirstina had sent her address. He talked of waiting until the autumn, when he would be back again, and either he or Patrick Shea could travel to Montreal.

In October he arrived, gray and tired, and undecided as ever. He caught cold, and sat coughing in his house, in the shadow of Johanna's brooding silence. Then, quite suddenly, the cold turned to a congestion of the lungs, and he died. Helga was shocked and wrote Kirstina. It was some time before Kirstina replied.

Johanna Warre was left alone in the Charlestown house. She refused all offers of company, all overtures from her friends, and stayed alone week after week. Late in November she received a letter from Michael, from Santa Fe. The letter had been six months on the way. He knew nothing of the sinking of the *Canton Queen.* He spoke of having left the ship at San Francisco on her return journey, and he mentioned a letter he had sent from there and which had probably gone astray. Johanna did not understand too clearly. She gathered that he had started home overland, reached Santa Fe and there joined the army. That was where he was now, fighting Mexicans and Indians and in no hurry to leave. "Tell my uncle," he said, "that I will write to him soon." He did not speak of his wife, and Johanna rejoiced.

All that was important to her was that he was alive. She had this word from him, for her alone. It was a miracle that it had come after Erik was dead. There was no one now with whom she needed to share it, no one who would force her to fetch Kirstina back. With the help of fate, she had finally achieved her end and she was rid of Kirstina for good. If Johanna had been a normal woman—normal even in her possessiveness—she would have thought far more about Michael's son. Even when she had believed Michael dead, she would have seized on the child, wanting to make him her own. Instead, in her hatred of Kirstina, the child had almost passed from her recollection. She did not remember him now. She thought only of how Kirstina was gone and how at last, now that no one but she knew that he was alive, Michael had become peculiarly her own.

Presently, and with great care, since she did not wish to bring him home and have others know that he lived, she answered his letter. Later, with equal care, she answered the further letters that arrived. After some time she let him know that his uncle had died, and she became very clever in the impression she built up of a Kirstina who was living there in his house, who was well and very self-sufficient, who burned unopened the occasional letters he addressed to her because she did not care either to hear from him, or to reply.

When Mr. Robert Walker and his wife Mary passed through Boston and stayed at Nordrupp's inn, they were on the last lap of a long journey. Only a little while before he had been a captain in Her Majesty's forces in India. He had sold out of the army because an uncle in Canada—his mother's only brother—wanted to make him his heir, and desired him to come to Montreal. As Mary Walker was expecting a baby, they broke their journey in England long enough to visit her people and to get her confinement over. Then they embarked at Liverpool on the steamer *City of Dundee*, bound for Boston. Their party consisted of their two selves, the infant Harriet, and the latter's nurse. No one on board was aware that the year 1847 when they were traveling would go down in history as the Great Cholera Year, but on the *City of Dundee* three people, one of them the child's nurse, died of that disease. It was called, euphemistically, "ship fever." Robert was chiefly concerned because it meant that he and his wife would have to wait over in Boston to find someone else to look after the baby.

The city was very full and the Tremont Hotel where they had been told to put up had accommodation only for gentlemen traveling alone, and these were being put three and four in a room. Robert thought himself lucky in getting a room at Nordrupp's inn. It was so thoroughly decent and clean and in the end it was through the hotel-keeper's wife there that they found the young Danish woman who accompanied them to their final destination.

As they ever afterward recalled, the last part of their journey was by far the worst. They were jolted in a coach over rough roads, through mile after mile of virgin forest. The inns were incredibly bad and the manners of their fellow travelers coarse and even hostile.

Across the border they were met with a disquieting rumor. Montreal was in the throes of an epidemic—whether of ship fever or of typhus no one seemed quite sure. The city was half evacuated and in the plague sheds which had been erected on the banks of the St. Lawrence sixty to a hundred persons were dying each day. Robert made inquiries and discovered that his uncle was among the refugees. He had a summer place at Lachine, some nine miles up the river, and there at long last the Walkers arrived and found themselves at home.

The fever epidemic continued all through the hot months and it was the end of September before it was considered safe to allow Mary and her baby into the city; then they moved into an imposing town house of cut stone, not far from Dalhousie Square and the barracks. John Farquharson's wealth was nothing if not substantial. He was an importer or—as he preferred to call it—a trader. He owned a number of ships and these carried corn and lumber and furs to

England and to the West Indies and brought back sugar and manufactured goods for the Canadian market. He also had money in one of the city's breweries and he was busy now buying up stock in a new railroad. "The railroads are going to open up this country," he kept repeating. "Wait until the trunk line goes through to Toronto."

Even in England, Montreal would have been considered a handsome town. There was over a mile of stone wharves; all the main streets were wide and paved and lit with gas; the public buildings were fine and the shops showy and interesting to visit. There was no lack of wine shops. There were fine horses and carriages in the streets. Robert looked up what regiments were in garrison and was fortunate in finding some old acquaintances among the officers. It was pleasant to be no longer irked by the duties which still bound them, to have money enough to be able to entertain them as well as to share in their pursuits. Society naturally revolved round the governor and his staff, and Robert found Lord Elgin very civil. Montreal, in fact, suited the Walkers down to the ground. Robert began to think of settling there for good and perhaps even carrying on his uncle's business, but he never got to the point of discussing these wishes in detail. One very cold day at the end of January Mr. Farquharson died from the same type of attack that had warned him the year before that he was growing old.

After the will had been read and the extent of his inheritance ascertained, Robert told Mary of his decision to remain in the Canadas. She was content and they both considered the matter settled.

They had not, however, reckoned with the effect the Canadian winter would have on Mary's spirits. When February and then March passed and still there was snow on the ground and no abatement in the cold winds, she began to flag. A cold she had taken in January did not leave her; a nagging little cough forced her to keep indoors even when the sun shone. Robert was making progress in the skating he had not practiced since he was a boy in England; he went on snowshoeing expeditions and enjoyed driving his uncle's horses in a brightly painted cutter. But Mary was cooped up in the house and her face became pinched and drawn and smote him with compunction whenever he came bursting with health into her room. When at last the thaw began and the first overseas mail reached them via Quebec (for the Montreal harbor was still frozen) she had letters from her people telling her of an early spring in England, with the snowdrops and primroses carpeting the woods. Several times Robert

73

came home to find her with her eyelids reddened from weeping. At last one day he said, "Mary, do you very much want to go home?" and she burst into tears before him and confessed that she did not think she could bear it if every winter were to be like this.

However much they had enjoyed the life of the place, there could be no point in remaining in Montreal unless they were both going to continue to be happy there. They talked the situation over, and then Robert set everything in train to realize his Canadian assets and reinvest in England. Then he went down to Commissioners' Street and booked passage for himself and his family on the first suitable vessel out of the port of Montreal for Liverpool.

All this time Kirstina Brandt had been in charge of the nursery, bringing up her own child along with theirs. Naturally, since this arrangement answered so well—though they all knew that later different provision would have to be made for the boy—Mary was anxious for Mrs. Brandt to accompany them to England. But the young woman did not want to go.

Robert did his best to persuade her. He asked her if she had not been happy with them, and then asked why, in that case, she did not wish to go on as they were?

"I told Mrs. Walker, sir, that it was because of my boy."

Mary had mentioned some such thing but had not seemed to have it quite straight. Robert said helpfully, "Yes?"

"I have never been in England, sir, but I think I know how it must be there. Owing to Mrs. Walker's kindness and your own, for a few more years I should be able to keep my little boy with me, but after that I should have to put him out to board. He would be brought up to touch his cap to gentlemen, and as soon as he was old enough he would be set to learn a trade. Because I was a servant he would never have a chance to be anything else but a servant."

Robert nodded. "You are quite right, Mrs. Brandt. That is the way it would be, and not only in England."

"But it would not be so here, sir. Here, as he grows up, nothing will be forbidden him. No one will hold him down. His father was an American. I feel it would not be right for me to take him back to the Old World."

"How will you manage when we are gone?"

"I'm a good needlewoman, sir; Mrs. Walker's friends have promised me work."

74

"Well, then, if you will not change your mind, the least we can do is to wish you luck."

"Thank you, sir."

He told Mary of his unsuccess, and she was disappointed but not surprised. "I told you, Robert. Heaven knows how she'll get on, but she's so bent on being independent I think even if we stayed she'd leave us soon. You will have to give her something substantial when we leave."

Robert gave her fifteen pounds. The Walkers set sail at the end of April with a marvelous quantity of luggage, a manservant, and a new English nurse who had originally come out with an officer's wife and was as homesick for England as was Mary Walker. All their friends came down to see them off and stood on the wharf waving until nothing more could be seen of them but the white blur that was Mary's dress and parasol.

Montreal remembered the Walkers for a little and then forgot them; only upon Kirstina was their influence indelible. But for the Walkers, Kirstina would never have arrived at Montreal; never have come in contact with a way of life until then totally unfamiliar to her; never, perhaps, have been left to fend for herself in a city where she was unknown.

Further even than that, the Walkers had given her a long period of tranquillity in which to recover from the shock of Michael's death, and it was they who had finally taught her to speak English. When Robert Walker thought she expressed herself well for a person in her station of life, he did not realize how much more unusual he would have found her manner of speaking if he had not known she was a foreigner. To the end of her days Kirstina would speak English with a Danish accent, but the English she used was the English of Mary Walker, and was unimpeachable.

She found lodgings through the girl who had come to the Walkers' to help with the laundry. Lizzie Bridie was an amiable, soft creature who liked to fondle Rudi. When she said that she lived with an older woman who was also a laundress and who had a room to let, Kirstina went to see. The room was of moderate size in a house and street that were no worse than others in the poorer parts of the town. It was not clean, but that could be remedied. A more serious objection was the dislike Kirstina took to the landlady, a fat, stale-smelling old woman of whose Cockney good nature she was suspicious. She hesitated, but she could afford very little and she had to stay among the English-speaking minority in the town because as yet she knew no French. In Montreal most of the poor who were not French were Irish, and among the latter she knew she could not bear to be. In the end she decided to accept the room, and to take Rudi about with her as much as she could.

She still had a trunkful of clothes, all the trinkets and gifts Michael had bought her, besides the remainder of the linen she had originally prepared for her trousseau. She moved all of these into Mrs. Cannon's house, scrubbed out her room and spread her own linen on the bed.

Through May and June ladies of every age and position were engaged in restoring and adding to their summer wardrobes. The households to which Kirstina applied welcomed her eagerly and she had as much work as she could manage. After the first few weeks, however, she realized that she was not going to amass a fortune quickly. The wives of the Montreal businessmen, were they English, Scottish or French, were as thrifty as their husbands, to whom each month they had to render account of their expenditures. They paid for the work done for them, but they paid not a penny more than they needed to. Kirstina made enough for her rent to Mrs. Cannon, to buy food and a few necessities of clothing, after which she had a dollar, perhaps a little more, saved at the end of each week. She had a trinket box with a lock and key in which she kept this money and she hid it always in the depths of her locked trunk. She was not too anxious. It seemed to her that she could not expect to do well so soon, and later would be the time to see what more it was possible for her to undertake.

But at the end of June she discovered that for about two months she was going to lose her customers. All the wealthy families of the city, and most of those moderately well-to-do, went to the country for the summer. If Kirstina had been working for a full year she might have been able to cope with this; she would have had some savings and enough commissions to enable her to carry on. As it was she was ill-prepared and by the third week in July she had used up the last of her saved dollars in paying Mrs. Cannon, and the week after that she had to break into the Walkers' parting gift.

Molly Cannon was in a talkative mood that evening. She stood with one hand on her massive hip and the other weighing Kirstina's coins and said jocularly, "Had to pinch yerself to get this lot, didn't yer? Yer spend too much on the brat."

"I don't give him anything he doesn't need."

"Laws! I'm not saying 'e can't use it! Brats' stummicks is made without bottoms if yer arsks me! But it don't do 'em no 'arm to keep 'em a bit short—keeps 'em quieter like, fer one thing."

"Does Rudi's noise disturb you, Mrs. Cannon?"

"Nah, not me! 'Aven't yer got 'im off 'ere by yerself? But if yer was me hit'd get on me nerves to 'ave 'im allus scamperin' abaht like that, worritin' at things and never still fer a minnit. Not 'ealthy, it ain't. Give 'im less to eat and a nip aht of a bottle onct in a while—that'd calm 'im down."

On one or two occasions when Kirstina was in the neighborhood shops the men and women there looked at her in a sidelong fashion she did not like, but her reserved manner and lady's speech kept them from making any direct comment, and it was only by degrees that she became sure of what had been Mrs. Cannon's profession when she was younger and less rotten-ripe. Mrs. Cannon herself made it quite certain one evening when, after she had for some time been watching Kirstina's labors over a piece of embroidery, she said, "If yer was to arsk me, there's ways I could get yer a sight more than that bit uv flimsy'll bring in."

It took Kirstina some time to persuade her that her good offices were not in demand. "Yer needn't be insult," Molly kept repeating. "I wouldn't make yer the offer if I didn't think yer could 'andle it."

Kirstina was still going out almost every day to people's houses to work, but it was to families who neither could nor would pay as much as those for whom she had worked at first. Often she got as little as fifty cents for a day's work, and, since in such houses they did not want to feed Rudi as well as herself, she had to pay Mrs. Cannon extra for the food the woman said she gave him. When she stayed home and worked in her room she made meals for herself, but though all food was cheap, with meat at five cents a pound, and butter at fifteen, it still took more than she wished.

Lizzie Bridie had become her admiring slave. No one knew where Molly Cannon had got Lizzie, but she treated her as if she owned her, cuffed her about, confiscated her earnings, and paid her for her labor only with her food and bed and an occasional dram of gin. It was when Mrs. Cannon had herself drunk enough to go comfortably off to sleep that Lizzie would leave the damp linen lying and slip upstairs to Kirstina's room.

This was usually in the evenings. Rudi would be already tucked away in the bed and his mother would be sewing by the light of the oil lamp she had bought when she left the Walkers. She had needed it (how could she work at night without a steady light?) but now the memory of what it had cost could make her blench and, since tallow was so much cheaper than even lamp oil, the moment she had finished sewing for the evening and had only to make herself ready for bed, she would light a tallow dip and blow out the lamp. It was before that, while she was still working, that it was a comfort to look into Lizzie Bridie's great, owlish eyes and see that someone still thought her so fine.

All the time she felt terrifyingly alone. When she had first heard from Helga that Captain Erik was dead, though she had never expected to see him again and had intended to evade his pursuit, she had grieved bitterly. Now, more and more, her responsibility toward Rudi weighed on her. She kept remembering how it was she who had deprived him of his father, and had then brought him away from all those who might have helped him for his father's sake.

One day late in August she went to some people for whom she was accustomed to work remarkably long hours for very little money. She reflected with satisfaction that this was the last time she would go there; next week would be September and the worst of her troubles would be over. She worked away alone in the little room set apart for her, and her luncheon was brought her there on a tray in the early afternoon. Shortly after that the two daughters of the house came to be fitted and Kirstina was working on the second one when she was suddenly aware that she felt unwell. A fit of dizziness passed through her; her body felt heavy and swollen and broke out into sweat. It was over in a moment and she thought confusedly that it must have been something she ate. A queer, sickish headache remained, however, and stayed with her all afternoon, while periodic dizziness made her blink her eyes at her work. She was sure after a time that she had a fever, but she was anxious to finish the task in hand and stayed with it until at six o'clock it was done and she was paid and could go home. Her employer remarked that she looked pale. Kirstina said it was because of the heat and she would be thankful to get out into the air.

But she was still standing on the steps of the house when she was suddenly doubled up over the rail with a cramp in her stomach. Her knees bent under her and she clung with her hands, gasping and running with sweat. Again, once it had passed, she felt weak but almost normal. She thought, I need some sleep; it has been very hot and I'm overtired and something I ate has disagreed with me. She had never been ill with more than a childish indisposition, never felt real pain except when her baby was born. It did not occur to her now that this could be something beyond her experience.

Again and again on her way home she was forced to lean against railings and shop fronts for support. She had no idea how she must look; dizziness and pain made her almost blind. The cramps attacked her with increasing rapidity and each was like a snake sliding through her bowels and tightening into a knot. Vague memories of tales she had heard of the fever epidemic the year before came into her mind, with fragments of Mary Walker's account of her maid's dying on shipboard. "Cramp," she had said, "the poor thing was in agony." That must be what it is, thought Kirstina. It is ship fever. She no longer wondered that no one stopped to help her—perhaps they knew she had it and were frightened. All she wanted, all she had strength to keep on walking for, was to reach her bed and lie there in peace. Then, insistently, something else hammered its way into her brain. Rudi. She should not go home where he was; should not lie in the bed with him. Rudi must not get this. Rudi must not be near her. "Keep him away from me," she said out loud. "Keep him away from me. Lizzie, keep him away."

She could not prevent her feet from taking her back to Molly Cannon's house. She knew nowhere else to go. Only, when she got there, she did not need to go in. Must not go in. Rudi was inside. She sank down on the doorstep and then rolled forward till her head touched her knees as another cramp assailed her.

Molly Cannon was in the house drunk. Lizzie Bridie was upstairs crooning to the small Rudi who had fallen asleep in her arms. It seemed to her that she heard something knocking, thud-thudding against the door. She stood up and carried the baby over to the bed, where she gently slid him under the blankets.

She went downstairs. As she opened the door, Kirstina fell in against her knees, and went on rocking herself to and fro. Lizzie caught her breath, for the fever was no stranger to her. She bent and put her arms about Miz' Brandt and tried to draw her up, but Kirstina pulled down. She breathed thickly, "No . . . no . . . Not inside . . . Rudi . . . Lizzie, not inside . . ."

She did not seem to understand that to go anywhere she still had to stand up. Lizzie had to come out to her and pull the door to before she could get her to her feet. The street was quite deserted, though behind the windows there were some who watched. Lizzie Bridie with the courage of the kind and simple-hearted, fetched Kirstina by slow degrees down to the fever sheds by the river.

The year before there had been so many ill that the dead and the living had lain side by side on the wooden bunks in the sheds with scarcely anyone to tell which was which. The government, which had built first three sheds, had built eleven before the end and still the latest comers had had to lie out of doors on the ground. The cloistered nuns had come out to nurse, but hundreds of the sick had died untended and been driven nameless to the great charnel houses on either bank of the river.

This year it was not like that, though every year fever struck in Montreal. Sometimes the emigrants brought it; sometimes it seemed to rise up from the ground. It was of many types, but to doctors who had never been East to see the cholera in Calcutta, or to the Southern states to see the malaria in New Orleans, it seemed safest to call them all "ship fever." Since they knew so little about the disease, it was only natural that the treatment should vary with the doctor, and even more with the nurse.

Kirstina was lucky. The numbers of sick this season were manageable, and she was not left alone. She was wrapped in blankets and bled and given as much water as she could drink. The taciturn French doctor who attended her was a man of logic; he had had time to think since last September, and he had reasoned that since in this type of ship fever the body lost so much moisture through copious sweating it must be necessary to replace this water. Further, since sweat is salt, let the patient who sweats be given salt with the water he drinks. The doctor's success had not so far been phenomenal and he watched Kirstina with anxiety to see if she at least would respond to his theories. She was a bad case, a very bad case, but she had a magnificent constitution. It went to the doctor's heart to see what illness could do to such a body as hers, and he felt she had been mutilated when they clipped her hair. But she did not die. Whoever she was—and no one either knew or recognized the language she spoke—she still did not die.

Anyone who had heard and understood her ravings would have found them jumbled and yet oddly coherent. The images were muddled, but the mood was always the same. She cried out in Danish about the ten thousand kroner, and about Michael who had cheated her. She had been promised so much. First of all there was the money and it was to buy her what she wanted, and she wanted to be safe. And then she loved Michael, she loved Michael, she loved Michael. And Michael she could have if she would give up the money, and with Michael she would inherit the earth. Now Michael was dead. Michael was dead because he had left her, and because Michael was dead she had nothing that she had been promised. She was robbed and pushed down into a pit. They were throwing stones down upon her, and all the stones were round gold plates. The sea was pouring over into the pit and she was drowning, was drowned, and so there again was Michael, but he would not know her because she had two of the gold plates still in her hands. But if Michael was gone couldn't she have back what she had paid for him? My ten thousand kroner, she screamed, my ten thousand kroner! And she was scrabbling under her stepfather's table for the coin that had run away.

Very, very slowly, after days of this delirium and of abysmal weakness, she began to mend.

The morning when she finally asked for water in her pure, refined English it would be difficult to say who was the more surprised—the nurse, who did not really understand her, or the doctor, who did. She was a mystery to them always. No one knew where to send her and she said nothing to help them, and so she stayed in the hospital much longer than most patients. When at last she left, it was on her own feet, and after the briefest of farewells.

She felt extraordinarily weak as she stood in the street; her height and thinness made her a gaunt scarecrow, while her face was weird in its pallor, with her cheeks sunk in and her hair clinging in lifeless, inch-long threads. It took her a long time to reach Mrs. Cannon's house. She knocked. Molly herself opened the door, with Lizzie Bridie behind her. They both paled as if they saw what could not be there.

"Christ!" said Mrs. Cannon. She crossed herself.

Kirstina leaned against the doorjamb, unable to speak or to move further.

"Yer didn't die," marveled Lizzie Bridie.

"Liz, help her," said Molly.

Between Lizzie's arm and the banister, Kirstina slowly climbed the stairs. She went into the doorway of her room. Inside stood the bed with the mattress, and nothing else. Her trunk was not there, nor her linen, nor the curtains she had hung at the window, nor her oil lamp, nor her clothes.

With a wrench of panic she turned and cried out, "Mrs. Cannon! Where have you put my things?"

Molly was halfway up. "Christ!" she said again. "Didn't yer know we thought yer was dead?"

A crowd of horrid images whirled up about Kirstina's head from the floor. She let go of Lizzie to press both hands to her eyes. Then she lurched sideways and spun round in darkness as she fell.

When she came to herself, Rudi was there beside her, dirty and pale, but her own child and unharmed. Mrs. Cannon was also there. Fortified with gin she was on the defensive; her light eyes bulged with a mixture of alarm and defiance.

To do her justice, it was not out of ill will that she had sold her lodger's belongings and forbidden Lizzie to return to the plague sheds. She had had no reason to suppose Kirstina dead except that she had taken the fever, but she had considered that ample, and she had not wanted to see her slavey dead of the fever also.

She stood talking at Kirstina, her aggrieved tones making clear what she thought her ill luck. Again and again she asked, " 'Ow could I 'ave known? I 'aven't done nothin' but wot was natcheral. It ain't right fer me ter be put in the wrong. Makin' me out a thief, that's wot it is, when I didn't mean no 'arm. I 'aven't even got rid uv the brat. Meant ter bring 'im up as me own, I did, and give 'im 'is milk reg'lar as yer please. Never expected nothin' fer wot I done, but I did feel 'ow I 'ad a right to the bits and pieces as was left. Though the little they brought in yer'd 'ardly believe after yer lettin' on they was so extra.

"An' now 'ere yer is back from the dead, so ter speak, and like as not wantin' yer things back. Well, I ain't got 'em. It didn't oughter 'ave 'appened. Puttin' me in the wrong like this! But 'ow could I 'ave known? I thought yer was dead."

Kirstina sat on a wooden chair, staring ahead of her, her face frightening in its steady, white intensity.

" 'Ere," said Mrs. Cannon, "wot yer needs is a little nip."

When she brought the two glasses she was relieved that Kirstina took one and drank. She wanted the atmosphere eased.

But Kirstina still sat without speaking. She looked into her empty glass, round the empty room, and last at Mrs. Cannon.

"You owe me a lot of money," she said.

"Nah look 'ere—!"

"I could have you sent to prison."

Agitation rose in Molly. She was afraid of this and afraid to show her fear. With noisy contempt she began, "Them bits an' pieces—"

"There was also the money, Mrs. Cannon. Ten pounds in gold in the box in my trunk. You made away with everything I had. I think my story would be believed. I could very easily have you sent to prison."

"It wouldn't get yer nothin' back!"

Kirstina knew that well. She realized that she was neither frightened any more nor angry at what had occurred. She was not even vindictive towards the creature who had robbed her. She had only two thoughts in her mind: to assess what she had lost and to get it back.

"With the money," she said, "what you took was worth at least a hundred and fifty dollars."

"I never saw no hunderd fifty!"

"Then you did not do very good business. You will have to do better now. I want to be paid, Mrs. Cannon."

Molly sniffed. " 'Ow?"

"As quickly as may be possible. From now on Lizzie shall bring the money she collects to me and not to you. I will pay for what we need. The rest I will keep."

"Like 'ell yer will! Do yer think I'm goin' ter stand fer anythin' of that sort right 'ere in me own 'ouse?"

"You have no choice. Unless you prefer to have me go to a magistrate?" She spoke as calmly as ever. Her last words were almost a courteous inquiry, and it was this self-control which intimidated the other woman. The two of them stared at each other, watchful, coming to terms. At last Molly shrugged.

"Nah," she said. " 'Ave it yer own way, then."

Kirstina's little sigh of relief was imperceptible. The wave of fatigue she had been staving off flooded over her and she broke out into sweat. She turned from Molly to the open-mouthed Liz. "Bring a pair of sheets," she told her. "I need you to make up my bed."

She remained in bed the greater part of the next three weeks, gripped by the weakness the cholera had left. When she was up she staggered about her room; if she managed to get downstairs she turned sickish and threatened to faint. She could not afford to give way to this helplessness; she had to dominate Molly Cannon and that could not be done from a sickbed. If it had not been for Lizzie, she would already have been defeated. Lizzie looked after her and Rudi, cooked, did everything for which Kirstina had no strength. Meanwhile Molly sulked, nursed her bottle of gin and let the dirty linen pile up in the kitchen.

Her business had always been haphazard. Lizzie Bridie collected the bundles of laundry from nearby hotels and inns; when she and Molly had dealt with them she trundled them back in the same handcart, and was paid. To make up for slipshod work they charged very low prices. Trade was never brisk, but work of a kind always came in.

Kirstina knew it would be a long time before she was paid in full unless she herself took a hand, and anger did a lot to spur her recovery. From her upbringing there was nothing she did not know about laundry work and when she gathered up the reins she was well able to drive. Molly found herself kept hard at work for hours, washing and starching and leaving much of the finishing for Kirstina. Lizzie began delivering days earlier than she had been accustomed. Not satisfied with that, Kirstina went out to solicit business from houses farther afield and, having put up her charges, she was glad to see Molly's earlier, riffraff customers melt away. As soon as it was at all possible, she kept Lizzie at home and hired a boy to do the fetching and delivering and they were able to handle still more custom.

She discovered that neither Molly nor Lizzie could work well without liquor. She had to spend on it for them and to save herself from complete exhaustion she also was often glad of it, but she kept strict control of all other expenses. In December the establishment was showing good returns, and by the end of January the hundred-and-fifty-dollar debt was paid off. Thereafter she divided the earnings equally with Mrs. Cannon, who was loud with satisfaction.

"Ter think," she would say, "that I thought yer was done fer proper that day yer turned up again. Nothin' left of yer, so ter speak. An' me as had thought onct ter make somethin' good out uv yer with yer fine big breasts and yer 'ead of 'air. Full uv juice, yer was. Well, nothin' like that doin' now, if yer gets wot I mean, but oo'd a thought yer'd fix us all up like this? Partners, that's wot you an' me are, dearie, and goin' ter stay that way."

Nothing shook Mrs. Cannon's belief in her own kindliness and popularity, but it was the possibility of this partnership continuing that reduced Kirstina at times to paralyzing despair. She knew she had only herself to blame for her situation, and yet it seemed to her that at least after the cholera she had had little choice. Molly Cannon had made away with her decent clothes and her working tools, and had told the people who inquired after her that she was dead. To have gone back, destitute, to those who had helped her before, Kirstina could not have borne. Nor could she altogether regret the loss of her former occupation since she was already making far more money.

It was Rudi who was the center of her disquiet. He was a baby still, needing only her presence and love to keep him happy. But how soon would that change? How soon would the things he saw, the people who touched him, begin to leave their mark? Old Mrs. Cannon's corpulent, spirits-soaked flesh, Lizzie's vacant devotion: day after day she felt herself grow more used to them, better able to control them and more degraded by their familiarity, and she knew that for her son's sake she must escape them.

One of the hotels with which she did business was a respectable house some distance away. Like the majority of the better hotels in Montreal at the time, it was run by an Italian. Signor Luigi Rossa called his establishment the Milan House, after the city of his birth. He kept a hotel because he liked to cook; the more exalted the tastes of his patrons the better he liked to feed them. It was his misfortune that to entice a sufficient number of persons into his dining room to provide him with profit enough to go on preparing their food, it was necessary as well to keep books, and make up bills, and train waiters and housemaids and bootblacks. Signor Rossa could cook, but he could not do these other things, and he never seemed able to employ anyone more capable of them than he. As a result the Milan House was not in the same class with Rasco's Hotel and Donegani's, and Signor Rossa in moments of stress often lamented that he had not remained in Milano, where an artist of his caliber would have received a more just reward.

Kirstina had visited the Milan House often, for there was always confusion over the laundry from Signor Rossa's hotel. She also remembered having heard Robert Walker remark that the best food in Montreal was served at that place of Rossa's, but how the devil could one take a party there when one knew there would be wine stains on the table linen and at any moment the waiter might tip the soup down one's neck? The day she decided to go to see Rossa she felt she already knew the man with whom she would have to deal.

She had made herself a gray dress that was presentable, and she bought a new gray bonnet and gloves. She washed her hair. It was not yet of any length, but it was thick again and had some of its former luster and curl. When it was dry and brushed out it framed her face softly in the shadow of the bonnet. Her reflection in the glass still made her sigh, but she had done what she could.

She entered the Milan House at the main door, and to a boy lounging about in what passed for a livery she said that she had business with Signor Rossa. She would like to know where she could wait until he was free?

She spoke in her precise, clear-cut English. Under her calm eye the boy made a startled effort to collect himself and hurried off. When he came back he escorted her through the saloon into a small office where was a wild melee of papers, open books and ink blots. Kirstina removed a pile of papers from a chair by the window, laid them on those already on the table, and sat down. Above Signor Rossa's desk hung a crucifix and a pair of crossed palms. By the inkwell stood an open box of cigars, and on the carpet was an undisturbed pyramid of ash. The flakes were large and white. Apart from these items the only thing distinguishable from the general muddle was a bunch of incredibly dusty artificial flowers stuck in a colored china vase.

The door opened and Signor Rossa came in. In fantastic contrast to his habitation, he himself was meticulously neat. He was a short man, solidly built but not fat, who held himself very erect. He had gone bald on the top of his head; all around this spot his graying hair was kept rather long and it showed a tendency to curl. His neckcloth was dazzlingly white, his black coat was well brushed and smart, his gray trousers fashionably tight and strapped. He looked more placid than usual and his eyes, which were dark and rather prominent, ran over his visitor with bright curiosity.

He said, "I believe I have not the honor—"

Kirstina had risen. She answered, "I do not expect you to recognize me, Signor Rossa. But for the past several months you have been sending me the laundry from your hotel. My name is Kirstina Brandt."

Though his expression did not change, he quickly looked her over again. Then he asked, "Mrs. Brandt? Have you come to see me with any special business in mind?"

"Yes, I have."

"Then perhaps we should sit down."

He waited to see that she had done so before he seated himself on the chair that was half turned away from his desk. His hand went to the box of cigars. She had the impression that he was about to offer her one and then recollected himself. Instead he closed the lid.

"You said," he prompted, "that you have been working as a laundress. May I ask why?"

"Because I could find no other work. But I have not always done that, and it is because I do not wish to do it any more that I have come to see you."

"You are looking for work?"

"Yes, I am."

Rossa hunched himself forward on his chair and stared at her. Suddenly he smiled with shrewd and engaging humor. "Mrs. Brandt, you must already have given this matter far more thought than you can expect me to have done in these few minutes. Will you be good enough to tell me just what you want?"

Kirstina swallowed. Though she wanted to be composed, she had to pause and say, with a telltale tremor, "You are very kind. I have been afraid I could not make you listen." Then she collected herself. "I have to work. I am a widow and I have a little boy to bring up. I would not have been reduced to the straits I have been in lately if I had not been ill. Before I was ill I was a seamstress. But that is all behind me now. I came here because I want to offer my services where I can be of the most use."

"You feel you can be of use to me?"

"Yes. Signor Rossa, when I have visited your house before I have stood long enough in your back kitchens to hear how it is with you. You are plagued with work you do not want to do. Your servants neglect everything they are told, and officers will not come here to eat because they say that your hotel is dirty. But all the things that are such a trial to you, I know how to do well. There is no house I cannot keep clean. I write a very clear hand and I figure accurately. I could keep those books where you can never find anything written. And I could see to it that your waiters serve food as they should, so that you would not have to change them every month."

Rossa's smile had become grim. "Then you think my hotel is a pigsty and I am an idiot?"

"No! Oh, do please try to understand! I have heard you make these complaints yourself! Housekeeping is only what every woman is supposed to know. I do not want to offend you and I need help most desperately."

"What do you know about running a hotel?"

"I have a friend who is married in Boston to a man who owns one. I have stayed with her there."

"What is it like?"

"It is quite big. My friend is Danish, as are her husband and I. The inn is an old house with big windows. It is very clean and bright. My friend's husband has a Swedish woman to cook; he keeps himself busy organizing the rest of the business. Everything is counted and numbered. Herr Nordrupp gives out the oil for the lamps himself, and the candles. He goes round to all the rooms every morning to see that the maids have changed the linen early enough and cleaned the rooms. He checks the stores. He is always on hand to talk to the guests and see that they get what they wish. He does not let in anyone he does not want. He keeps the names of those who come often in a big book, with a list opposite of the things they like best to eat and drink, and of what they don't like at all. Then when he sees them and can't remember he can look it up. He keeps all his accounts himself in separate books for the saloon, for the restaurant, and for the sleeping quarters. Then he knows where he is making most money, and where he is losing. But he doesn't lose much. He is getting quite rich."

Luigi Rossa said succinctly, "I have no doubt. Are you able to perform all this?"

Kirstina reddened and said, "It was what I had hoped."

"If you could, you'd be worth your weight in gold. How much would you demand?"

Under the suspicion that she was being mocked, her control suddenly went, and she drooped. "I am not able to demand anything. I believe, to get away from where I am now, I would do it for nothing."

"Where are you now?"

"I live on St. Peter Street, with a woman called Molly Cannon."

"Who also takes in the washing?"

"Yes."

"How did you first come to Montreal?"

"I came with the wife of an English officer."

"Who said that my rooms were dirty—*Sapristi*, girl, don't cry! I know it is true! What did you do for the wife of this officer?"

88

"I was nurse to her little girl. Their name was Walker. It was just after my husband died. He was a sailor—an American. He was drowned."

"How old are you?"

She halted a moment, and then owned, "I am twenty."

Luigi Rossa stood up. He came over in front of her and she looked up at him with apprehensive eyes.

"When did you say you were ill?"

"Last summer. I had the fever."

He reached out and pulled a strand of her hair. When he saw its length he nodded quickly, as if in confirmation.

He said, "Is all that you have told me true?"

"Yes."

"What will you swear it by?"

Her eyes darted to the crucifix and the palms but she knew that was not what he meant. In her own heart there was no item of faith. She said finally, very low, "By my little boy."

Once again he nodded. "You will have seen," he remarked, "that I am not wholly an idiot."

She was silent.

"What did you mean when you said you would work for nothing?"

"I meant—just what I said."

"Then it must be you who are foolish."

Again she did not answer and there was silence.

Rossa said, "It will be best for us to make an experiment. Shall we say, you lend me your services—for a month? For that time I will house you and your small son. After then we can see. It will take at least so long to discover which of us stands the most in need."

That night she crooned over Rudi as she washed him and tucked him into bed, but she did not exult. More and more she was coming to feel that it was better to be steel-sure and very cautious rather than happy or gay. Now that she had begun again, that for the time being she was going to be safe, she intended never to forget that it was through no one's efforts but her own.

She made one quixotic gesture when, on leaving Molly Cannon, she tried to take Lizzie Bridie with her. It released a weird phenomenon. Molly was roused to tearful and indignant lament. Was she, who had been good to Lizzie all her days, to be left lonely in her old age? Was it not enough that Missus Brandt should desert her? Must she also entice away her one prop and stay? Lizzie, to whom she had been a mother. Lizzie, whom Missus Brandt had poisoned against her. "Don't I love 'er like me own child?" intoned Mrs. Cannon. "Didn't I bring 'er up ter be a good, obedient girl, an' teach 'er ter clear-starch better nor I can do it meself? But no, nah she's gotter up an' leave me. Not that I'd ever 'ave the 'eart ter blame my Liz. Hit's only along o' me bein' left so lone." She took a nip of gin. She wept and the tears chased down the wrinkles of her cheeks.

Lizzie was appalled. It had never occurred to her that she could be so precious in the light of anyone's eyes. It was useless for Kirstina to insist that Molly wept only for fear of losing her slave. Lizzie put her arms about the old harridan. She put her own lips to the bottle. And she stayed.

Kirstina, though she had tried her best, was glad to have failed. She wanted all that she had suffered at Mrs. Cannon's to be something else she could put behind her. She could not keep it from her nightmares but with no ever-present reminder it would at least not haunt her waking hours.

At the end of her first month, Rossa agreed to pay her a small salary. At the same time he said, "But I want you to understand that it is not necessary for you to work so hard. I often see you look more tired than is right."

The Milan House had originally been two adjoining houses built in the style typical of French Canada: stone, with two rows of windows under a high gabled roof and a row of dormers. Enormous chimneys at either end, with another in the middle where the two houses met, rose from cavernous fireplaces within. The stone was rough-cut and the walls twenty inches thick, with deep window embrasures; the interiors of the rooms were finished in tinted plaster. Rossa did not think much of it; to his Italian eye it was a primitive and clumsy mode of architecture and he could quite see why patrons should prefer the smarter, more modern appearance of Rasco's and Donegani's. But Kirstina found her new dwelling comfortably familiar. There was Italianate and French architecture in Denmark; there were palaces in Copenhagen built in the finest rococo style, but these were not common in North Jutland, where even the towns had preserved a medieval air. Kirstina did not know enough about such things to evaluate the Milan House, but she did know she liked it.

She liked, too, bringing it into order—even if, for the first half year, she worked harder than she ever had before. Her main difficulty at first was language, for the employees as a matter of course were

French or Italian. With the Italians, unless they had learned a little English or French (though one who had not was rare) she could have no contact through words. To the French she could by this time make herself understood, but she was often unable to understand more than half their reply. However, the French girls knew how to work when they had someone over them who knew how work should be done, and when all else failed Kirstina could always teach by example. She made beds and showed how springs should be dusted. She washed windows and starched curtains. She polished brass until she made the boy whose job that was appreciate how it should look, and she did the same by the patrons' boots. She had her staff of Italian waiters into the dining room between meal hours and made them practice, until they were ready to throttle her, the correct, English fashion of serving a meal—as she had heard Mary Walker explain it to her servants.

With Rossa's sanction, she gave all the employees a full two months to learn and adapt themselves to her ways. At the end of that time she dismissed those who either could not or would not comply. In this way she got rid of the old headwaiter, of a dishonest bartender, and an insolent and dirty chambermaid. The rest of her people stayed on, and on the whole they liked her. Under her direction they worked harder than they used to, but because their work was organized it took less time. The hours they were supposed to have free, they got.

The city as usual emptied in July, but not before the change in the hotel's management had been remarked and the clientele somewhat improved. Before the September influx, Kirstina persuaded Rossa to put up his prices. "They will not think they are getting as much," she said, "if you do not make them pay at least as highly as at Rasco's." Luigi shrugged as if she were more likely to know than he, and did as he was told. He was continually delighted at the way things were going. He had come to the point of letting Kirstina take over the books and he was always amazed when she made him look each month at the balance. "Never did I know I made so much!" he would exclaim. "Did I?" Then he would listen with gravity while she explained just how his profits were increasing— "It is not only that we are taking in more money, it is because now we do not waste anything."

When the new year came round he gave her an interest in the business. "I already owe you a lot of money," he said. "It is only justice for me to see that you benefit from your efforts." He did not tell her that what had pleased him most during this first year of their association was to watch her slow restoration as a pretty young woman.

Two years more brought them to the time when the Milan House was not infrequently referred to as the foremost hotel in the city. Rasco's day of glory was over—had been dimming, if they had only known it, when Kirstina and Luigi first formed their partnership. Donegani's was gone altogether, destroyed by fire one August night in '49. The Walkers, had they come back, would have found the city much changed, for '49 had also seen the mob setting the Parliament Buildings alight and so driving the gay, viceregal society away from Montreal forever. Only the military remained, but so long as there was a redcoat left to parade in the Champ de Mars there was likely to be custom for a house that offered good wine and food. Kirstina no longer needed to do much physical work; she supervised, she gave out stores and checked accounts. In her well-made gray dresses, with her hair braided into a crown, she presided at mealtimes at the cash desk in the dining room.

In the spring of 1852 a young man named James Collingwood arrived off one of the first ships of the year from England, and registered at the hotel. Like many young men staying alone he was attracted to Kirstina Brandt and she knew it, but was undisturbed. Experience had taught her that her genuine indifference was enough to secure her from really unwelcome attentions.

James Collingwood had not so far had much success with women, but since he was anxious to set this down to anything but his own deficiencies he usually told himself that it was because he had yet to meet one who embodied his conception of womanhood. From much reading, and dreaming about what he had read, he had evolved an image of the ideal woman as a sort of mother goddess, possessed of simple, natural beauty, fecundity, and the wisdom of all the ages. It was this image that, as soon as he saw Kirstina Brandt, he believed she might fulfill.

For three weeks he haunted the public rooms of the hotel. He chose a table in the dining room as near as possible to her desk and he sat there eating, with a copy of the *Illustrated London News* before his nose, lowering the paper whenever she passed by. He did not speak to her, but he listened to every word she said to anyone else.

Rossa noticed this and asked her if she were annoyed. Kirstina said, No, Mr. Collingwood did no harm and he paid his bills. Privately she thought him a little mad.

He had no particular business in Montreal and no friends, but he had an acquaintance among the officers of the 20th Regiment whom he saw fairly often. Young army men were not much in his line—they were interested in neither books nor theories, and he went about with Captain Charlie Jeffries in the spirit of one trying to make the best of a bad job and of proving that he was a good sport. Captain Charlie in turn thought him a queer duck and spoke of him to his friends as the poet who was moonstruck over Kitty Brandt. In the fourth week of James's stay, Charlie Jeffries came in for what he termed "a bit of a windfall"—a legacy from an ancient uncle who had died in England. Charlie held a celebration to which James Collingwood was invited and where he became a victim, for the celebration consisted largely of meat and drink, and James, though he had a reasonably strong head, had an extremely weak stomach to which he was ashamed to own. From infancy he had had gastric attacks which he had learned to avoid only by keeping to a rigidly plain diet. After Captain Jeffries's banquet, he returned to the hotel in the early hours knowing that he was in for a bout of agony.

It was infinitely worse than anything he had anticipated. He was disgustingly sick. The cramp and shooting pains in his stomach made him almost lose consciousness. He was sure he needed a doctor and he rang his bell in vain. Eventually he staggered out into the hallway and he was there discovered by the night porter, who at once called Mrs. Brandt.

Kirstina thought he looked almost as ill as he believed he was. She was ready to send for a doctor until she gathered that such attacks were usual. Then she shepherded him back to bed and did everything she could herself. She was imaginatively sympathetic, for the spasms of cramp he was having reminded her horribly of the beginning of her own cholera. She was not nauseated by his sickness. Because he shivered as much from cold as from pain, she had bricks heated for the bed. She gave him hot water to drink and she wrung out cold cloths in cologne to lay on his forehead. By the time the dawn was breaking she had succeeded in having him warm and soothed enough to fall asleep.

After he had wakened, around noon, she came in to see how he did, and when she had ascertained that he was better and feeling only tired and weak, she said in an admonishing tone, "If you know the things you should not eat, don't you think it would be less painful to avoid them?"

He twisted on his pillows like an irritated boy. "You don't know how tiresome it is when fellows expect you to take whatever they do."

"Perhaps I don't."

"Mrs. Brandt, I haven't said how grateful I am. Do you know, you make a damned fine nurse—I beg your pardon!"

"You need not. I appreciate what you mean. I was very ill once myself."

"You don't look as though you could be!"

She smiled without saying anything more and turned to go out of the door. A sudden twinge of fright made him call her back.

"Mrs. Brandt?"

"Yes?"

"If Captain Jeffries should call—you won't feel that you have to tell him?"

As if he had been Rudi, she shook her head with a look of kindly reassurance.

In retrospect, James found it a mortifying occurrence. It was not thus that goddesses should be wooed, and he burned with shame to think of the light he had been placed in. He was not perspicacious enough to guess that the way, which would have been closed before to any advance, was now open. Kirstina had ceased to think him mad, and she was sorry for him.

Even his appearance seemed to her pathetic. He was extremely thin and had he held himself erect he would have been over six feet in height. In profile his head was fine, with an aquiline nose and a sweep of dark hair from a pale forehead, but from the front his face was too narrow, and his mouth had a droop which suggested despondency as well as discontent. She thought he was about twenty-five or -six. Actually he was only two months short of thirty.

In the afternoons it was Kirstina's habit to take Rudi out walking. Usually she made her purchases first, and then, if the day were fine, she would make her way to one of the gardens in the public squares and let the child run about while she sat and watched. Sometimes she went to the Place Viger; other days she sat in the garden of the Place d'Armes, where there was a fountain. She was here some few days later, enjoying the spectacle of Rudi feeding the pigeons from

a little parcel of bread crumbs he had brought, when James Collingwood passed and raised his hat. She bowed and, after watching him
hesitate, smiled.

He came up to her at once and sat down beside her on the bench.
"This is a very pretty square," he said.

"Rudi likes it. We often come here."

"How old is he?"

"Five and a half."

"He is a fine little fellow."

Kirstina looked pleased. James asked her what he had long wanted
to know.

"Mrs. Brandt, am I right in supposing you are not English?"

"Quite right. I am a Dane."

"And you learned English from your husband? Excuse me, but I
have been wondering how you come to have no colonial accent."

"I learned to speak English from an Englishwoman."

"And you speak French also," pursued James.

"I took lessons in that after I came to the hotel. It was necessary."

"It must have been very hard for you to be left in the position of
having to earn your living."

"Very hard." And how little you know what that means! she
thought.

"Do you have any relatives in Canada?"

"No. I am afraid not."

For a few moments he was quiet and then he opened again with,
"I suppose you think I am English?"

"Why, yes. I do."

"I am not. I was born in Canada."

"Really?"

"Practically in the wilderness. Ten miles from Toronto."

"Is it long since you went away?"

"Nearly ten years."

The thought seemed to fill him with gloom. He leaned forward,
his elbows on his knees, staring fixedly at Rudi and the still un-
satiated pigeons.

Suddenly he straightened. "Mrs. Brandt, I haven't much to do
these days—" Merciful heaven, she thought, what a way to begin!
"I was wondering if . . . that is, whether you'd mind . . . perhaps
you wouldn't . . . That is, after . . . But I do admire you very much!
Would you like to bring the little chap for a drive one day?"

"Why, Mr. Collingwood, that would be delightful! Rudi and I will love to come."

"When?"

His abruptness made her swallow. "Well, in the afternoon. Tomorrow, perhaps?"

"Thank you. Mrs. Brandt, thank you very much. I'll see to ordering the carriage." He stood up, lifted his hat. "Thank you very much indeed."

She was relieved next afternoon to find that he handled the reins well. It was late in May, a very warm day with a cloudless sky. The trees were tender green and the road had finally reached a stage of firmness after the spring slush. Kirstina, in a smart braided pelisse and a gray straw bonnet, enjoyed bowling along, sitting high up with Rudi wedged in between her and their host. They were almost halfway along the Lachine Road before the axle broke.

She had a few seconds of panic as she clutched Rudi and was hurled sideways into the ditch. She was shaken and she supposed bruised and there was mud on her skirt and petticoat, but she was not otherwise injured. Rudi let out a wild shout of excitement and when he had landed on his mother pulled himself up pummeling her and laughing.

Mr. Collingwood was in despair. He scrambled from his collapsed carriage and hung over Kirstina, made as if he would feel for broken bones and then withdrew his hands in embarrassment and would not believe her when she said she was unhurt. In the midst of her annoyance—for she was annoyed—she felt constrained to comfort and assure him that she wanted him only to assist her out of the ditch. It occurred to her that no one but he could have managed to hire a carriage from a reputable livery stable and still have it prove defective.

Fortunately they were able to commandeer a cab returning empty to the city to carry them home. Their carriage was pushed a little farther off the road; the horse was hitched to and trotted along after the cab. The accident had been ridiculous rather than grave, but Mr. Collingwood would not have it so and was extravagant in blaming himself. "The little chap might have been killed!" he insisted. "You might have been seriously hurt! What a fool I was to suggest such a trip!"

"Nonsense, Mr. Collingwood. Such an accident might have happened to anyone. I hope you will be severe with the stables."

"Are you sure you are quite all right? No pain anywhere? Your ankle—your knee? Are you sure you didn't wrench yourself?"

He kept it up until they were at the door of the Milan House, by which time she was too bored to be amused any longer and made a final gesture only because she knew his suffering was genuine.

"Mr. Collingwood, will it convince you if I ask you to please hire another carriage tomorrow? If you accept the responsibility, I assure you I shall have no fears."

She was standing in the open doorway, extending her hand. He began to color.

"Mrs. Brandt, how good of you! Yes, of course, if you would like it—if you are sure you are not afraid—"

"That is enough," she said firmly. "I am not going to reassure you again."

The second expedition passed off without mishap. They went up Mount Royal. The weather was as fine and the day as auspicious as before. James did drive well; when she remarked on it he told her he had been taught to handle horses almost as soon as he could walk.

From then on he began to take her about a good deal—driving, to walk in the gardens, to see the occasional military parade. Luigi Rossa looked upon him with the gravest suspicion. More and more Luigi was inclined to treat Kirstina as if she were his daughter.

"What does he want with you?" he demanded. "Why hasn't he got a business?"

"I don't know."

"Hasn't he any family?"

"If he has he has never mentioned it."

"Then you can depend upon it he has, and probably a wife as well. Kirstina, child, don't have anything to do with him. His kind are better left alone."

Now that he had been assisted over the initial barriers, James was much less clumsy. He knew how to escort a lady; he could be an interesting companion. He talked of subjects that were entirely new to her and, though she did not always understand him, she liked to listen. He would take her up to Guilbaut's Botanic and Zoological Gardens at the corner of Sherbrooke and Bleury Streets, almost at the edge of town, and while they walked about the promenades and arbors he would tell her about the Botanical Gardens at Kew in England, and about the Regent's Park Zoo. Kirstina would listen very attentively, poke the tip of her parasol into a cage for a monkey to prod, and laugh. When they went there they usually had Rudi with them and they always finished up in one of the arbors eating Guilbaut's renowned ices.

Or he would take her alone to Julien's restaurant and there talk for hours about books she had not read, or quote from poets of whom she had never heard. She had started by pitying him; now she was inclined to like him, and she relied on his attendance far more than she realized.

During June, Montreal was very much alarmed by a great fire which started in a carpenter's shop on St. Peter Street and burned a whole area in the center of the city. At one point thirty buildings in three parallel lines were aflame at once. The military removed the sick from the Hôtel Dieu, the historic old hospital. It was a miracle that the loss of life was small.

The city was the perpetual victim of fires. Two years earlier nearly the whole of the Irish settlement of Griffintown had been destroyed. In the same year another blaze had started in a Craig Street livery stable and been carried eastward by a high wind until a hundred and fifty houses had been burnt.

Luigi Rossa, who was congenitally nervous about fire, said irritably that it was the people's own fault. There were no city laws about building. Fine stone dwellings were flanked with ramshackle wooden hovels. There were timber yards in the center of the urban section. What safety could one expect in a place where half the private houses were still built of wood? And what houses! Haphazardly erected, one story high with a garret; in winter overheated by stoves, in summer dried to tinder by the fierce sun.

A great many other persons who owned property were beginning to get restive and to demand that the city council lay restrictions on building and make provision for improving the water supply. At the beginning of July the council decided to act, and to start by putting down conduit pipes of larger caliber to distribute the water through the city. In preparation the largest water reservoir was drained. Early on the morning of Thursday, July 8, workmen began to dig to lay the pipes; at the same hour, in a house just east of St. Lawrence Main Street, a small fire started.

It was an attack at the city's heart, for St. Lawrence Main divided Montreal into two nearly equal parts.

The little fire burned briskly. It had wooden houses on which to feed in its infancy, and a strong westerly wind. The fire fighters were hampered by the poor flow of water, but still not much alarmed. No one remembered that directly in the path of the flames was a timber yard; when someone did remember it there was no time left in which to take down the piles of dry wood. Next after the timber yard the fire feinted towards the General Hospital, but that was saved through the efforts of volunteers who beat out patches of flame on the roof with blankets while the 20th Regiment stood ready to evacuate the sick if these measures were unavailing. The hospital stood in a large garden. About half past eleven the fire, blocked by the garden from going westward, turned south.

It was then that Luigi Rossa, who had been out marking the advance of the flames and smoke, returned to his hotel and told Kirstina Brandt to put together whatever she wished to save.

Kirstina looked at him aghast.

"If you don't want to believe me," said Luigi, "come up where you can see."

He led her to the top story. There, from a dormer window at the back, she saw the flames advancing unimpeded on a front hundreds of yards wide, with a tower of black smoke behind. She and Rossa where they stood were directly in its line.

In horror she could only mutter, "I must get Rudi."

"It may be stopped," said Rossa.

Kirstina looked at him as if she would laugh.

She collected Rudi from her room on the way down. Already the door of every room in the hotel stood open. Behind each were excited men and women hurrying to fill portmanteaus and carpetbags, shouting for a porter to help with their trunks. They cried to her as she went past, "Oh, Mrs. Brandt, isn't it dreadful?" "Mrs. Brandt, what do you think will happen?" *"Madame, il faut vous sauver!"*

She went downstairs and there she met Collingwood coming towards her. "Mrs. Brandt, you mustn't stay here. Tell me what I can help you take away?"

She said dully, "It is of no use. There is so little we are able to carry."

He made her accompany him back upstairs and disappeared into his room to fetch his two portmanteaus. When she realized he intended both these for her she expostulated and followed him into his room to see him pack away his initialed ivory toilet set, a few books and a couple of freshly laundered shirts.

"That will do," he said. "Now let us see after you."

In her own room she looked about her with a sensation of complete futility. So much that she had worked for was here, but no one thing was worth more than another.

"What shall I choose?"

"At least some clothes for yourself and Rudi. Aren't there any things you especially value?"

"No. I lost all those before."

Because he expected it of her, she opened drawers and took out some clothes for Rudi and all that was strictly needful for herself. While they were busy Rossa came in and said, "I am going to the bank. Have you any valuables there?"

"No. Only a little money."

"That will be all right. I've got the men taking out a few things from below—not that it will do any good. What misfortune! Didn't I always say it would happen?"

As he went out the smoke which they had been tasting in the air for some time suddenly got thick and uncomfortable and Rudi began to cough.

"Come on," said Collingwood. "I really think we should get out."

He picked up the two portmanteaus and stood waiting. Kirstina, who seemed capable of doing only as she was told, caught up her newest pelisse and bonnet and passed through the door. The hotel was emptying fast. A great deal of the furniture from the downstairs rooms was piled in the street outside and three of the waiters, laboring with admirable loyalty, were spreading the carpets over the pile. As they got them arranged they proceeded to throw bucketfuls of water over the whole, going back into the building each time to refill the buckets.

"But we could help with that!" exclaimed Kirstina.

She folded her pelisse about the bonnet and, leaving Rudi to guard both them and the portmanteaus, she and Collingwood went back into the building and made themselves a part of the chain of bucket slingers. The same scene was being enacted all up and down the street and continued for about an hour, until the sparks and burning flakes were falling thickly on the mounds of possessions in the street and the rear parts of most of the houses were taking fire and so putting the kitchen pumps out of commission.

When the water at their source failed, Collingwood came and took Kirstina's arm. "I don't think it is any more good," he said. "I think we had better go and see after the little fellow." He was alarmed when he saw her face with its look of dazed despair. She would have been unable to explain the emotions roused in her at being forced to labor so frantically in such an utterly useless pursuit.

As they came out again into the street they could see that the whole row in which the Milan House was situated was going. The roofs everywhere were showing patches of flame and smoke was already belching from some of the upper windows. The street however was wide, and householders on the south side still had hopes of preserving their property, for there they saw swarms of men up on the roofs with blankets and buckets, pouring water and beating out sparks wherever they fell. Kirstina, with Rudi pressed against her skirts and looking about him with wide, unafraid eyes, stared fixedly at every part of the scene, as if she wished it to be forever ingrained in her mind. She saw those who still worked to save some possessions; she saw a detachment of soldiers arrive to keep the people at a safe distance from the fire; she saw the first yellow tongues of flame flicker through the windows of the Milan House and round its gilded sign. It was only then, when large burning flakes were drifting down about them and the air was becoming painfully hot to breathe, that she consented to go.

Collingwood had commandeered a small handcart that had been part of the equipment of the hotel. Into this he put their portmanteaus, her pelisse and bonnet and his own coat; with Rudi on the top they made their way, traveling slowly eastward, before the flames. As they progressed, the streets gradually filled with a crowd of people, laden and traveling as they were. Some bore traces of fierce fighting with the fire; there were blackened faces and burned and bandaged hands. A few were driving wagons with horses nearly out of control and neighing from time to time in shrill terror.

They came at last into the open space of the Champ de Mars, where they stayed. The crowd gathered there was immense, and everywhere there were mountains of furniture and baggage. It was impossible to judge how much of the city was burning. The fire seemed to be to the west and to the north, but a column of smoke was also rising to the south, by the river. They heard that the Roman Catholic cathedral had gone, and the just-completed Bishop's Palace. They learned that the smoke to the south was from Sim's lumber yard, ignited half a mile away from the main blaze by a wind-blown spark. By five o'clock they thought it was nearly over. The fire had not continued south of the street where the Milan House had stood; it did not move farther eastward along St. Catherine Street. There was time for bitterness among those whose property had been the last to catch.

Then at six it broke out again and was blazing at the east end of Notre Dame, and suddenly the buildings just north of them were alight and immediately afterwards Dalhousie Square. It was worse than before. The sun went down west of Mount Royal; the sky was a mass of reddened smoke and the flames mounted toward it. The buildings that were burning now were all new—solid stone, the Hays House Hotel, four stories high with a theater behind it, everything of the city's finest and best. "It must be like the burning of London," said James Collingwood. His face was awed but glowing; he felt he was living history. Kirstina, unable to see beyond her own personal drama, sat in silence, hour after hour. She was neither horrified nor impressed; all she felt was desolation, and a nausea that was the forerunner of panic.

They had not seen Rossa since he had left them in the early afternoon but at about ten he appeared.

"You are very well known in this city," he told Kirstina. "At least six people told me I should find you here."

Though like everyone else he had been pushing his way through the crowds and smoke, Luigi still managed to look dapper; also, now that the fire he had always dreaded had come, he did not seem overwhelmed. He leaned over to where Rudi was peering at him from the handcart and pinched the child's cheek. "Still out of bed, young man?" he inquired. Rudi chuckled.

Kirstina was sitting on an upturned box. Luigi stood in front of her and rocked to and fro on his toes. "Well," he said at last, "this settles it. I shall go back to Milano."

She looked at him with blank eyes. Luigi turned to Collingwood. Then, realizing he was not going to get any response, he said, "I'll be back again if you don't move," and departed as quickly as he had come.

"He has always wanted to go back to Italy," said Kirstina. "I know it is for that he has been saving his money."

How much, she was trying to remember, had she saved? There was some, she knew, but it would not last very long. She said to herself, I must not think now. If I think now, God knows what I shall do! But it was not easy not to think; in the noise and confusion, with everyone staring at the flames, she was as much alone as if she were shut away in her room. I believed I was safe, she thought, I believed I had made us safe!

"If Signor Rossa goes back to Italy," James Collingwood asked suddenly, "what will you do?"

Oh God! Why did he have to ask? She said flatly, "I have no idea. Once before—before I came to him—I worked as a laundress."

"That is not true!"

"Yes, it is. I delivered laundry to Rossa's hotel in a handcart, very like this one here. You might have sent me your shirts."

There was no questioning her passionless voice. He was appalled, and at the same time oddly excited.

"But that could never happen to you again," he said.

"Why not? What do you know about what can happen to a woman left alone? It is better to take in washing than to starve."

"But you . . . I never dreamed . . . You should not have had to do that!"

His inability to comprehend suddenly bored her. In the fitful, unnatural light she shrugged her shoulders and would not speak.

James looked down at her and struggled with his confusion. Invariably he found any glimpse of reality shocking and tried to cover it with the mantle of his romanticism. Now he was stirred as he had very rarely been. All day he had been thrust into an unaccustomed role of action. He was aware that he had acquitted himself well, that he had taken and been able to hold the initiative.

He came round and stood in front of Kirstina as Luigi had done and he had wit enough not to speak until she turned her eyes on him.

"Mrs. Brandt," he said, "Christine—if you are so afraid of that, and you are going to be left alone again, wouldn't it be better to marry me?"

"You romantic fool!" she said.

He did not answer her; did not even, for once, look embarrassed.

She went on, "Do you think because I have aroused your pity that you could bear to have a wife who had done the things I have had to do? Gentlemen do not marry laundresses, Mr. Collingwood! And before that I was a servant in the house of an Englishman you might have had as a friend. If you had come to his house, I would have called you 'sir'!"

"I am not asking you to marry me because I am sorry for you! I admit that if so much hadn't happened today I might not be asking you just now. But you must know how I admire you. I have from the very first!" His voice became troubled, his words hurried and half coherent. "You are so beautiful . . . so fine and strong . . . I have made you my ideal. I love you. I have never loved anyone else. You do not know anything about me. If you don't marry me I might as well be dead. Doesn't it mean anything to you that I love you?"

She was impressed not so much by his words as by his manner. Never had he been so intense, or so wild. Sure neither of herself nor of him, she said, "I will not decide anything tonight. I am sorry if I misunderstood you. But you must realize that I do not feel as you do."

"That does not matter! I should love you if you hated me! I have never minded your being out of my reach. But now that you need me, you must be my wife!"

Rossa's coming back saved her from further importuning. "I have found you a room," he told Kirstina. He nodded to Collingwood. "You'd better come, too. If we can't do much we can at least sleep under a roof."

When they looked into the handcart they discovered that Rudi was soundly asleep.

Luigi led them to the house of some Italian friends, and though they were already crowded they gave Kirstina a room and fussed over her comfort. She wanted only to be left in quiet.

But after she had wakened in the morning and had had time to think, she was amazed at the disinterest she had shown. She had no idea of the extent of James Collingwood's resources, but he acted like a man of substance. If she was not able to think of her own advantage, what was she doing to neglect Rudi's?

About nine Collingwood knocked on her door. When she opened it she saw at once that wherever he had spent the night he had not slept. His eyes were circled with black and he looked ghastly pale and disheveled. He leaned against the wall by the door and said, "You must be kind to me. I need you so."

She was shocked at his appearance and shepherded him over to the window seat. She said then, while he sat staring up at her, "I think we need each other."

There was a moment in which he seemed to make sure of her meaning. Then he lifted his arms to clasp her and pressed his head

104

against her body below her breasts. His eyes were closed. She looked down and brought one hand to stroke his hair.

Luigi was very well pleased. He believed every woman was the better for a husband and he had no objections to Collingwood once he had declared himself. Luigi was also very anxious to see Kirstina provided for before he left Canada. Now that he had decided to go he was in a hurry, and maintained that he was overjoyed not to have to face the prospect of another glacial winter. He planned to wait until his claim for insurance was settled—though he was pessimistically certain the company would declare itself bankrupt—and then set sail.

Collingwood also had no reason to remain longer at Montreal. He did not explain now why he had lingered so long, but he did admit that he ought to have gone before, and he wanted to conclude his marriage quickly and set out for the home near Toronto which Kirstina had only once heard him mention.

They were married by the chaplain of Charlie Jeffries's regiment, the only clergyman in the city with whom James had an acquaintance.

Their wedding night was all that James had anticipated, but it left his wife in a strange state of unease. Long after he had fallen into final sleep she lay awake beside him. It seemed to her incredible that she could pass a second time through an experience and feel nothing the same. How was it possible to duplicate all the motions, perform the very act of love, and not be roused to warmth? She was glad if she was able to give James what he wanted—whatever that might be. But what would this bring to her?

She lay in the dark and for the first time in many months wrestled with the aching misery of unfulfillment. Her skin was hot with fever. As she pressed her cheek against the pillow she found herself whispering, "Michael . . ." Then she was shocked. Michael was dead; half a world away his body had gone down into the sea, and he had drowned. It was wrong that this knowledge should hurt her more desperately now.

I V

THEY began their journey to the West at once, taking the cars as far as Lachine and there embarking on the steam packet *Jenny Lind* for Ogdensburgh. The newly completed canal system sped the voyage considerably. At Cape Vincent they changed to the steamer *Champion* and continued through the night and next morning past Kingston, Cobourg and Oshawa, arriving finally at Toronto about midday.

Until then James had been in the best of spirits, enjoying Kirstina's pleasure in the voyage, and showing Rudi the workings of each successive ship. But as they sailed past the mole into Toronto Harbor he suddenly became moody and was uncertain how to proceed. Since there were only ten miles more to go Kirstina had naturally supposed these would be completed before nightfall, but James decided in the end that it would be better not to go farther that day and accordingly they put up at a hotel.

Through the evening James's unhappiness increased. In their room, after Rudi had been put to bed, he strode restlessly about, unable to say what distressed him but pausing every now and then to look at Kirstina as if it were mainly connected with her. At last he said with great effort, "There are things I should have told you."

"About your home?"

"Yes."

"You do not have to tell me. Tomorrow I shall be able to see for myself."

"But I should have told you." He repeated himself obstinately, getting no further.

She wanted to help, and asked, "You have some family?"

Again he said, "Yes." He thrust his hands down into his pockets. "My father is dead. My sister Margaret runs Prospect. You will not like her. There is no one else except my mother, who is—ill."

"Prospect is the house?"

"Yes—Prospect House. My father named it. It stands on a point above Port George."

"You sound as if you do not like it."

"I don't. I liked living in England. Prospect is wild—as the country is wild. But I could not stay away forever."

"No."

"And now—with you—it will not be so bad. Only promise me you won't be shocked."

"Why should I be?"

"I don't know . . ." He looked at her and in her composure found reassurance. She had been sitting on the overstuffed settee at the foot of the hotel bed, and he came now and sat beside her.

"It is a very big house," he said. "My father built it to make himself important. He was like that, and Margaret is like him. They have always said I take after my mother. Only the center part of the house is kept open. There are two servants, an English couple called Raikes. Don't ask if they have ever had children. They won't like you either."

"You mean they won't like having a new mistress?"

"Yes, that is it. It will be very uncomfortable for you. You will wish you had not married me."

He sounded so dejected that amusement overlaid her apprehensions, and she tried to comfort him. "You should not be afraid of that, James. Didn't I tell you that we needed each other? It is your home and you are offering to share it with me."

"I didn't warn you before, because I was afraid. That is also why I didn't ask you sooner to marry me. I wanted to make love to you—I wanted to be married to you—but I do not want to bring anyone to Prospect."

"James—you will be there to help me."

"It is I who will need help. Don't you understand? I hate the place!"

Remembering that he had left his home when he was twenty, and that for all his uncertainties he was now thirty years of age, Kirstina believed that once he had returned he would find he had outgrown whatever fears the place had once inspired. She told him this, and eventually persuaded him to stop worrying and to come to bed.

Next morning they went on board the clumsy stagecoach which ran through Port George on its way to towns farther west. The road lay partly alongside the lake, which, as the day was calm, had scarcely a ripple; at other times it passed through portions of forest in which at intervals there were the clearings and the log houses of newly arrived settlers. Presently they crossed a river which James said was the George. The wooden bridge was very narrow and at the far side the road turned left suddenly and dangerously. For another mile they wound beside the river, which gradually became wider. Then, where it opened into an estuary and harbor, the road ran into the village, the coach stopped and they were set down.

It was a settlement like many that they had seen along the lake shore as they passed in the steamboat. There was an inn where the coach had stopped; farther along were the saddler's and shoemaker's shops and a church built of stone, with a tall, simple wooden spire; opposite were the smithy and a few houses—the single street was neither long nor wide and became open road again beyond the last house. Where Port George differed from other such places was in its situation, which was singularly attractive. It was built on the low-lying ground at the point where the river emptied itself into a circular sheet of water over a mile wide. On either side the land rose toward the Great Lake beyond, and stood finally in two high bluffs guarding the exit from the symmetrical bay. In the sunlight Kirstina gazed about her entranced. Several sailing ships were anchored in the bay and she saw a long wharf where even steamboats might tie up.

James, who had passed into the inn, now reappeared to say that Hobart, the landlord, would lend them a rig to drive out in. Behind him came Mr. Hobart himself to shake Mrs. Collingwood's hand and to hope she would be happy. He was a large man with shrewd dark eyes as affable as his manner. Kirstina thanked him for his good wishes and said that she thought she had never seen a prettier place.

"Ah," said the landlord, "wait until you've seen the view from Prospect Point."

James was frowning and fidgeting with his hands. A boy came round with the rig—an affair on two wheels with a high-slung seat; Kirstina was helped up, Rudi and the baggage were lifted in, and James drove off.

"Which is Prospect Point?" she asked.

Her husband pointed with his whip to the bluff on the east side of the bay.

"Is the house up there?"

He nodded.

She thought she could see the outline of a roof above the trees, and became filled with excitement.

To cross the river again they did not have to go back to the bridge;

a ferry was run across its mouth—a raft slung on a rope cable and poled through the water. While they were on the raft James recovered his presence of mind. He mentioned several items of interest. The small shipyard belonged to a man named Munro. There were trout in the river. When he was a boy he had kept a boat on the beach and gone sailing in the bay.

The road climbed steeply up the far bank and turned to the right. After a while they came to the point where a pair of high stone pillars guarded the entrance to the Collingwood land. Just beyond on the right were the foundations of a small house never completed.

"My father was given a grant of a thousand acres," said James. "He wanted to make an estate. That was to have been the lodge."

"How much farther is the house?"

"Another mile."

Now the way lay wholly through forest. It was dark and cool. They drove in silence, the soft clopping of the horse's hoofs and the rattling of the wheels the only continuous sounds. Suddenly they came into the open again; rough grass grew on either hand and led on to an overgrown garden; the drive divided about an oval stretch of turf; beyond stood the house.

It would have been remarkable for size even in Montreal. The central block was two stories high; on either side stretched long, one-story wings; because the basement ran under the whole and was everywhere half above the ground, the house gave an illusion of more height than it actually owned. There was a low hipped roof from which rose four groups of chimneys. James had said that only part of the house was open, yet there were curtains at every window. Every window was shut. Nothing stirred, either within or without.

James laid aside the reins. He came to help her down and lifted Rudi. A flight of half-circular steps led up to the gallery. They went up and waited there while he rang the bell and then pushed open the door. Still there was no answering sound.

"Stay here a minute," said James, and disappeared inside.

Kirstina walked to the railing and looked out. She sensed the strangeness of the place; its grandeur set in such isolation; its stealthy quiet. Because of the trees she could not see the village nor even where the cliff edge must be. She thought, From the upper windows I will be able to see, or from the roof.

Footsteps were approaching. She turned and saw James coming out with a woman and saying, "Margaret, this is my wife, Christine."

She was almost as tall as himself, the sister; a dark woman with strongly marked, arrogant features.

They went inside to a vestibule and then to a hall lit by a tall window over the stairs on the far side of the house; midway the hall was crossed by a passage which presumably—though the way was blocked by doors—led to the side wings. In a small sitting room at the back and to the left of the hall there was some attempt at comfort; the room was lived in, yet the fine and delicate furniture was scratched and uncared for, the carpet was gray with ground-in dirt and the curtains were falling into holes. Margaret invited Kirstina to sit down and told James, "The Raikeses will be downstairs, if you look. Raikes will have to take back Hobart's trap and you can ask Mrs. Raikes to bring tea."

It was a casual way to treat him after an absence of ten years, but he passed no remark. For a little while Kirstina was alone with Margaret, who asked about her journey; then James came back and presently an elderly woman appeared with a tray and they had tea in cracked porcelain cups, poured from a silver teapot that was black with tarnish.

After tea they went through the rest of the lived-in portion of the house: the library, a room on the other side of the hall, corresponding in shape and position to that which they had just left and possessing a large collection of dust-laden books; a pair of small sitting rooms on either side of the front door, one of them arranged as a makeshift dining room. Then upstairs, the first door at the back, Margaret's room; in the front right corner, one that had used to be James's; one over the front door with a bow window and a little balcony. Then another room, a corner one like James's, before the door of which Margaret paused and said with a significant look at her brother, "Mother is just the same."

They went in. The room was again untidy and dirty. The two windows were draped in shreds of lace curtain, the four-posted bed the same. In a low chair by the empty grate sat a little woman with a delicate, unlined face. Her white hair was very clumsily dressed; her clothes were haphazardly chosen and put on. Her small hands were folded in her lap and, though she had turned her head toward them as they came in, her eyes were quite without understanding.

Margaret, paying no attention to this blankness, said, "Mother, James has come home," and James went forward and kissed the little woman's cheek.

110

"And James's wife, Mother. Her name is Christine."

The daughter's voice was exaggeratedly clear, as if by speaking so she might hope to reach that absent consciousness. Kirstina looked from her to the mother and to James standing behind the low chair. She could think of nothing to say.

Meanwhile the little woman's eyes had found a level in which something made them sparkle with life. She spoke in a high, light-timbred voice.

"Why, there is a little boy! What is your name, little boy?"

Kirstina glanced down at him, expecting he might be afraid to answer. But he was already saying without hesitation, "Rudi."

"And mine is Estelle. Tell me, do you like sweeties?"

She had forgotten anyone else was present. She spoke as if she and the boy were two children alone. Rudi nodded.

"I'll give you one," she said. She began to pull at her skirts until she found a silk reticule and felt within. There was nothing there; so her hands darted out to a small china box on a table. The box also was empty.

Appallingly then her eyes filled with tears. She looked up directly into Margaret's face and held out the empty box. "There aren't any left," she said sobbingly. "Someone took them all away. See, Margaret, I haven't any bonbons."

Margaret went and took the box. "You shall have some if you don't cry." Her voice was furiously cold; she turned to Kirstina and and went on, "This must be very distasteful to you. But James will have told you of Mother's unhappy condition."

Kirstina was instantly aware, first, that Margaret knew very well that James had not, and second, that she was glad to attribute this failure in him to cowardice.

"We will go," said Margaret.

Rudi, who had stood looking upon Estelle's tears with commiseration, said suddenly, "I have some sweets." It was true; James had bought them for him in Toronto. He thrust his hand into his pocket and drew out two fat, sticky lumps. "Here," he offered, "you can have one."

Estelle's sobbing halted. She examined his outstretched palm with care, chose one lump and stuck it in her cheek. Rudi took the other.

"Good-by," he said, "I have to go now."

He followed his mother cheerfully to the door, but turned there again and waved before he went out.

What rendered Kirstina far more uneasy than the mindlessness of her husband's mother was her instant recognition of the place's state of decay. It would have disturbed her less had James shown any distress over it but, even without his complete lack of surprise or indignation, she knew that the deterioration she saw was the mark of more than the ten years he had been away, of more than slovenliness on the part of those in charge. The house could not be more than thirty years old and almost from the moment it had been built it must have been allowed to rot. Dirt and carelessness had done their worst within, frost and snow without; the masonry had stood up well but patches of damp on the ceilings upstairs showed where the roof had failed and everywhere outside the paint was cracked and peeling. The wooden guttering had broken away and caused long water stains on the walls.

At the back, in what had once been a planned garden, there was a wild tangle of flowers and rose briars; the weeds grew as high in the paths as on what had been lawn. One small patch was cultivated to grow vegetables and a small field beyond was planted with potatoes. There was an orchard where those trees that were still living were full of dead wood, and a rough pasture where a horse and two cows stood grazing.

There was no stable large enough to match the pretensions of the house, but as they approached the small wooden barn James pointed out to her that it stood within the foundations of an earlier structure. "The first one burned," said Margaret, "and all the pedigreed stock burned with it, and my father's thoroughbreds and carriages." In the new little barn there was space for only a pony trap and a sleigh and very few animals; chickens ran about on the earth floor and in a pen outside were two thin and ill-tempered pigs.

Almost a quarter of a mile away, on the tip of Prospect Point itself, was a little summerhouse. It was delicate and pretty, with grooved, wooden pillars weathered to a soft gray. The path to it led now in the clear, now through woods, in some places so close to the edge of the cliff that it was possible to look down almost directly upon the waters of the bay below. The drop was not sheer; small bushes and even a few pine trees clung to its surface, but Kirstina disliked heights and the rustic handrail which had been built for protection was now crumbling away. Only when she had arrived and seen the views from the summerhouse, both across the bay and to the village, and out over Lake Ontario itself, did she feel it had been worth coming.

112

At length they went back to the house and ate supper in the small room at the front. Margaret sat down at the foot of the table, facing her brother, so that Kirstina sat in the place of a guest. At the meal she saw the man Raikes. He waited on them in a black coat which in the lamplight had a tinge of green. In these surroundings his air of austere dignity was comic but not unpleasant, and he would appear to be more capable than his wife, if one could judge by the cookery, for which presumably she was responsible. The soup they were served had little taste; the pork swam in grease; the potatoes were a glutinous gray mass; the dessert when it came was leaden. Kirstina and James, who had had no midday dinner, were hungry and ate what they could. Rudi followed suit. Margaret only picked at her plate.

It was taken for granted by everyone that Kirstina would occupy the center bedroom in front, the one with the bow window. The bed had been made up there, and the one in James's old room next door for Rudi. Kirstina took the little boy upstairs almost immediately after supper and when he was in bed undressed herself and finished unpacking and putting away the few things she had with her—all that she had bought since the fire. Somewhere downstairs she knew James was talking with Margaret and she hoped when he came up he would not be worn out, for now there were things she herself had to find out before she could sleep.

When at last he knocked and came into her room she was standing by the open doors that led onto the balcony and she asked him without turning round, "James, do you suppose we could have enough trees cut so that I could see the village? It would be so pretty."

He came across the room behind her and placed his hands on her shoulders. "Does that mean," he said, "that you feel you will be able to bear it here?"

She knew that though, since it was not strange to him, he could have no real idea of the impression Prospect had made upon her, still he was afraid to learn what she thought. She leaned back and turned her face up to let him kiss her before she spoke again. "Now that I have seen it, there is so much I want to ask."

"I should have told you about my mother."

"She has not always been like that?"

"Oh no! Only since my father died. You need not be afraid, you know. She would not hurt anyone."

She thought of Estelle lying in her bed next door, her tiny figure and girlish voice, her immature face, and she said on a note of surprise, "No, I could not possibly be afraid of her."

"Christine, you are so charitable! I believe, with you here, things will be better. I have told Margaret that of course tomorrow you will sit opposite me at table."

"If you wish."

"But of course you must!" He left her side and began walking about the room, very much as he had the night before at the hotel. "I want you to have everything you should have. Naturally my wife is mistress of the house even if Margaret has been cock of the hoop for the past twenty years! She must get used to it. Kate would have made her step aside."

"Kate?"

"The cousin to whom I was engaged to be married in England. She married someone else. Don't imagine I am sorry! I wasn't then and I certainly am not now. But it is not as if Margaret were not expecting me to bring home a bride."

"I see." While he was speaking she had walked quietly over to the bed and seated herself upon it. "James?"

"Yes?"

"Why is the place in such a state of . . . neglect? It must have taken a fortune to build and now it isn't even in good repair."

"I know."

"Well, why?"

"Because we haven't the money."

The leap in her suppressed fears made her titter. "Don't be ridiculous, my dear! You know how I have seen you spend money."

"While I had it."

Again the chill rise in fear.

"What do you mean?"

He came up to the bed, so that he stood beside her. "We have never had any money, Christine. My father used my mother's fortune to build this house. The last of her money was lost the night he died. After that we had only this estate, and the only thing of value on it was the stock, which burned—as Margaret told you today. Fortunately, my father's sister in England had married a wealthy man who when he heard what had happened made us a yearly allowance. When he died he left us enough principal to continue it. It isn't very much—about eighty pounds a year divided between Margaret and me. I don't think he wanted to provide it at all but his wife made him. It was her idea that I should marry her daughter Kate, who has the rest of her father's money."

Still struggling to keep the issue clear, Kirstina said, "But when you were in Montreal—"

"While I was in England—I lived there at my aunt's expense—another cousin died and left me a small legacy. It was just enough to keep me one more year away from home. Even without the fire I could not have stayed any longer at Montreal."

"How much have you left now?"

The concrete demand made him look blank. Then he stuck his right hand into his pocket and drew out a purse. It was an absurd gesture. She had seen the purse open earlier that day and knew that among the few coins it held, only one was gold.

Kirstina began to laugh. She stared up into his face, saw its bewilderment, and lost all control. She laughed and laughed, her mouth taut and wide, her eyes open and very bright.

James thrust the purse back into his pocket and seized her arms. He had no idea what caused her hysteria but he was obsessed with the dread that she was laughing at him. He cried out, "Christine! Christine! Why do you laugh?"

The note of panic in his voice reached her. Her laughter stopped while her mouth was still open. Her eyes met his only a foot away from her own. Her body lost its tenseness. As he let her go she shuddered and sat hunched and silent.

In her mind the bitter laughter remained. No matter where she went to hide herself, there her own peculiar devil found her out. Because in the beginning she had thrown away what was hers, was she never to have any part of it back?

"Christine—please, Christine—will you tell me why you laughed?"

"I must be very tired, James, or I would not have. I think it was because I am not afraid of your devils, and you would not understand mine."

In the early hours of the morning, James awoke with a painful gastric attack. It was nothing comparable to the one she had seen him in before, but still distressing. Not being in her own place she did not know where to look for anything to relieve him and he would not let her wake his sister. "She thinks I've grown out of it," he gasped and held onto his wife lest she should leave him. Remembering the appalling meal he had eaten, Kirstina thought indignantly that it was probably the long succession of such feeding, combined with nervous excitement, that had caused or at least encouraged his weakness. She felt no contempt, but was pitifully reassuring when he became easier and asked, "Christine, do you suppose you will be able to see that I get food I can eat?"

The first thing she embarked upon was the cleaning of the part of the house that they used. She started on her own room and when James came in and found her down on her knees with a bucket of water, her arms covered with soapsuds, he was horrified. She sat back on her heels and laughed at him.

"Dear James, you are going to have to get used to seeing me working!"

"Yes, but not like this! Let Mrs. Raikes do it."

"She was here. I sent her down to the kitchen." She paused, looked down and traced a circle on the wet floor with one forefinger. "James?"

"Yes?"

"Would it be possible to send the Raikeses off?"

"You don't like them?"

"I don't like her."

"The trouble is," he said, "that I doubt if we could get anyone else. We pay them very little, you know. And in some ways they have not been so bad. My father brought them out from England and they were the only ones who stayed with us after he was gone. Raikes was his valet and Mrs. Raikes was my mother's maid, but they have done everything for us here ever since. And . . . there are other reasons also why I think we could hardly get rid of them."

"I see."

"Are you very disappointed?"

"No. I expected you would say something of the kind."

"If Mrs. Raikes is insolent or won't do as you ask her, I'll have Raikes speak to her."

"No," she said again. "It will be all right. I would not choose to work with someone who dislikes me, but I can manage."

Everything was as dirty as her first impression had led her to expect, and her standards of cleanliness were high. Curtains that could not be made clean or mended were burned; carpets that were stiff with dirt were taken out of doors and scrubbed there by Raikes; chandeliers were washed; ceilings were swept free of cobwebs, wallpapers sponged over and floors, after they had been scrubbed, were polished. Mrs. Raikes found herself making unheard of quantities of soap and beeswax cream. The fervor of cleanliness swept James into its wake and he himself took down and wiped off every book in the library. Rudi thoroughly enjoyed it all and so did Estelle, who sat exclaiming with wonder while her own room was put to rights, and thereafter wandered about with a duster or brush in her hand and was occasionally given tasks she was able to manage. Only Margaret took no part; she would inquire with a thin smile how they were getting on, and disappear into the garden.

Because of Mrs. Raikes's abominable cookery Kirstina had feared that she herself would have to undertake the work of the kitchen, and it was with relief she discovered that the woman could produce decent meals when she was forced. The one thing she dreaded was an invasion of her own quarters below—for she and Raikes lived in the basement, where the kitchen, pantries and supply rooms were. Once Kirstina had been down there, and made it plain that unless the food improved she herself would take permanent charge, Mrs. Raikes changed her ways. The best she produced would still make anyone who had eaten at Rossa's hotel wince, but at least she condescended to do her best.

Finally the orgy of cleansing was over and the light had been let in. It shone through the sparkling, freshly curtained windows and struck glints from the lovely pieces of furniture in the house, from shield-backed and Chippendale chairs, from inlaid cabinets, little tables of marquetry and elegant settees. Kirstina knew little of their value; what she had hated was the waste and neglect. A spinet, stored away in the ballroom in the right wing, had become warped with damp and was badly out of pitch, but when they had brought it into the sitting room they used, James undertook to tune it. Kirstina could not play it, and Margaret, if she could, had no intention of trying. However, one morning Kirstina heard a little tinkling melody and discovered Estelle playing the notes of a well-remembered piece with the earnestness of a good child.

Soon after his arrival, James had received his and Margaret's half-yearly income. Already Kirstina understood what he had meant when in Toronto he complained to her that he could not have remained away forever. Nowhere but at Prospect could he have lived on such a pittance—let alone have supported his household—and so it was here that he was compelled to stay. At Prospect a roof was provided, and his few pounds sufficed for what had to be paid for in cash; they had enough animals and vegetables for food, enough wood for fires.

James had no thought of struggling to better his condition. He and his sister were alike in their belief that however little money they might have it behooved them as gentry to live on it without suffering the indignity of labor. Kirstina's conviction was that any situation could be improved by hard work. In those early days she was too busy and confident to argue, or to mind the complacency with which they enjoyed the comfort she worked to provide, but she was steadily learning that whatever she was to gain from her new life would have to be of her own making.

In September she knew she was to have another baby. James was overjoyed and touchingly grateful. Kirstina, though glad that he was pleased, felt that just at present she had no time for such a hindrance. Irritation at her coming disability chafed her, and she worried James with her questions and plans for the future.

"Is the timber on the estate of any value?" she asked.

He said unhesitatingly, "Yes."

"For what?"

"Principally for shipbuilding. There's a good deal of white oak— nothing is better than that for ocean ships."

"Then if we sold it we might make a lot of money?"

"We might."

"Well, why don't we?"

"You can't sell timber standing—at least not in this part of the world. We should have to cut it and get it out ourselves, and we have neither the labor nor the teams."

"But if we did it a little at a time?"

"Christine, how many trees do you imagine Raikes could cut alone?"

"I meant if we got men from the village?"

"Laborers are expensive; we should have to pay them at least five shillings a day. And we couldn't get them. There isn't a man in Port George willing to hire out—they have all got their own places. And in the winter they go to cut wood in the wilderness where they know they can make their own profit."

"I see."

"Don't imagine I haven't made all these inquiries before, Christine. I have gone over them again and again. There is no way out."

She was horrified when, as the weather turned cold, he sent the two cows to be slaughtered for meat.

"But, James! We need the milk."

118

"I know, dear. But we haven't enough feed for them through the winter."

She thought back to all the uncut grass turning brown and withered around the house and said, "But we could have had!"

"How do you mean?"

"Look at all the hay we could have cut! And we could grow turnips and grain."

Tolerantly he asked, "Who is going to do it? There is only Raikes, you know."

"James, when one hasn't enough servants to do things, one has to do them oneself."

"Not if one doesn't know how." He said it with great good humor. "You may know how to plow and sow, my darling, but I'm afraid I never learned."

"It is not too late. No, James, don't laugh! I am in earnest. On my stepfather's farm in Denmark, where I grew up, we kept our cattle alive through as long a winter as we have here. And though the land was poor, everyone worked. Why can't we at least try to make full use of what we have?"

"Christine, I am not joking. If you can think of any way to improve our situation I shall be glad and not hinder you, but don't imagine I shall ever be of any use working in the fields. It isn't what I was brought up to."

She felt suddenly that his lethargy was too inherent for her to combat. Temporarily she gave up. James bought a pair of goats to provide milk for the household through the winter months.

At the southeast corner of the property, along the cliff above the lake, there was the suggestion of a path that led off into the bush. Kirstina found it one afternoon late in the year, when the leaves on the trees had finished changing color and were growing thin. She walked some distance, with the sun filtering through upon her back, avoiding the half-wakened memory of a woods outside Boston. Suddenly the trees came to an end and she found herself out in the open again and looked down across two cleared fields to a house and outbuildings in the hollow beyond.

She was very much surprised. She had not known nor ever heard speak of a property adjoining Prospect. This house, moreover, was a big one—not comparable in size to Prospect, but built of the same stone and larger than any other she had seen in the neighborhood.

119

She wondered how it was reached and supposed there must be a fork which she had not noticed in the road from the village. She would have liked to go on to satisfy her curiosity, but, suspecting she was trespassing already, she turned home instead.

At dinner later she mentioned her discovery, and said, "I had no idea there was another house so near. James, you should have told me."

She was aware immediately that she had caused offense. She kept her eyes on her husband but it was Margaret Collingwood who answered, "That is Murray Fraser's place. I say his name this once since you have asked, Christine, but you must understand that we do not speak of him in this house."

James said nothing at all. Furious anger struggled in Kirstina. This sort of thing had happened before. James, who with difficulty could be made to discuss the future of his estate, nearly always refused point-blank to discuss its past. On this occasion both Rudi and Estelle were present and she held her peace, but as soon as the meal was over she went after James, protesting, "You cannot expect to treat me like a child! What is the matter with this man? Is he a criminal?"

"No, Christine. It is a private matter. Some years ago he offered my sister a deadly insult. We have never spoken his name since."

She stared at him. "Is that all?"

"Isn't it enough? My father would have killed him."

"James, is this your judgment, or Margaret's?"

"In this we think alike. And believe me, now that you have heard, it will be wisest for you to do as we do and forget the whole matter. If I had thought of it in time, I would have warned you."

No doubt she could have insisted and dragged from him piecemeal all she wanted to know, but she did not really understand him and she was apprehensive of what she might discover. Both James and Margaret reveled in the petty mysteries they created about themselves.

Inevitably, Kirstina began to find the restricted life she was leading distasteful as well as foreign. She had come to it straight from the management of Rossa's hotel, and at Rossa's she had each day seen twenty or more new faces, had been in touch with a hundred or so different minds. Never had one day duplicated the last, never had she been able to foretell exactly what would be in the next. Since James did not care to drive her about, the necessity of seeing something more than the house and its clearing made her begin to drive out herself. Sometimes she took Rudi, sometimes she went alone. She had not driven since she was on her stepfather's farm, but she loved holding the reins and was moderately skillful. When she went through the village she smiled on everyone she met, and would have welcomed an opportunity to stop and talk. But the people were shy of her—shy of anyone or anything to do with the Collingwoods—and she herself felt ill at ease and unnatural: neither kin to the family at Prospect nor to the townsfolk of Port George. She was completely strange and alone; a word or two with the landlord at the inn, or with the parish vicar, was the most she was able to accomplish.

Once the snow had come, she drove herself in the sleigh and, because she liked it best, very often at night. James remonstrated with her; he thought she should be taking more care of herself; also, since he did not enjoy going out in the cold, he could not understand how she might. Kirstina, wrapped in a buffalo robe, with a fur hood and thick mittens, did not feel the cold at all; she loved to see the white smoke of the horse's breath and her own on the frosty air, to hear the sound of the bells and the muffled thudding of the hoofs in the snow. It was exciting to drive fast in the darkness under the stars, or through the streaks of black shadow on a moonlight night.

On just such a night in January, clear and white and without a wind, she had an adventure. She had driven to the village and had crossed over the ice on the frozen river on her way home. As she came up the slope beyond and turned into the road again, she met a man standing in a patch of brilliant white light and singing towards the moon.

> Wi' a hundred pipers and a', an' a',
> Wi' a hundred pipers and a', an' a',
> We'll up and gi'e 'em a blaw, a blaw
> Wi' a hundred pipers an' a', an' a'.
> Oh, it's o'er the border awa', awa',
> It's o'er the border awa', awa',
> We'll up and we'll follow to Carlisle ha'
> Wi' its yetts and castles an' a', an' a'.

He was in the middle of the road; she could not force her way past and she had to stop. He had a strong, rich voice. As he sang he marked time with sweeps of his left hand, which held some object she could not identify, and he was magnificently unaware that he presented a picture in any way out of the ordinary. He turned round with a flourish and made her a sweeping bow. Then she saw that what he held was a flask. He lifted it and drank.

Her horse's head was on a level with him. As he took the flask from his lips he flung his right arm over the animal's neck and asked her, "Do I know you?"

She could not be alarmed; rather, she was curious. She said, "Do you think that likely when I do not know you?"

Still looking at her he despondently shook his head. "It is a pity. If I knew you I would let you drive me home."

"How far might that be?"

"Farther than I care to walk in my present state— And, mind you, I am no' drunk."

"I did not say I thought you were."

He considered her. "That is true. Another woman might, but you did not. I am sorry I do not know you." With his bright eyes examining her face, he took another drink.

A suspicion crossed her mind and at once became certainty. "Are you Murray Fraser?"

"Ma'am, at your service." He drew himself upright, made her another and more formal bow. "May I have the honor—?"

"I am James Collingwood's wife."

"Ah—!" It was a long-drawn sigh of understanding. With no more ado he stepped back out of her road. "Then pass, friend, and do not say I kept you."

She saw then that he was actually as far from being drunk as he had claimed. He stood quite steadily and while she watched he felt in his pocket for the cap of his flask and screwed it on with ease. He was a very big man, tall and broad in proportion to his height. He had a large, handsome head and a crest of thick, graying hair.

When she had finished her examination and still did not move he looked up again and met her eye. Deliberately she said, "I will drive you home if you will tell me the things I want to know."

After they had set off together he had to prompt her to begin. "Come on now. As I judge it you're as ready to be frank as I am, and it will not hurt either of us to say what we think."

"What was it you did to insult Margaret Collingwood?"

She looked full at him as she asked; he seemed amused and then immediately thoughtful.

"Is that how they put it to you? Well—I suppose they might. I will

122

tell you the whole and you can decide for yourself. In the beginning I wanted to marry her—that was long before there was any question of insult. Margaret was nineteen and I was going on twenty-five. She was never beautiful, but she was exciting—more like a reckless, temperamental boy than like a girl. I used to think how I would marry her and then beat her, and I was sure she would be a better woman thereafter. I am still inclined to believe that.

"But when I proposed to her, Margaret was good enough to ask me who I thought I was, and threatened to appeal to her father. That I didn't want—not that I was exactly afraid, but if ever a man rode a devil all his life that man was Edward Collingwood and I preferred to keep out of his way. My sorrow! but I was angry with Margaret! She looked at me as if I were her groom, while in honest truth there was nothing to choose between us. My father came out in the same year as Edward Collingwood; they built their driveways with the same labor and got their stone from the same quarry. My property— and it was my own even then, for my father had died—stands acre for acre with Prospect.

"Obstinacy would not let me give up and year after year I went on farming my place and riding over to Prospect and after a while Margaret, though she wouldn't marry me, made me welcome. After her father was gone, I asked her again. Heaven knows why save that all their other friends melted like snow and I had to prove that it was not only the money and consequence that had counted with me. I would still have taken her if she had been willing, and a good shaking and a pack of children might have rid her of the notion that she was different from other women. But Margaret would not listen to me then any more than she had done before. So at last I stopped wasting my time and I up and married her maid."

Kirstina beside him gave a little gasp. He repeated emphatically, "That is the truth of it. I married her maid—Ellen Raikes. You will have met her parents."

She suddenly recalled James's voice: "Don't ask if they have had children." She began to laugh.

Murray Fraser said, "I have never regretted it an instant. A prettier, rounder, more comfortable creature than my Ellen you couldn't find. We have four sons and we're very much content, for all that Margaret got poor James to forbid us his house."

Kirstina rocked with helpless mirth. "Oh," she gasped, "how could you?"

"It was no trouble at all. I did it to please myself. And, believe me, with no thought of insult."

"No, of course not—of course not! But why couldn't James have told me?"

"Och, puir Jamie! You must not expect too much sense from him."

She said more seriously, "What of your wife's parents? What did they do?"

"Her mother was as angry as Miss Margaret. She said my Ellen did not know her place. That, mind you, in this free country! But Ellen misses her father."

"Has she not seen him since?"

"Once in a while. The old man is fond of our boys. I am always expecting him to escape for good one day and come to stay."

The story filled her mind, so that she was scarcely prepared to answer when he asked, "And how do you find yourself at Prospect?"

"I am—well enough."

"Puzzled?"

"A little less so now."

"They are a queer lot, you know. The father was someone not lightly forgotten."

"How did he die?"

He stared at her. "Have they not even told you that? He was killed. He had a high perch phaeton he imported from England, not the thing for our roads, ever, and he always drove himself too fast. So one night he drove out from Toronto and the thing overturned on the bridge across the George and pitched him into the river. He smashed his skull on the rocks."

Kirstina sighed with the relief of knowing. "And Estelle lost her mind," she said.

"She had every reason. It was 1837—the year we had our rebellion. You will not have heard about that and it came to nothing, but it was a big thing at the time, with a pack of rebels gathering to march on Toronto and everyone in a fever of fright. Edward Collingwood was in town. He had no liking for revolutions and no faith in the militia's ability to protect his property; so he drew all his gold out of the bank and packed it away in his strongbox on the phaeton to drive it home. Instead, he went into the river and, so far as I know, the strongbox went in after him. No one even knew of its existence until young James went in to see the bank."

"But—how is that possible?"

"Och, how should I know? The thing has been argued up and down Port George these sixteen years. Collingwood's horses came tearing into the village after midnight, with shreds of the English carriage dragging behind. I was there at Hobart's inn—we all turned out and followed up the road to the bridge and some of us climbed down and got the body. It was dark, and the night before a rebellion—we had been drinking and arguing about our rights and our liberties. We were shocked to see Collingwood dead, but if we thought anything much it was that he had come by his just deserts, and not one of noticed a box, nor any glimpse of a gold coin. Or perhaps there was someone soberer than the rest who did notice and went back later. Or, if the box fell into the deeper water, it may have floated clear out to the bay."

Another box of treasure, she was thinking. Another heritage gone astray.

"What is certain," pursued Murray, "is that there was none of the money left. And Margaret was like a wild thing, accusing us all of murdering her father and stealing his gold. We were sorry for her at first. Then there was Jamie, white and shaking with fright at the suddenness and terror of it all, and at Margaret, and even at the specter of his own freedom. Estelle was wise, puir thing, to let herself run mad."

"I see."

"I doubt if you do. It is a crazy story. It could not happen to reasonable people, like you and me. And the Collingwoods know it is crazy and hide it away. They are all of one blood, you know—the father and mother were cousins."

The horse was plodding along. They heard the soft stepping of his feet, the creak and jingle of harness and bells, and they half listened while they thought. Murry said, "Did you find the place falling to bits?"

"It seemed so."

"The land is as good as any you'll find from here to Toronto. Even today the timber is worth a pretty penny. You could make changes if you wished."

"I!" she exclaimed, her voice suddenly hard with scorn and surprise. "I am more than helpless, Mr. Fraser! Will you tell me what is the use of pricing timber you can't cut? And I can't sow even the land that is cleared!"

"Did I say that was for you to do?"

"Who else will do it at Prospect? There is Raikes, Mr. Fraser, who is your sons' grandfather. And there is James."

"There are those whom you might ask for help."

"Are there? Listen. If I were to fetch you in to bring order to Prospect, James would no more forgive me than would Margaret."

"Well?"

"I am his wife."

"And I am his friend. Yes, I was always that—or I would not now be trying to offer him help through you. He was fond of me when he was a wretched, white-faced little lad, and Lord! he needed someone to fight his battles for him then!"

In their progress they had come to the fork in the road. As she started to turn down to his place he caught her hands and the reins and pulled to a stop.

"No, I will walk the rest of the way alone. But I want you to let me speak. It is not fair to expect too much of James Collingwood. He was a weak, unhappy boy and, as I judge, must be weak still and happy only in having found a woman such as yourself for his wife. James uses his pride as other men use backbone. He will let his house rot and fall about his ears sooner than lift a hand to hold it together. But you might persuade him to accept help from me."

"No," she said. "He would hate me for it. I want to have peace and I will not make trouble."

"Will you sit and do nothing to cure the trouble there is already?"

"I will do everything I can do alone."

"Then you will do nothing."

"That is not my habit."

Looking at the firm, stubborn line of her mouth he shook his head. "You have notions of pride yourself."

"Like James, I have had need of them."

"Before long, you will be ready either to throw them overboard—or, to leave Prospect."

She watched him climb out of the sleigh and thought what a relief it had been to talk with a man whose strength was his own. She gave him her hand and said, "I am sorry we can't be friends."

She did not meet him again, nor see him as she passed through the village. When the snow began to melt she was forced to give up her lonely drives. She was carrying this second child as easily as she had Rudi, but as she grew heavier she found that her daily routine about the house was enough to make her tired and by nightfall she was glad to sleep. Margaret and Mrs. Raikes were contemptuous of her good health and James more than a little puzzled. To him, as to the two women, it was the part of a lady to be ailing from the moment of a baby's conception until a month after its birth, and he would have understood her far better if she had reclined every day upon her sofa.

Several times as the spring advanced she made her way through the path in the woods and looked down across Murray Fraser's farm. Once she saw Raikes there when he was supposed to be on an errand in Port George. It was not yet time for planting and sowing, but some of the earth was being turned, and the sight of the well-marked, neatly fenced fields roused her envy. Murray had had some more trees felled through the winter—not enough to sell, for the wood was being sawed into lengths for his own use—but the space where it had been cut, already partly cleared of stumps, would be rough pasture this year and cultivated field the next. To turn back from the contemplation of Fraser's progress to the unkempt desolation of Prospect was bitter pain. She ached with her longing to accomplish all that lay at her hand, and with only a little more help than she had so much would have been possible.

In April one morning she came down and found that Raikes had gone. For several weeks he had been on increasingly bad terms with his wife; apparently at length loyalty and patience had snapped together. She knew quite well where he had taken refuge; it amused her to see that so did his wife and Margaret and James. Their conscious airs and silence were absurd. But Raikes's departure was disaster for herself. He, at least, had been willing; while he was there she had not needed to go and see if the ground he had said he was going to dig was dug, if the wood was chopped, the animals watered and the goats milked. Now these and a hundred other tasks she had either to supervise or do herself. Some she could teach Rudi to do, some thrust upon Mrs. Raikes. Inevitably the time came when she hardened her heart and said, "I am sorry, James, but you will have to chop the wood for the fires."

He was in the library, and she knew that if the ceiling had descended upon his head he could not have been more astonished.

She explained, "I really can't, and Mrs. Raikes has too much to do."

"But I never have!"

"I know, dear, but you have always had Raikes before. You must have seen him do it often enough."

When he saw that there was nothing else for it, he said he would try. And then she had nearly as much work in showing him how it was done as she would have had in doing it herself.

Raikes did not come back. James continued to chop wood. He also, when it was necessary, harnessed the horse. He had no notion how to groom the animal but he did it, under Kirstina's direction, with a very bad grace. She realized that he held her responsible for anything he was thus forced to do. She, and not necessity, was blamed, and she knew it would have been useless to argue the point with him even if she had had time to waste in argument. She drove James because she had to, but she also worked patiently and steadily herself and kept it up all month. Then she could do no more, and utterly worn out she took to her bed and slept. Early next morning James Collingwood's son was born.

He was a small and handsome baby. His hair, which was unusually profuse, was much darker than James's—almost black; it clung to his head in close, round waves. He had a high color, but was not a florid red. Even his features were neat and well-defined, and his hands, with long fingers, had an air of elegance.

Margaret Collingwood, when she came in to view him, lost her smile of condescension and turned pale. She bent over the cradle and exclaimed, "Oh God! It is my father over again!"

James, who had been watching proudly from Kirstina's bedside, started, and went to stare at the child.

"Nonsense! You are thinking only of the coloring."

"It is my father," insisted Margaret. "Look at his hands—and the flat, small ears."

It was curious. Ridiculous of course to see a strong likeness in a baby only a few hours old, but James was made uneasy.

"You will call him Edward," said Margaret, as if it were asserted fact.

Her brother shuddered. "No! Anything but that."

They called him Geoffrey. It was a name long in the family and Margaret had to be content. From the start she regarded her nephew as her own peculiar property; wherever he was sleeping, there she would be beside him; whenever he cried she was there ready to pick him up. The only times she left him voluntarily were when he had to be fed, for she could not bear to see him at his mother's breast.

So long as his wife kept to her room, James perforce and in his own fashion did the outside work. As soon as she reappeared he gave it up. He was not being deliberately callous. He did not reason that what he left undone she would be forced to do—it was more that he took it for granted that she would expect to: that what was hardship for him was her natural occupation. Kirstina's increasing powers of perception showed her that he lacked imagination, that in matters of practical behavior he was stupid, and the time was coming when his unfeeling complacence would make her as angry as his incompetence.

All through that early summer, no matter how much she did in a day, she could still see there was more that should have been done. She would not allow the house to be left again untended; she insisted that everything else be cared for as well. But it was impossible. The house was big and the land was wild. All her helpers save the child were unwilling. There was her baby to be nursed. There were the animals and the garden and the potato patch. There was Estelle. There was the hay which should have been cut and the wood that ought to be sawed and stacked, and these two latter tasks, with their premonition of winter, hovered over her consciousness like an evil cloud.

With so much threatening her she worked far too hard, until she became used to being always tired. She no longer cared that she had no time for Rudi, that she was letting James feel cheated. She started without hesitation on tasks that once she would never have attempted.

Near the end of July, when the grass in the open before the house stood tall and ready to cut, she drove into the village and inquired everywhere if there was a man for hire, but she found James had been right. It was the busy season for all and whether they needed the money of not there was no man free for twenty miles. Next morning she went out and took the scythe to the grass herself.

She had never handled one before and she was afraid of it, but she had watched many men scythe, and she knew she had to have feed stored for the winter. At first the weight of the blade threw her off balance and she found herself following after the swing of her arms. But presently it grew easier and she worked steadily, careful of the precision of each stroke. The rhythm of her work bound her and the sound of the cutting became after a while identified with breath. Drops of sweat gathered at the nape of her neck and began to run. The cut grass steamed as she left it behind under the sun. She did not notice that the blade grew blunt, that it began to pull; nor did she notice how long she had been at work, nor that through heat and fatigue she began to move in a daze. Near the drive she came to the end of one lap and straightened up as she made ready to turn. Suddenly she felt weakness sweep upon her. She had just time to heave the blade aside before she spun round and fell.

When she came to she was lying on her face and felt deathly sick. She vomited as she pushed herself up and she hung there, supporting herself on her hands while she tried to gather strength to crawl away. She knew she had had too much sun; by the bushes at the drive she could see a patch of shade. When she could, keeping it before her eyes, she started out and as soon as she came within it she lay flat again. The sudden cold was like a douche of water and quivered along her spine. Her weakness was horrible and humiliating. She could not have moved again from where she was; she lay very still and by degrees she brought her hands up under her forehead. Then, making no effort to stop herself, she began to cry.

It was not alone the wretchedness of the moment; it was because suddenly she could see no end. Here she was at last, impotent; nothing stood between her and the long line of failures. She saw herself as a child; with Michael; alone in Montreal. She was sick almost to death in a shed among people she did not know; she confronted and subdued Molly Cannon; she forged her courage into a hard shield and found shelter for herself and her child; she watched what she had built up burn, and she tried again with new weapons on new ground. It all changed, yet it was all the same. Nothing she did ended anywhere but in her own defeat. Oh God, she begged, let me keep what I get! Let me make something and keep it this time! She was not conscious of whether she was praying, and if she was it was only because there was nothing left in herself to which she could turn. She was so utterly without strength that her tears were childish, first weak and then stormy, and when they stopped she lay shivering with an occasional long, sobbing sigh.

After a while she became aware that someone was watching her. She stopped shivering as she wondered who it could be and why he did not speak. Then she rolled over and lifted herself on her elbow.

At her head, about three feet away, sat a man, and beside him, a dog. They were looking at her with an air of grave concern and as he saw her face the man said slowly, "How should you be in such misery—you that have hair like a king's own daughter?"

The strangeness of the expression passed her by. He was nearly an

old man. His hair was thin and gray and rather long; a little fringe
of it stood in a wispy beard along his chin. His face was the color of a
ripe nut and crisscrossed with deep lines, while his eyes were set so
far back it was not possible to tell their color. They sparkled a little
as he squinted in the sun. And he was small. Even when he stood up
he would be small; now, sitting cross-legged as he did, he looked no
taller than his dog, which was a huge, shaggy beast with a head like
a wolf and a coat the color of a smoky blue cloud. The dog's ears were
pricked up, his eyes were full of sly humor and the end of a very red
tongue lolled sideways from his half-open mouth.

Bewilderment seized Kirstina. With the faintness still on her and
her eyelids stiff with half-dried tears, she seemed to be translated to
her childhood, and a vague memory floated to her of a man from the
moon with his dog—only then there should have been a lantern and a
bundle of wood, while on the grass here lay nothing but a knotted
walking stick and an ancient, battered hat. She was sure she must be
dreaming. Not one of the three of them made a sound. At last when
she spoke her words sounded odd and meaningless.

"I thought I was alone."

"You were that until they sent us from the village."

She lifted herself further and sat round facing him with her knees
drawn up. "Why did they send you?"

"They said there was a great house, and they were right indeed. I
think it will be too great for me and I will not stay."

The lilt in his voice was at once puzzling and strangely familiar. He
looked at her all the while he spoke and suddenly she placed what
teased her and said, "You are Irish."

"From Ireland I came a long time ago. It was in a ship—a little
ship from Cobh. There was a storm and it was like the dark of hell
with the devils' shadows moving on the walls and the lights never
still. But when the sun shone it was a good ship. There were the sails
puffed out white like a swan's breast, and birds resting on the ropes.
And there was whiteness on the waves, but the ship rocked like a
cradle in between."

"Yes!" said Kirstina. "Yes! I have been on a ship like that."

"It is a good thing to remember." He nodded at himself and at her.
"Yes. That and a few others are good."

Kirstina looked down again and was quiet.

"Will you have been trying to cut the hay?" he asked.

"Yes."

131

"Have you not a man in such a great house?"

It was a stern question and she flushed. She said lamely, "My husband is busy with his books."

The little far-set eyes stared at her so long that the sparkle disappeared. "Indeed," he said, "with his books. And who beside you both lives there?"

"My sons—one is a baby. And two women."

"Perhaps truly it is a poor house?"

"You will not find many poorer."

"You will be needing me," he said. "I'm thinking I will stay."

He stood up as he spoke. She saw that he was actually as small as she had thought—probably no higher than her shoulder.

"What do you mean?" she asked.

"That I will be staying. Did you not be asking yesterday in the village for a man?"

"Yes—"

"And I came today." While he talked he had moved over to where she had thrown her scythe. He picked it up and ran his thumb along the blade.

"But I have no money! At least enough only for a few days!"

He dragged the scythe back and stooped to rummage in a bundle which had been behind him out of her sight. He pulled out a hone and drew it in a long sure stroke against the blade.

"But you will be needing me?" he asked.

"I cannot pay you!"

"Begad," he said, "how do you know what will pay me? Will I be comfortable in your house? Will you be easier that I am here? Will I carry sweetness away with me when I go? I never had but one gold piece in my life and that one bought me a day of misery before it was gone. I will be cutting your hay; do you go in out of the sun."

The dog cocked his ears and listened to the even strokes of the honing. When the blade was sharp enough to cut a floating hair the Irishman turned it on the grass and presently the sweep! sweep! of his scything began. Kirstina sat on and watched, but when he reached the end of the first lap she got to her feet and walked dreamily to the house.

When she told James, he asked only what the man's name was and she did not know. James went off and came back to tell her. "He says his name is Patterson, and a more idiotic name for an Irishman I never heard yet."

Rudi said Mr. Patterson's name was Andy, and the dog with the smile was called Argus.

That afternoon Kirstina went to her room and slept. She had told Mrs. Raikes to feed the man and the dog and make ready a bed, but when in the evening she went out to the barn she found Andy there spreading a blanket over a bed of hay. In answer to her question he said, "Yes, I have seen the woman. I will eat the food she cooks for that will be only breaking your bread, but I will not sleep in a bed she makes. . . . It is in my mind that I will build a little house. That I have never had, and it would be a good thing to remember."

In all the time Andy Patterson was at Prospect, Kirstina never learned exactly what he had been and done before. Fragments of his past would come out in his talk, sounding a little as if they were tales about other men or things that had happened more than a lifetime ago. Sometime, perhaps when he was still a boy, he had sailed from Ireland. He had been in New York. Always he had wandered, stopping now here and now there, leaving each place as soon as it had no more need of him.

"I do not starve," he would say, "and if I did, it is better to starve where you are alone than where people will be offended because you starve in their sight."

Andy never hurried, but he worked with the precision of a man who knew what he was doing and did not intend to let it waste his time. What he lacked in strength of body he made up in cleverness and it amazed Kirstina to see the way in which he used his balance to put weight behind his arm, so that he drove a saw as hard as a man twice his size.

He was very strict in his notions of what was fitting for her to do: she was allowed to milk, but if she lifted a pail to carry water Andy would ask severely if she were thinking he had forgotten to do it; she could weed in the vegetable garden, but if she touched a hay fork she would be told to put it down before she got hurt. She found herself spending her time picking fruit with Rudi, churning butter, fussing with the pans of cream she had set in the cellar, and trying to remember how to make the goat's-milk cheese she had used to eat as a child. She had enough to keep her busy all day but she was no longer irked desperately by the knowledge that if she sat still for a moment nothing was being done. Whenever she wished she could go out and see how the hayloft was being filled and the wood stack growing long and wide.

An hour before sundown Andy would finish everything he would do for her that day, and go off to work for himself on his little house. He built it of logs, neatly axed and laid, on the very edge of the cliff to the right of the big house. It was square; there was a door, and three windows, and a chimney in the center where the roof rose to a point. It was not built for a man of normal size and the doorway when he stood in it made Andy look big. "For indeed," as he said, "I am not building for anyone else at all." About the house he made a fence of split rails woven together with withes. To come upon his domain in the twilight gave one a strange feeling: it was so small and so new, and yet looked as if it had been there always, between the forest and the edge of the land.

It was Rudi who insisted that the dog Argus could sing. Andy, who had had so little with him when he came that he had carried only one bundle tied up in a blue cloth, had had in that a sort of flute—a short, fat pipe made of horn with a few stops. He did not play tunes. He liked to sit cross-legged on the ground outside his house while the stars came out, and blow little groups of notes very inconsequentially, with pauses in between. Sometimes the notes were not even in groups, but one slow, soft one after another, each allowed to die away in its own time. After Andy had been blowing in this way for a little while, the dog Argus, who sat in front of him, would lift up his head and begin a long, musical howl. It was neither quite animal, nor quite human. Andy's notes would go up and down, and so did the melancholy voice of the beast.

Kirstina had understood in a measure how James had felt no obligation towards the Raikeses; they had at least owed him (or his father) something for their passage from England, and they had stayed with him largely because they had no ambition to go. Mrs. Raikes had the true servitor's attitude; she preferred the derelict grandeur of Prospect to anything she could have achieved on her own. Andy Patterson was different. Andy stayed at Prospect not for what it gave but for what it demanded from him, and Kirstina was willing to accept his help only because she saw it as necessity, and because she knew that he was pleasing himself. James, however, believed that if people served him it was because they liked to serve and because they enjoyed the shelter of his superiority. He resented Andy's squatter behavior on the estate and asked Kirstina how she had come to allow it, and he had no hesitation in giving him orders and criticizing his work and his condition.

"The man looks a tramp," he would say. "Those Paddy Irish are all the same. My father would never allow them on the place." Kirstina would grow hot with shame.

She bitterly resented also the increase in James's patronizing attitude towards herself. His memory was short and his first respect and diffidence towards her had been overlaid by the more recent sight of her laboring in the fields. Gradually he had ceased talking to her about his own intellectual interests and always brought their conversation to what he supposed to be her level of practical domestic affairs. Once or twice he lapsed into asking Margaret to see to having something done in the house, automatically classing his sister with himself, and his wife with those to be ordered. He was treading on very dangerous ground.

Kirstina was aware that she had been lured to Prospect under false pretenses; if James had not actually lied to her, neither had he been frank. She had been disillusioned too late to help herself, but still she had done the best she knew for him. In order to save his pride she had spurned the only offer of help she had received from outside.

One October evening she made time to enjoy herself and sat in the drawing room taking tea. Rudi was there, and Estelle, and Margaret with the baby Geoffrey out of his cradle in her lap. Kirstina had changed her dress to the one of gray silk she had brought with her from Montreal. Her hair was freshly done and it shone in the light from the fire and the lamps. Presently James came in. She gave him his tea and he settled himself with a look of smug complacence.

He said, "You see how much pleasanter it is, Christine, when you content yourself with not doing so much unsuitable work. A gentleman likes to feel that his wife has time for himself, and for gracious living."

He was perfectly serious. Kirstina looked at him from under straight brows and felt acrid and unexpected amusement.

An hour or so later she went out and asked Andy to harness the horse. She drove herself with quiet determination down the drive, and along the road she had never yet taken to Murray Fraser's farm.

When Murray Fraser was still very young it had appealed to him to think of marrying Margaret Collingwood and then taming her; in the end it had suited him far better to marry Ellen Raikes. Now he had a comfortable home, he had his family of sons, and he was left alone to pursue his own amusements. He had liked the look of Jamie Colling-wood's wife—a fine, upstanding girl with courage and humor of her own. If she had not attracted him he would never have offered her help at all, and neither would he have offered her any if it had not somehow made him indignant to see such a creature caught in Jamie's lethargic web.

Now when she came to his door he welcomed her with expansive satisfaction—"Though I expected you long before," he said. "I thought surely Raikes's flitting would bring you."

Looking at him she thought it likely that he had schemed to bring that about. She examined his surroundings and liked what she saw. Ellen Fraser greeted her without self-consciousness and did not apologize for her father, who bowed and mumbled awkwardly from one corner. The four boys also were in the living parlor, the eldest a tall lad of about fifteen, broad-built like his father, and the youngest a round, inquisitive child of seven. They were not allowed to stay listening. Ellen packed them off and her father went too. Then she sat calmly knitting while Murray and Kirstina eyed each other and started to talk.

"I hear," he said, "that you found the man you needed at Prospect."

"It would be better to say he came and found me."

"Ah!" He leaned forward where he was by the fire and began to poke it up.

"Mr. Fraser, you were right when you said I would be able to do nothing alone."

"Well, at Prospect it would be hard for you to know where to start."

"I cannot start at all without your help."

"Now, have you told Jamie that?"

"Not yet."

"Do you remember what you told me would happen if you did?"

"I thought he would hate me. Now I have changed my mind, and I do not think James will hate anyone long for adding to his comfort."

"What do you wish me to do?"

Her eyes clouded and he saw the new look of irony deepen. "You were right again," she told him, "when you said it was difficult at Prospect to know where to start."

"I know that."

"Mr. Fraser, I must have more money."

"Yes."

"But I have only the estate and the one man to work it. I have come to ask you what you think there is I can do."

Ellen Fraser had set down her knitting and was listening. She and her husband glanced at each other.

"At Prospect," said Murray, "you have only one standing asset, and that is the timber."

"But who is to cut it?"

"Wait a moment—and don't let yourself be frightened. You have been thinking of this too closely; Ellen and I look at it from outside. I suppose James has told you you have to cut the trees and get them out yourself?"

She nodded.

"He got that from his father. In Edward Collingwood's day it was true. But today already—how much virgin forest do you see along the lake from here to Toronto?"

"I thought it was all forest."

"Not compared to what it was, and most of it is second growth, thin small stuff, no good yet for building. To get hardwood today you have to go up the rivers. The men do it—cut the wood all winter and float the rafts down after the spring thaw. You must have seen them, if not here then at Montreal."

"Yes, I have seen that. When we came on the steamer we passed very big log rafts, with houses built on them."

"Exactly. But your timber stands right on the lake shore, and it is good stuff. You have white oak there and maple and plenty of straight, well-grown pine. It would be no job at all to cut it, make a chute on the cliff face, and send it down to the bay. And then—well, I may as well admit that I have this all thought out. It's been in my mind ever since I spoke to you. D'ye know our shipbuilder in Port George?"

"No."

"Name of Alec Munro—Scots, and a friend of mine. Never does anything but grouse over the price of timber. Can't get any more round here—the logging fellows take all they cut to Toronto or farther east to get a higher price. Munro has to compete there and buy it away from home and tow it back. He doesn't see the point and in his place neither would I. My idea is that we should talk to him, tell him he can have all he wants from Prospect if he'll buy it as it stands. He can send his men to cut through the winter, when they have their dead season. You should get a fair price."

Kirstina, looking at him in the firelight, had gone white. "Are you telling me what you really believe?"

"I am. I see no reason why we shouldn't pull it off. Ask Ellen here if she hasn't heard me talk it out before."

His wife's placid face was earnest. "That is the truth, Mrs. Collingwood. It has been on his mind for months."

"But ye wouldn't come to me, ye stubborn woman! I could do nothing without your letting me in. And now listen, we're making a bargain, you and I . . ."

"Murray—" said Ellen softly.

"Let me alone, my dear. Listen," he told Kirstina again. "I've had to set my cards on the table—couldn't do anything else. And because I've had to do that you can diddle me altogether. You can go down to Alec tomorrow and he'll jump at the chance you offer him—though I doubt you'll get so good a price as if you had me by—and, after, you can tell Jamie Collingwood you are saving him entirely on your own, and earn yourself no trouble at all. Do you follow me?"

"Yes, I understand."

"Then you will know what I mean when I say that if you do that it will be a dirty, rotten cheat!"

"Yes, I know. You want me to tell James and to tell Margaret and to have them know that it is you who had to show them how to save their necks in a way they could have very easily thought out for themselves."

"You have put it better than I could. I have a score to settle with Prospect for myself and for my Ellen—who'd never in her life ask to have it paid—and if I choose to write it off by doing them good rather than evil that is my affair. I only want to be sure you are not going to spoil sport."

"You can be sure," she promised him. "You and I, Mr. Fraser, are alike in this—that we both, always, pay our debts."

When she got back she found James in the library and she said to him at once, "I have been to see Mr. Murray Fraser."

He started, and hurriedly looked round.

"No. Margaret is not here. I waited to tell her until after I had told you."

"Christine, do you know what you are saying?"

"Yes, I think I know. Are you angry, James, or are you frightened?"

He suddenly became angry. "What is the matter with you? Are you mad?"

138

"I went to see Mr. Fraser about selling our wood. He does not think it will be hard." She paused a moment and went on slowly, "You see, James, you were not able to help me. We must have more money, because I cannot go on forever as I have been doing, and there are the children to bring up. So we are going to sell our wood to Mr. Munro, the shipbuilder. He should be very glad to get it. Mr. Fraser says it is good wood, and we shall sell it as it stands."

Her husband said wonderingly, "Have you arranged all this already?"

"Not quite all. We have simply talked it over. Tomorrow morning he is coming here and we are going together to see Mr. Munro."

"Murray Fraser . . . is coming here?"

"It is more convenient than for me to go to meet him."

Her tone was as cool as it was reasonable. James made no more effort to speak. He kept looking at her. Then he began to laugh.

Kirstina started. She watched him narrowly and it was not long before she realized that his mirth was wholly malice. "It is Margaret!" he gasped at her. "Margaret! Don't you see? After all these years! Oh Christine, this time you have given me what I want! Margaret! My God! You shall let me tell her myself."

It was then that for the first time, underlying her surface relief, Kirstina felt a threat of the evil that existed at Prospect. She felt it again when, after James had wakened Margaret up to tell her, she met her sister-in-law's baffled and vindictive eyes.

When Murray came in the morning James suggested accompanying them to Port George, but his genuine antipathy to business later changed his mind. He shook Murray's hand, told him not to stay away so long again and to "forget whatever I said before I went abroad. I was only a pup then and very much under petticoat rule."

Margaret was not in evidence. Murray Fraser, who was enjoying himself, swept his inquiring gaze over everything and on the drive going away asked Kirstina exactly what had happened. She told him.

"Are you a good enemy?" he asked.

"I don't know."

"Because Margaret is a bad one. I'm a scoundrel, you know—as Ellen told me last night. I should have contented myself with helping you and let it go at that. Now there is no telling where this will end."

But the chill that had floated over Kirstina the night before had gone with the new day and she would not be dismayed. They drove straight into Port George and to the office on the bank of the river where she met Mr. Alec Munro. He was a middle-aged man with a sedate, formal manner. She was surprised, for Murray had told her on the way that the Scotsman had a baby daughter, and it was only later she learned that Mr. Munro had married very late in life.

He greeted her punctiliously, dusted off a chair before his desk and begged her to sit down.

"Mrs. Collingwood has come on business, Alec," said Murray, who leaned against the window frame. "It is wholly to your advantage, so you'd better listen. Jamie would be here also if it wasn't that with his head for figures he prefers to trust to his wife."

"Anything to my advantage, Mrs. Collingwood, I shall be very happy to hear. But you must allow me to say I hope I can also be of service to you."

"Don't you believe him," interrupted Murray. "Alec never gave anyone the better of a bargain yet."

Mr. Munro looked hurt. Privately he might be proud of his reputation as a sharp man of business, but before a new acquaintance he would have preferred it to be ignored.

"Mr. Fraser is a better friend to you behind your back than to your face," Kirstina told him. "When I asked his advice he said at once that I could not do better than to come to you. My husband and I have decided to sell the timber at Prospect."

Mr. Munro expressed surprise, but Murray grinned at him tactlessly and hurried him along.

"You know as well as I do what that stand is like," he said. "James Collingwood will have no trouble disposing of it anywhere he tries, and it is easy to get out. But when I heard it discussed last night I naturally put your name forward. It seems only fair that Port George timber should be offered first to a Port George firm. You can always say you don't want it."

With Murray standing over him, that was exactly what Mr. Munro could not say. His finger tips pressed together, he stared over Mrs. Collingwood's head with a bland expression and irritation in his heart. He did want timber; whatever he bought would be green; that at Prospect would be as good if not better than what he could find anywhere else, and a great deal easier to come by. Only he knew that Murray meant to make him buy it standing and at no less than he would pay anyone, and why Murray should suddenly want to help the Collingwoods, God alone knew!

"How do you come into this?" he asked his friend suspiciously.

"Mrs. Collingwood being a stranger, she naturally wanted an opinion from someone who knew the country. Jamie, you know—Jamie would never know how much to ask."

Savagely Munro agreed. He eyed Kirstina with some of the belligerence he felt for Murray. Then his annoyance began to fade. She was a remarkably handsome woman, widowed once already and now married to Jamie Collingwood, the poor lass!

"How much?" he asked. "Mrs. Collingwood, how much did you think your timber might be worth?"

When Kirstina left they had still not managed to say. Mr. Munro was to come up and look for himself, and Murray Fraser was to be there to help. "Among us all we shall reach a fair price," said Murray. Alec Munro feared he was correct.

The chute that Murray had advised building was made on the cliff face just by Andy Patterson's little house. All winter, while Munro's men were chopping in the woods, the horses strained through the snow dragging the tree trunks up to it and the logs were levered into position and sent crashing down upon the ice below. The whole of the bay did not freeze, but the shores were ice to about fifty feet out. The great piles of logs lay there, looking small and brittle from the heights above, waiting for the spring when they could be maneuvered in the water and towed to the river's mouth. It was fascinating to watch the work. Rudi spent day after day in the snow admiring the woodsmen and riding the horses to the chute. Kirstina went to see the logs fall; she did not like it, for the cliff's height still terrified her, but she wanted to see what went on. Alec Munro paid her for what he took; next season he planned to do the same. To clear the whole estate would take a long time.

With the little extra money on hand came Kirstina's chance to try what she could do. As soon as the ground thawed she hired another man in Toronto and so was able that year to make use of all the old cleared land. She went into town again to buy sheep, which could graze where the trees had been cut and the land was not yet free from stumps. All through the Canadas wool was still far more expensive and difficult to obtain than fur. Woolen blankets came from England and in the settlements the few families who raised sheep did so only to provide for their own home spinning. It had seemed to Kirstina that a surplus of wool should find a ready market and her first clipping proved her right; as the Prospect flock increased each season thereafter, so did her profit.

She thought back often to the farming she had seen as a child, drawing upon a store of half-forgotten knowledge. That first year she planted one field with yellow turnip, and next winter it was obvious how the animals benefited from the variety in their diet. She increased the number of goats and made the cheese, which she had previously used only for her own household, in quantity. It went to Toronto to be sold. She found a way to make use of James when she asked him one day what books there were on farming and whether people had ever written about sheep-breeding and stock. James had to send to London for information but what he eventually got was of value and he, who had never learned anything of the land from living upon it, began to find it interesting in print.

Behind all Kirstina's driving energy was her determination that this time at last she was going to build strongly and safely, and to keep what she made. She looked at Murray Fraser's farm, which paid its way, at the farms of all her other neighbors still struggling to independence, and she knew that hers could do better and would never satisfy her until it did.

Her first sale of timber had been in the winter of 1853. Not until the second spring after that did she begin to have any sense of permanent achievement and even then she was careful not to exaggerate —she merely felt that she had reached the point where her worst days must be behind her. In June of that year she sat down and wrote to Helga Nordrupp. She had known for some time that she wanted to do so, but it was characteristic of her that she could not write while she was still in difficulties, and she had sent Helga no word since the cholera in Montreal. Even now she was not frank. She asked for news of her friend, and about herself said only that she was well and happy and that Rudi was growing into a strong, handsome boy.

Six weeks later she had a reply. Helga had not changed; she wrote:

DEAR, DEAR KIRSTINA,

How I thank God that you have written at last! All our fruitless inquiries have made us fear you might be dead. We never were able to trace you beyond Montreal. I have to give you news that will make you glad, that has been waiting for you these three years. It is hard for me to write. I am so happy, yet I want to weep.

Your dear husband is alive. It is he who has been searching in Montreal—who has never ceased to search since he came home. Oh Kirstina, if you could have seen his grief to find you gone! But now all such troubles will be at an end. He is away in Canada, but Aage is writing to him of your address. If I could see your joy as you read this! So soon now you should meet. Then you will write to me again.

I am well, and Aage also. God has been kind to us. We have never been in want and we have three strong children. Always, dear Kirstina, I remember that it is to you I owe all that I have.

I send you my love and am always your faithful friend,

HELGA

Your husband's aunt, Johanna Warre, is dead.

Kirstina read this. It was too utterly incredible for her to believe. Here she sat in her own house; the sun came in at the window; she was alive; she was well: this thing was not possible. She did not read the letter again. She folded it up ready to tear, changed her mind and put it away in her writing table and went out.

In the garden Rudi and the baby were playing with the puppy Murray Fraser had given them. The hired man was cutting grass in the field beyond—in the field she had once tried to cut herself. She saw the land that was hers, the children that were hers, the house that was hers. She walked out beyond it and along the path above the cliff. Her hand followed the rough handrail. When she reached the summerhouse she went in and stood looking over the lake. Suddenly she found she was gripping the balustrade, bending back and forth over it. She took her hands away and sat down on the seat.

I have had a shock, she thought; naturally it has given me a shock, but there is nothing to be afraid of. Helga has made a mistake. That is all. Perhaps Helga is not well. People sometimes have odd fancies. It certainly is not true. Michael Shea is dead. He has been dead eight years.

How could a man stay away eight years? A man who had a wife and son? That was not reasonable. . . . Michael had not known he had a son. . . . But a man had a home! If he were alive he came back to it! He did not stay away eight years—nine years, all together, since he had left her. If a man did not come back, anything might happen. . . .

She found her hands pressing her temples, and her mouth as

143

taut as if she had screamed. Once again she placed her hands in her lap and forced herself to think.

It had to be possible. Michael was a sailor, often in danger. . . . There were sometimes false reports. . . . She could see that it was possible. But how could such a thing happen to her? What had she done to deserve this? . . . I loved him, she thought; I loved him, and they told me he was dead. No one said, Perhaps he is not, perhaps this is a lie. They said he was dead, and I believed them. I believed it was my fault that he had died, and that was why I ran away.

If Michael Shea were alive there had been no need for the many things she had suffered. It was because she had thought him dead that she had left Boston and but for that she would never have been forced along the bitter road she had come, never have married James, never have lain vomiting in the grass, beaten by her own impotence. . . .

It had never been of any use to blame a man who was dead. She had grieved for him when she thought he was dead. But if Michael Shea were alive then he could be called to account for all she had had to bear. Let him come, she thought; I am not a child now; he will find out how I have changed. . . . She began to brood over what she had once been, over all that she had learned, over what she had become.

She sat so long that when she stirred she was stiff and the shadows had begun to lengthen. She was as bitter as she was unresigned, and equally without hope. How could it profit her to be strong, or to resolve to keep what was her own? The law would be against her now, as fortune had always been. Once, she had married Michael Shea, and Michael Shea was alive.

V   FOR three weeks Kirstina went about Prospect steeling herself for the disaster. She knew she could not have long. The worst that could happen to her was that Michael should come striding up to the house unannounced, and she persuaded herself that that would be like him. What she prayed was that he would write to her. She was thankful that when Andy went to the village he always brought the letters directly to her.

In the end Michael wrote from Toronto and his letter came addressed to her as Mrs. James Collingwood.

> MY DEAR KIRSTINA,
>
> It is difficult to write much after so long and under these circumstances. I have thought that you would prefer us to meet first alone. I am staying at this hotel, and if you can arrange to come here that will be best. Or if you prefer I will go anywhere else you suggest.
>
> I know this is hard for you but nothing can be gained by further delay.
>
> MICHAEL SHEA

This letter surprised her by being totally unlike anything she had expected, but it was full of assurance and it heightened her tension. She replied that she could come the following Friday, choosing that day because it was market day and so least likely to provoke question at home. When the time came she drove herself into Toronto with Andy, let him down at the market and went on from there to the hotel.

Michael was waiting for her. He showed her into a small private room at the back. There was a table in the center with a green baize cloth and chairs round it. He pulled a chair out for her and she sat down.

He struck her at once as being much quieter than she remembered. Much older also—but then, so was she. I am twenty-seven, she thought, and he is thirty-three; it is eleven years since we were on the *Kronborg*. He had an air of well-being and his clothes were good. But he seemed ill at ease and this gratified her. She thought him foolish to say, "It is good of you to come."

"I have every reason for coming. It was not hard to arrange."

"You are looking very . . . well."

"I am well. . . . I had Helga's letter three weeks ago. I suppose you had yours from her husband?"

"Yes . . . though I had found you before that. From an advertisement. It was finally answered by the family with whom you stayed after the fire."

Relief flooded her, for then at least this catastrophe was not of her making.

"The advertisement had been repeated off and on for two years. But only one member of the family read English and he did not see it before. . . . After I had talked with him I knew where to look. I found the record of your marriage at the barracks, and your address. Then I didn't know how to tell you . . . how to write to you. Until Nordrupp's letter came, and I learned you already knew."

"Yes," she murmured quietly, "I knew." She stiffened her back. "Michael, I am not going to waste your time. I don't know where you have been, nor what you have done. I don't know what you expect, but I will tell you at once that I am not coming back to you."

"Not—?"

"I do not feel myself to be your wife. I am married now to a man whom I do not love but whom I at least know. I have my own life. I am going to keep it."

Michael said very slowly, "Are you sure you know what you are saying?"

"Yes. And I know you will tell me it is impossible. Perhaps it is. But I have a right to fight for what I want, and what I have at Prospect is mine. I am safe there. I will not let myself be torn away."

"Kirstina, listen. . . . You don't need to be afraid of what you will have to give up. I can take care of you. You will never have to fear poverty again."

"I know I shall not—because I have learned to look after myself."

He swung out the chair beside him and sat down. "I don't think you understand. . . . You have no choice in this matter. Your present marriage is no marriage at all. In law I am your husband. Don't you see that you cannot stay where you are?"

"I will stay until I am driven out."

"There would be only one way to arrange it. I could divorce you . . . then you might remarry. But that way you would be certain to lose your son. You are forgetting him."

"I never forget Rudi. Rudi is mine. You did not know you had a son."

"I know it now. . . . Kirstina, please—I think you must realize that this is no sound argument. All the force is on my side. I want to spare you whatever distress is possible and the break will be much easier if it is quick. I want you to bring Rudi and come back with me to Boston at once. . . . If you insist you want to marry this other man, I will go to law and arrange the divorce. But I have been looking for you for over two years and I mean to have my son."

She said stonily, "I will never come. And I will never give up Rudi."

Michael sat frowning and silent; after a few moments he stood up and walked over to the one window at the back. She looked at his tall, still figure and her muscles ached from the stiffness with which she was holding herself. At last he turned and came back. "Kirstina, is it because you hate me?"

She was looking full up at him. She opened her mouth. Within her something broke and her face twisted as she cried, "Oh God! Why didn't you die as they told me you did?"

She sank back shaking, strangled with sobs, but without tears. Michael's hands clenched at his sides; he had gone white. "I see," he said. He sat down again facing her. "I was not on board the ship when she went down."

"Where were you?"

"I got into a fight in San Francisco and couldn't go back to the ship. I went overland to New Mexico to join in the war . . ."

"What war?"

"The war with Mexico—I see you have never heard of it. I was there the better part of two years. Afterwards, I went back to California. Gold had just been found. Men were coming there from all over the world. It seemed like the chance of my life. I stayed . . . until two and a half years ago I returned to Boston."

Her eyes were so bewildered they were pitiful. "You could—if you had wanted to—have come home before?"

"Yes."

"Nothing . . . kept you?"

"No."

"I . . . don't understand. I . . . thought—"

"I know, Kirstina. I know what you must have thought. But I have no excuses. Nothing kept me . . . only, believe me, I did not set out to desert you. I never knew the ship went down. I wrote to you. I never dreamed you would hear I was dead. . . . And try to remember that it was eight years ago. I was twenty-four. I was caught up in something so new and so absorbing I could not bear to leave it."

"You say you wrote. I never had a letter."

"The first one was lost. I wrote others. I sent them to Boston. My aunt . . . got them, and she kept them there."

Kirstina suddenly laughed. She bit her underlip. Then again she began to titter, staring at him all the while. "Your aunt kept them! . . . Were you happy while you were away, Michael? Were you leading such an exciting life? . . ."

"Is it amusing?"

"It is to me. I remember what I was doing. What did it feel like when you came home?"

"I was still in New Mexico when I heard my uncle was dead. I was not surprised that you did not write to me. I knew how much you would resent my staying away. Much later, in San Francisco, I wrote asking you to come out there and join me. It was after that, when I could put it off no longer, that I came home. . . ." He stood up, and began to move about the room, stopping between phrases, speaking in jerks. "When I arrived in Boston I learned we had a son. My aunt had all my letters, but she had told no one I was alive. She was so much afraid you would come back. . . . I did not think, at first, that it would be hard to find you. I went to Montreal. I traced you easily to the hotel, to the night of the fire. I talked with hundreds of people who had seen you, who told me things about you and about our son . . . but I couldn't get any further. . . . My aunt became ill in Boston. I had to go back to her. I think she loved me, and I was sorry for her, but even when she was in great pain, and dying, I could not bring myself to forgive her. It seemed to me that I had to find you first."

"Did it really?"

"I knew all you had once had to go through. I was so sure that while I was searching you were again destitute and in want."

"Yes! That would have suited you, wouldn't it? If I had been in want I would have had to accept you. I would have had to give you Rudi, and take whatever you offered." She stood up and went behind her chair as if to put a barrier between them. She laid her clenched fists on its back. "You! How can you possibly know what I suffered? You are a man. You had a wife and child but you could run away and leave them for years. You could forget I existed. You want me to remember that you were young—yes, but I was younger! I was driven out of the only home I had. I worked day and night to get food for my child. I learned to drink gin in a laundry in Montreal. I crawled with lice in a fever shed—"

"Kirstina—"

"Do you want me to be sorry for you? Because you came back and had to learn what you had done? Because you knew it was your fault? I don't pity you, Michael Shea! I wouldn't pity you if you were dying as miserably as I nearly died."

The silence that fell between them spread and grew deep, until Michael's eyes left her face and he said, "I do not want to fight you. I hoped I would not have to. I know I am to blame. I have already faced up to that many times, and it has not made me change my mind. I have looked for you, and found you, and I want my son. If I go to law I will get him. If you choose to come with him, I will look after you. The choice is yours, and no doubt I sound very cruel, but it would not help for me to make protestations and beg you to forgive me."

Kirstina said, "I have two children now. They are half brothers, and they are mine. All that I have is mine, and I will neither leave it nor let you take it away from me. You can go to the law if you want to, and it may give you your son, but before you take him I will see to it that he hates you as bitterly as I do. . . . I can do that. I am his mother and he loves me, and I have learned how to fight. . . . Will you want him afterwards, when I have finished with him?"

"He would still be my son."

"Rudi was born nine months after you left me. I took him away with me while he was still a baby. It was I who nursed him and watched over him. I fought for him. I married a second time to provide for him. All his life he has known me, and only me. He is eight years old and he protects me as if he were already a man." Bitterness and fear had begun to choke her. She stopped, and when she went on her voice became tormented. "Whose son can he be except mine? Whatever right can you have in him, coming again after so long?

Leave me alone, why won't you? Go away, and leave me in peace!
You have never done me anything but harm!"

Michael did not answer her and did not move, and she had not
the strength to stay longer. She turned and walked quickly to the
door, and went away.

Never in his life would Michael be able to forget the horror of his
homecoming to Boston, of discovering his aunt's mad and ruinous
deception. He had intended none of the things that had happened
to Kirstina, nor to the son of whose existence he had been unaware,
but for all of them he was responsible. He had begun his search at
once, and had continued it, with the burden of his responsibility
growing always heavier. If Kirstina had died from the cholera, if she
and his son had starved—and in the course of his explorations in
Montreal he had discovered how nearly that had been possible—he
would still have been to blame.

Some of his worst fears had begun to ebb as soon as he learned
where Kirstina was, and since then he had been able to remember
almost with amusement how near he had come to pursuing Luigi
Rossa to Italy, for it had seemed more likely that she had gone with
him than that she had vanished into the air.

Now that he had seen her he could measure the depth of his
earlier fears by the greatness of his relief.

He sat down slowly, looking at the chair she had used; he became
aware that all the time he was searching for her he had been thinking
of her not as his wife but as a victim, as the woman whom he had
injured, possibly beyond repair. He had not thought of her as the girl
who had stamped herself upon his memory the moment he first saw
her, standing on the wharf in that little foreign town, with her boxes
and baggage beside her. That was a long time ago, and the girl was
a woman, changed and grown, but she had still the sharp and independent quality that marked her off from other people and made
her impossible for him to ignore.

A vast curiosity seized him, to know about this life she was now
clinging to, about the man who was the father of her second child
and yet merited no more than the barest reference in her speech.
When he thought that she might be simple enough to hope she had
seen the last of him, he was sorry for her. He had come this far, and
he would follow her next to Port George. But though he had threat-

ened her with it he did not want to go to law; he resented the implication that this matter concerned anyone but himself and her.

When he made inquiries about Port George he discovered it was a very small place. The only industries were the flour mill on the river and the shipyard of Alexander Munro. As a stranger could hardly appear there without explanation, he went down to Toronto Harbor and looked for an official who would know Mr. Munro. Having secured a letter of introduction and enough information to meet his needs, he packed his valise and went out on the stage.

Alec Munro received him and read his letter.

"Mr. Reid told me you were the man I should see," said Michael.

"There is no one whose opinion I value more. John Reid came out from Scotland five years before myself."

"So I understand."

They went out into the yard and stood about there all afternoon, watching and shouting questions above the din of hammers and saws. The yard was small but well equipped. Munro built trading and fishing luggers, thirty to forty feet long: good, sound little ships of standard design. He was ready to build for steam also and eighteen months before had launched the *Insignia,* with an overall length of a hundred and five feet and a screw propeller imported from the Clyde. At five o'clock promptly, he drew out his heavy gold watch and said, "You'll come up to the house for tea?"

Michael went. His host's wife was a placid, capable young woman at least fifteen years younger than her husband. The one child, a thin, large-eyed little girl of six, stared at Michael over the rim of a blue and white china mug. There was a ham on the table, and cheese and jam and hot breads, and tea as black as ink. During the meal Michael talked freely of his travels and of his years at sea. He could feel Alec warming to him.

"Most men on the Great Lakes have come from salt water," said Alec. "I did myself." He told how he had started his yard, putting into it all the money he could collect after his father's death in Scotland. "I wanted to build my own ships," he said, "and I could never have done that at home. John Reid wrote that here I could break new ground, and so I came. I haven't regretted it. There are sound ships and good skippers on the Lakes."

"I've seen that. And nearly as many steamers as sailing ships."

"Yes. About half and half now. This has been the proving ground for steam, Mr. Shea. On the ocean the problem is more difficult, but here with fuel all along the shores it was easy to start and we've kept right along. It's when it comes to iron shipbuilding that we have to drop behind. Because we have no iron near at hand we have to import the plates from the Clyde and rivet them together here. It's done, mind you—don't think it isn't. The *Zimmerman* and the *Peerless* are both iron steamers, put together at Niagara. But it's not an undertaking I'd care to tackle myself."

"Why should you, when you have all the timber you could ask for?"

Munro grinned. "Ay, I can still say that, though not every man can. Good ship timber is getting as scarce round Lake Ontario as elsewhere. On the south shore there's none left."

"But you have your own source of supply?"

"For the next few years. I bought up one of the few good stands left hereabouts and it's nowhere near finished yet."

"And can you get more when that's done for?"

"I shall have to pay higher and go further afield, but in the back country it's inexhaustible."

"And you import only your marine engines?"

"That's right—when I have occasion to use them."

"Mr. Munro, it occurs to me that you're a pretty warm man."

Alec's caution abruptly returned. "Well, I'd no' go so far as that. These have been very good years. Traffic on the Lake has been growing heavier ever since I opened. We may already be seeing the end of that."

"Why do you say so?"

"Next year the railroad will cover the whole north shore. It will kill our passenger trade. I shall still have a market for traders and fishing smacks, but it's possible there'll never be another passenger steamer laid down on the Lake."

Janet Munro had begun to clear away the plates, with the child Clare sedately helping her. Alec said, "Do you care for a smoke, Mr. Shea? We will go into my room and leave Janet in peace."

The room that he called his overlooked the yard. In the evening light the waters of the bay were copper-toned and the wharf and the timbers of the half-finished ship stood out sharp and black. "It is not salt," said Munro, "but for all that it's a beautiful spot. Tell me, what brings you to the Great Lakes?"

Michael said, "Curiosity." He waited until his pipe was drawing before he went on. "Curiosity—and business. It is some years since

I was at sea and I have no wish to go to sea again, but ships are still what I know most about."

"And so now you want to start building." Munro's voice was expressionless, his eyes bright and alert. Michael looked at him thoughtfully.

"I'll be frank with you. I had fair luck when I was in California and I have a certain sum of money to invest. I intend to go into business, but like yourself I have no desire to be swallowed up by bigger fish. In Boston I would never stand a chance. I know nothing of inland waterways and this is the first time I have been able to come and look for myself."

"I see."

"In Montreal I met a man from Rochester who had come by steamer all the way through the St. Lawrence canals. He told me it would be quite practicable to build ocean ships on Lake Ontario and sail them to the Atlantic. He also told me, as you did just now, of the shortage of timber on the American side. It seemed to me that could not yet apply in Canada and a man who built his ships where the timber was close at hand and cheap, and sailed them to Boston or New York, could make a much higher profit than if he'd built them in either of those cities in the first place."

Mr. Munro took the pipe from his mouth. He looked at Michael speculatively. "That's a big idea you have."

"What I want you to tell me is whether it is a practical one. I'm not a gambler, Mr. Munro."

"What exactly would you think to build?"

"Ocean clippers. For sail, timber construction throughout. That way you'd take advantage of all you have here and not lose by what you have not. You'd scarcely need a larger dock than your own."

"A clipper ship is one I've never built."

"Ocean ships are all I know."

"Mr. Shea, is it a partnership you're proposing?"

Michael permitted himself a smile. "So far, I'm only asking advice." He had gone a little further than he had intended, but the idea he was propounding had come to him in the way he had described and had remained in his mind ever since. His inquiry was genuine.

"You've put me to think," said Alec at last. "Yon's not a thing I can answer in a hurry."

"I'm in no hurry."

Presently Alec asked him if he had arranged for a bed at Hobart's inn and offered to accompany him there. In the taproom when they arrived were John Hobart with Murray Fraser and the man named Ferris who owned the flour mill. They welcomed Alec and looked his guest over with curiosity. Hobart brought two more mugs of his cider. Alec saw Michael seated and edged himself onto a table just outside the circle. "Mr. Shea was five years in California," he said. Michael looked round and met the eyes turning his way. With rich amusement he understood that he was to be the lion of the evening.

When he went to bed at last it was with a feeling of pleasant exhaustion, and of having talked too long and too hard. His audience had steadily increased as more and more men who sauntered in, stayed. At one moment he had felt himself stared at from the floor, and looked down into the face of the fifteen-year-old who helped behind the bar; the youngster had listened open-mouthed to the talk of Indians and pistol fights in the night. Michael was moved to wonder if one of his hearers might by chance have been Collingwood; he reminded himself that he had come to Port George to gain information rather than to give it.

In the morning he breakfasted at the inn and then strode down to the wharf. There were only two ships anchored in the bay but several small boats were drawn up on the beach, and a couple of boys were working busily over one. His eye followed along the headland, through the gap to the open lake and on to the eastern bluff. He saw what looked to him an immense roof among the trees and he squinted to see again, sure that he was wrong. A building of such size would be an impossibility in such a place. More likely what he saw was an outcrop of rock. But as he looked again he thought he could see chimneys and a portico through a cleft in the woods.

" 'Morning," shouted a voice behind him. He swung round. Murray Fraser's was one of the few names he remembered from the night before. He waved and called back, "Good morning."

"I'm driving to town," said Murray, coming down towards him, "but my horse needs a shoe before we start. What were you staring at just now?"

"Perhaps you can tell me. I thought I saw a house up there?"

Murray looked and grinned. "Afraid it was the aftereffect of last night, were you? I don't wonder. It is a house. That's Prospect."

Michael stiffened. Murray went straight on. "Incredible great place. You should go out and see it close to. Poor Jamie would not like you but his wife might make you welcome."

154

"Who built it?"

"A man named Edward Collingwood—a cross between the devil and a banshee. He's dead now, God rest his soul."

"Who lives there now?"

"The banshee's son and daughter; and widow, too, poor thing. And young James's wife."

"Yes?"

"The earth's most goddamned determined woman. That great barn up there was falling into ruins when she arrived. There wasn't an acre of cultivated land round it, there hadn't been a tree cut in twenty years, there were bats in the chimneys and weeds pushing in at the front door. Young Mrs. Collingwood is mad, of course—any sane woman would have known she was beaten before she started—but she cleaned up the house and reclaimed the garden. She sold the timber to Alec Munro—for a very good price which I hardly had to suggest—she found a man to work for her and, before God, I believe she makes that place support them and will do far more than that before she's through."

"And that surprises you?"

"Will you tell me why such a woman should marry a puir ass like Jamie? That's the marvel of it, to me. If it were you or I, for example —but no, it's James Collingwood. Och, I'd better be going. I'll likely see you again?"

"I hope so."

"If I'm back this evening you must come out to my place—or we can make that for tomorrow."

Michael watched him leave. He felt that it was a long time since he had been so drawn to anyone: Murray Fraser had no hesitations, and when he offered his friendship it was with a large openhandedness that made you free of everything he had.

After a while Michael walked back off the wharf and over to the shipyard. Alec was on his dock, intently watching the work going on below.

"I've been hearing where you get your timber," said Michael, coming near. "Mr. Fraser tells me you were scalped by a lady."

"Murray Fraser is a liar," retorted Alec without heat. "I paid Mrs. Collingwood a fair price but not one penny more than I'd have paid anyone else. And I've only paid her for what I've cut."

"She sounds a remarkable woman."

"I wouldn't ask a better to do business with. For that matter, if I did go out of my way to help her it would be no more than her due. She has a hard time."

"No money?"

"Precious little, and the Collingwoods to hold in line. They're an unlovely collection and likely the child will be no improvement on the rest of them when he gets older. Luckily, she has her own boy."

"She was married before, then?"

"At sixteen, or thereabouts. The first child is nearly nine. He comes down here and he and my Clare chase about the yard and climb and fall into the bay and frighten Janet into fits. It's not wildness in Rudi —he's a good boy—but he has a passion for ships. Near every time he comes he tells me that his father was a sailor and a good sailor would always prefer to die at sea."

Michael's heart contracted. Without asking, he was hearing as much as—almost more than—he wanted, and all at once. New and disturbing ideas were rushing in on him; he needed time to digest them and yet he was afraid of taking too much time lest his purpose weaken.

Alec that morning was in the mood for business. He wanted details and facts and took Michael into his office, where they argued and drew up figures. It was constructive talk. It made Munro enthusiastic and Michael recognized that, quite apart from his other plans, he had hit on a solid investment.

It had not been love of adventure only that had held him so long in the West. Accident was what had first detained him—accident that at the time he had bitterly resented. Then, in New Mexico, he had fallen under the spell of a new world—a wide-open world of virgin territory, crying out to be used. In that atmosphere the ambition that Kirstina had once thought lacking in him awakened. In due course it drove him back to California instead of home to Boston. The chancy business of gold-hunting was not really to his liking but because of the gold money was afloat in the country. He had found himself a partner, a man older than himself, with something the same turn of mind. The two of them had used their first strike to open a store in Sacramento, and thereafter every enterprise to which they turned their hands had flourished. When Michael had left he had not known it would be for good. He had intended to settle his affairs in Boston and bring his wife back with him to California. He had not withdrawn all his capital, and the partnership of Surrey & Shea was still in operation in Sacramento and San Francisco. There might yet come a time when he would return to the West; meanwhile, he had money in hand and he saw no reason why he should not acquire an interest in the East as well.

He could afford to go halves in this venture with Munro, and the agreement they were considering—with Munro providing the working facilities and himself the cash needed for rapid expansion—would suit them both even if only Munro remained on the spot. At one point Munro looked up at him and said, "I have always worked alone, you know. I preferred it. But I am an ambitious man and if this succeeds we may find ourselves with one of the biggest concerns on the Lake."

They went up to the house again for their midday meal. The afternoon Munro spent in the yard. Michael stayed with him for a time and then took a notebook of blank pages from the office and set himself down in the shade outdoors to draw plans for his ships. It was so long since he had done this that his pencil felt awkward and stiff and he worked slowly, stopping often to look around him. The Munros' garden surrounded their house and ended at the beach. The house was behind him; on his right was the path to the office building and to the dock; just below, out of sight, were the men at work. In the hot, still air the noise of hammering sounded far away and faded. It occurred to Michael that Alec Munro's life was the peaceful, circumscribed ideal for which many men hankered. Alec worked at what he did best and lived within sight and sound of his work; he was happy in his home and in his wife, he was sure of himself, and his ambitions were reasonable and consistent. His was an enviable lot, and it brought home to Michael that what he himself had found hardest in the last two years was that there had been nothing positive he could achieve in them. As he thought about this he became impatient to start work, and he left off making detailed plans and began to rough in the lines of a completed ship, with a raking clipper bow and aft-leaning masts.

After a time he felt something breathe on him and looked round to see the child Clare at his shoulder. She had been on the beach and her dress was splashed with water, her bare legs and feet scratched and brown. With her thinness and lank, dark hair she had a wild look that amused him when he considered her as the offspring of Janet and Alec Munro. When he smiled at her she came round and dropped cross-legged on the grass, followed by the boy who had been on his other side and whom he had not till then seen.

Michael stared at his son and Rudi looked calmly back. He was not like Kirstina. His hair was as brown as his skin, and his eyes were gray. He was tall for his age and very sturdily built. He sat down on the near side of Clare and asked, "Is that a clipper ship?"

Clare said, "His name is Rudi Brandt. I told him you have been round the world."

"But China is only halfway," said Rudi, with the patience of one who has had to explain something several times already, "unless you went on from there?"

"No, I didn't. I came back."

Rudi gave Clare a brief glance. "But that is a clipper ship, isn't it?"

"Yes. Would you like to look?"

He handed over the sheet of paper. Both children bent over it, their heads touching.

"They go to China and back," said Clare.

"Four masts," counted Rudi. "Would she be more than a hundred feet?"

"About a hundred and ten."

The boy looked at him with admiring respect. "I have never seen ocean ships. I shall when I'm a sailor."

"You are going to sea?"

"Of course. My mother says I must wait until I am fourteen."

"Yes. That was when I went to sea."

Rudi's eyes rounded and he opened his mouth to speak again, but Janet's voice called from the house and Clare jumped up and ran. Rudi stayed a moment.

"Will you be here again, sir?"

"I will."

"Here is your ship."

"If you like you may keep it."

The boy's smile broke across his face in sudden, heart-warming surprise. "May I? May I really?" He stood poised, as if wanting to make sure of his treasure before he escaped with it.

"Yes, keep it," said Michael. Rudi turned and chased after Clare, but at the house he looked round again and waved before he went in.

Michael stared across the bay, at the roof of the great, half-hidden house. His eyes traced the line of the chute on the cliff's face, the scars the tree trunks had made. He had a kaleidoscopic picture in his mind and all the vague impressions of the morning were suddenly clear.

He could not settle again to work. He got up and put his materials away, shouting to Alec that he was going for a walk. Alec called back that there was an hour or more yet before tea.

Little lanes led out from the village in all directions and he supposed most of them must either lead directly to houses or peter out into forest tracks. In the end he walked back along the road he had traveled in the stagecoach, striding impatiently in spite of the heat. The river near its mouth was wide and deep-flowing, its waters colored with the brown mud that showed wherever the banks were undermined, but two and a half miles back at the turn of the road and the bridge it was running swiftly between boulders and ledges of rock. Well in sight was the small waterfall that turned the wheels of Ferris's flour mill on the one bank and the local sawmill on the other. By the time he came there Michael had slowed and he stopped for some time on the bridge looking upriver. Presently he climbed down to a ledge of rock below which, in a shallow pool, he could see a fat trout lying.

It was not true, as Kirstina had intimated, that he would have been glad to have discovered her in want. That was the nightmare that had haunted him and her accusation had been markedly unjust. Yet the last thing he had expected was to find her pre-eminent through her own exertions. He did not wonder at Murray's and Alec's admiration, and even they did not know her as he did. They knew nothing of her beginnings, of her stubborn besting of himself and of all her disparagers in Boston; they knew nothing of Montreal, and her struggles and disasters there. He wondered briefly what it would have done to him to have met so repeatedly with such reverses, but Kirstina's strength (so different from his own) seemed to lie in her inability to assess the odds against her, in her rash staking of everything she possessed on the thing she wanted, no matter what it cost her and no matter how impossible it seemed to be to obtain. On the surface, she might appear practical and even cautious, but when it came to the point she was always ready to cut her losses and start over again; in fact, she was the gambler that he had said yesterday that he was not.

He had reached this point in his thinking before he saw, suddenly, which way it was tending. The waters of the river at his feet ran swiftly, now in shadow, now in sun. He heard the rippling, pleasant sound, and excitement seized him and mounted within him. This, then, was why he had been waiting; why he had not been able to decide on the course of action to follow. He had imagined it was only the boy, but now he knew he wanted Kirstina as well.

He pictured her, entrenched in her great house, and defying him and any forces he might bring to bear on her, and the spectacle made him smile. He knew that now, long afterwards, it amused him to remember her initial struggle against him, how stubbornly she had resisted and then, in her own tumultuous and headlong fashion, changed her mind and run to marry him.

He had little sympathy with the type of decayed magnificence at Prospect described by Murray Fraser, and he did not believe it could appeal either, of itself, to Kirstina. There could be nothing positive to hold her there—even the second child belonged probably more to the place than to herself. If he laid siege to her position, sooner or later he would be able to make her want to leave and come away with him into the living world. When that time came, he thought, he would take her face between his hands and say, I will do the fighting now; be still, and I will take care of it all.

The confident trout caught his eye again before he turned away and he stooped and picked up a smooth pebble to flip into the pool. The water rippled; when it cleared again the trout was still there. Michael smiled and went to climb back to the road. As he did so he heard the sound of wheels. Murray Fraser was driving rapidly home from town, and pulled up beside him and offered to drive him to the village.

Arrived there, Murray came in with him to the Munros' and was invited to stay to tea; he promptly began to tease Alec about his new business enterprise. True to his habit of caution, Alec side-stepped every sally until Murray winked broadly at Michael Shea and said, "Alec, you crafty old humbug, why trouble yourself? I saw John Reid in town today."

"Did you now? And was he looking well?"

Michael began to laugh; Murray joined him and they rocked as they watched Alec's impervious face. "Keep your own counsel!" exclaimed Murray at length. "I've heard nothing and I know nothing though I wish you both every success. Will you come over with me now to my place?"

Alec, with dignity, agreed. Murray Fraser drove the three of them out. On the way Michael realized suddenly that they were following the road to Prospect. He saw the huge gateposts to the estate. He passed them again when it was very late and Murray drove them back as far as the river.

Next morning Alec came early to the inn with some letters to be picked up by the stage. It was a very fine day with the heat haze disappearing fast. A small sloop had come into the bay overnight and was lying tied up at the wharf. While they stood looking down at it a high cart came rapidly along the river road. Michael glanced up and saw Kirstina driving. She was pale and her eyes held concentrated fury. Beside her sat a man who could be only Collingwood.

Alec had turned with him and Kirstina drew up alongside them.

"Good morning, Mrs. Collingwood! 'Morning, James. You're out early."

"We've been to Ferris's," she said. "Now we have letters to leave with Hobart. I hope Mrs. Munro is well?"

"Very well. Will you allow me to present a friend from Boston? Mr. Michael Shea. Mr. and Mrs. James Collingwood."

Michael bowed. The stiff man on the driving seat inclined his head. Kirstina said, "I heard of Mr. Shea yesterday, from Rudi."

More expansive with her than with Murray Fraser, Alec volunteered, "Mr. Shea and I may shortly be partners in business."

"Indeed?"

"To our mutual benefit, I hope," said Michael. "I can think of no more promising place to settle than Port George."

James Collingwood suddenly leaned over. "This is the wilderness, Mr. Shea. Most of us would give our eyes to get away. But you Yankees will move in anywhere."

"Wherever we see something we can use."

James barked shortly, "No doubt."

"My husband is not a businessman," explained Kirstina. "He finds no interest in commercial enterprise."

She twitched her reins, smiled at Alec, and drove on.

"She is never herself when he is there," commented Alec. "Did you get a look at him?"

"I did that."

"Puir Jamie—as Murray Fraser would say! But you cannot blame him overmuch. I think myself he is only half a man: the rest was frightened out of him while he was yet a lad."

At noontime Michael received a note. An old man brought it—a little, spry man, brown and dry like a nut. Michael found him at his elbow when Alec was turned away. "What is it?" he asked.

"Will Michael Shea be your name?"

"It is."

"Then this is for you."

He held out the folded and sealed sheet of paper and Michael took it and slid it into his pocket. He looked the messenger over with mingled caution and inquiry.

The old man's eyes peered at him and glinted in the sun. "An Irishman you are," he said. "You should have come before." He turned and went away.

Michael went into the office and read his letter.

I never wished to see you again [wrote Kirstina]. Even now I can scarcely believe you have had the presumption to come here. If you are at the gate of Prospect at four o'clock I will meet you and make my intentions quite clear.

Michael folded the letter carefully and put it in his note case.

He went in plenty of time and she was not there when he arrived. The long drive curved away into the woods. The trees were very thick on either side of it and he could see neither the house nor any sign of the clearing that must be around it. When Kirstina came in sight she did not speak but beckoned him further in and led the way past the foundation of the unbuilt lodge, along a narrow path to an open space where Munro's men had worked the winter before. There she turned in the sun and demanded, "Tell me! I want to know the worst I have to fear."

Her eyes were dilated and he felt the agonizing suspense she was in. He said slowly, "You have nothing to fear from me."

"I think you must hate me, Michael Shea, as much as I hate you. Why else would you do such a cruel thing?"

"You forget that I have a right—"

"Right!" she exclaimed. "I am not speaking of right! In common humanity why must you hound me? Why can't you leave me alone?"

"I am not hounding you."

"I did not think it of you. Not after I saw you again. I thought you might do anything else. But to come here! What will you gain by it? What can you possibly hope to gain?"

"I would like to make you change your mind."

162

She struck her hands together in despair.

"Kirstina," said Michael, "I have listened a great deal to you. Now you must try to understand me. I know that I left you for years and almost forgot you, but as soon as I saw you again that was at an end. You are the woman I married because I wanted you for my own, and that is as true today as it was then. I am not going to go away. I am going to stay near you, and wait."

"You are mad!"

"I only know what I want. Why should I go where I don't wish to? There is nothing to take me back to Boston, or anywhere else. You are my wife and you are here, and my son is here."

"You would leave today if I would come with you. If I won't go, you will stay until I do. Is that it?"

"Yes."

"That is blackmail! Don't you see that? You are trying to blackmail me, you wretched coward!"

"Kirstina, I am not exposing you. I am not going into the courts and saying, 'This woman married a second time in ignorance. Now she knows her fault, but she continues to live in a bigamous marriage.'"

"Are you threatening me also with that?"

"No. I am reminding you that it is what I could do, and never will. My God! I am being cruel to myself rather than to you! Do you think I can enjoy seeing you day after day alongside that poor creature you cling to?"

"Why should I not cling to him? James was kind to me when there was no one else."

"And so you love him."

"Thank God, no!"

"He would cast you off tomorrow if he knew what you are doing."

"You're wrong. James needs me. If he ever finds out, I shall prove that. But he never will find out. . . . You shan't stay here, Michael Shea. I won't have you. You saw Rudi yesterday. I told you what I would do with him. Do you think I didn't mean it?"

"You meant it, my dear, but you will never do it. You love your son too much to be able to betray his trust in you."

"I will! I will!"

She raised her clenched hands as she said it, and he stepped in and caught her wrists. "What will you tell him? What have you to tell him about his father?"

"I will tell him you left me! That you didn't die, you left me to starve! That you left him to grow up in misery! That you were rich but you didn't care! That you have come back to torment me—"

"The truth will get in your way, Kirstina. You will have to say also that I want you, that I love him and want you both. It is you who are being unjust to him, you who are depriving him of what should be his. There is nothing for him in this estate of yours. That belongs to the other child, if to either one at all. But Rudi has a right to anything that is mine and whether you are willing or not I will see that he gets it. I will be here, and in one way or another he will come to me in the end."

Kirstina rocked on her feet, pulling away from him but helpless. His hands went to her upper arms. He held her still and dropped his voice. "Come with me now, Kirstina. What is it that you are fighting to retain? Do you want to spend the rest of your life working to help a man who will never be able to help you? You can have so much more than that."

"Let me go!"

He clasped her to him hard and forced up her chin and kissed her, trying not to think of what she said, nor to remember her hostile eyes, wanting only to reach down and wake in her what was forgotten, to draw up what had been lost. But when he raised his head he had not moved her. She stood like a dead thing until she felt him release her and then she tore herself loose.

She began to speak in a screaming whisper. "You fool! I am not a soft child now! Can't you understand? Do whatever you like! I am a woman—I can't hurt you! Take my son. Shame me every day by making me remember what I am. Stay here until we both grow old. I won't come to you! I would sooner live in hell than come one step!"

"Kirstina—"

"Now will you go away? Will you leave me alone?"

"You are what I want. I shall not give up."

She backed away from him slowly until she came up against a tree trunk and leaned there, saying, "Get out now! Get out! Don't ever come onto my land again!"

While he watched her, he went on speaking very clearly. "I was to blame at first," he said. "You have a great deal to forgive. But now it is you who are wrong and it is you who are going to be hurt again. You are trying to make yourself live with lies."

"Get out!"

He turned then and went along the path. Looking after him she cried out, "I hate you! I hate you! I hate you!" and as he went from sight she lifted her hands and clasped them before her mouth. Her teeth pierced her lip and she went down on her knees in the grass.

At the drive, Michael paused. The gates were on his left. He turned sharply right and walked fast until he came out beyond the trees. Prospect House lay before him. He looked it over from end to end. He looked at the garden and the sweep of fields, at the rise of land behind, on up to the bluff. He went no farther. He stood and looked. Then he walked back, not so fast, but without other deviation, into Port George.

That evening he signed his agreement with Alec Munro.

At the time when Michael Shea was first approaching Prospect, Kirstina's son Rudi had been busy in the hayfield with a hired man. In the midst of his labors he straightened up and caught sight of his mother walking off down the drive, and it occurred to him that she was probably going to visit the Frasers. Rudi liked the Frasers; he was thirsty, and he thought kindly of Ellen Fraser's fresh buttermilk; also, he enjoyed going anywhere with his mother alone. He shouted to Sam that he was leaving and chased off across the field.

Instead of following the drive he took a short cut through the wood, and when he arrived at the gateway Kirstina was not in sight. He decided then that she could not have come the whole way, she must only have started and then turned back, for she had not had time to outdistance him. He stood hesitating, stubbing his toe on the ground and considering going to the Frasers' on his own. If he didn't arrive with his mother it was unlikely anyone would make sufficient occasion of his visit to give him buttermilk. He kicked a stone with his foot and a small snake skittered excitedly into the grass. Nothing else moved, and at last he turned and started back the way he had come. Then he heard voices.

It was his mother who spoke first and he guessed she must be in the clearing. So he left the path and made his way there through the underbrush. He came out just as Michael Shea was saying, "I am going to stay near you, and wait."

Rudi stopped where he was, in the shadow of the trees. He recognized his friend of yesterday and he would have gone on, except that both grownups were so unconscious of his presence that he suddenly felt shy and would have preferred to run away. Then his mother spoke again and he saw her face and could not go.

My mother is never frightened, he thought; my mother is not afraid of anything. But he knew she was afraid now.

He became aware that they were speaking of him. He was miserably uncomfortable and his shirt prickled his neck. He heard Michael Shea lower his voice and saw him hold Kirstina and kiss her. He heard his mother's rage and he crouched down and hid in the long grass. Later, when she was alone, he saw her fall on her knees and he heard her begin to cry.

Rudi did not cry—he was too thoroughly shocked and dazed—but he was seized with dread lest she should get up and find him and ask him what he was doing. Like a small, scared animal he crept away and the moment he dared he stood up and ran, tearing headlong out of the wood and up through the fields until he burst through the cedar hedge into the safe familiarity of the garden.

Someone standing on the other side caught his arm and held him still and he looked up at his Aunt Margaret.

"Who was it?" she demanded. "Who was it in the wood?"

Rudi goggled at her, panic-stricken with the fear of telling what he had seen. "W—where?"

Margaret jerked his arm. "In the wood! Who was in the wood?"

"No one, Aunt Margaret!" shouted Rudi. "No one was there!"

"A man came and stood in the drive, looking up at the house. A very tall man with brown hair. Who was it?"

"I didn't see! I didn't see anyone in the drive!"

Margaret let him go and watched him as he tore away again towards the cliff. She had not meant to frighten him but she knew what she had seen and what she wanted to find out. She went into the house and sat by the window in the front parlor until she saw her sister-in-law Christine coming back from the wood.

Rudi ran on until he came behind Andy Patterson's little house, where he flung himself down on the ground. The terror that had come over him while he listened to his father and mother had been increased tenfold by the shock of Margaret's questioning and by the fashion in which he had instinctively lied.

Irrationally, the most startling thing was the one he easily accepted, for he had always secretly believed that his father was alive. Mr. Shea's name was Michael and he had gone to sea when he was fourteen; it seemed very possible that he and Rudi Brandt's father were one and the same. But the rest of the puzzle was hopelessly confused and at its root lay the thing he shied away from every time he came

near it. He was used to a world in which everything his mother did
or said was right, and yet he knew beyond a shadow of doubt that in
the talk he had just overheard it was his mother who had sounded
wrong.

The person who had knelt in the wood screaming and crying had no
connection with his mother as he had always known her. The thought
of meeting her again and looking into her face terrified him anew.
He twisted his body on the ground and began to sob, sure that he
would never dare go back to the house, never go anywhere for help.

At length the dog Argus came and found him, nuzzling him all
over in friendly inquiry. Presently Andy Patterson followed and squat-
ted down and asked, "What is it then? Is it a pain that you have?"

Rudi was no longer capable of the defense of lying which he had
used against Margaret. He sobbed agonizedly, "My mother! My
mother . . . I saw my mother . . ." but he was incoherent in his
misery and could tell nothing beyond that Mr. Shea had been with
his mother and he had seen them together.

Andy Patterson was a wise old man. He listened, and did not
speak. After a while Rudi quieted and pulled himself up with his
arms about the dog.

"That is better," said Andy, severely commending. "And what did
you think had gone wrong?"

With his head pressed against Argus's side, Rudi looked round.
Andy was observing him as calmly as if this were a most ordinary
occasion.

"Has your mother not had trouble before? Huh, that one! She is
like a child. She will always be hurting herself."

Rudi stiffened. Grasping after a fast-disappearing fact, he said,
"My mother is always right!"

"Then what for are you crying?"

Rudi wiped his eyes against the dog's shaggy coat and again on
his sleeve. He sniffed.

"Now for this Mr. Shea," said Andy, "I am in two minds. He is an
Irishman and for her that might be good. But he comes out of the
past, and that is never good."

"Don't you like him, Andy?"

"That I did not say, nor will I. I would be slow to judge any man,
and when I saw this one the dog was not by."

Rudi nodded. He understood and shared Andy's faith. Argus was
neither tactful nor diffident and his judgment with regard to persons

was unerring. His indifference to James Collingwood was so marked as to be offensive; whenever Margaret passed him the hair on his neck bristled and he sank his head in a growl; once he had taken Mrs. Raikes's ankle in his mouth and fondled it playfully while she screamed and screamed. Andy had come slowly to her rescue, and said later that "it was time the woman learned to look where she set her big feet."

"You saw what was not yours to see," Andy said now. "I would not be thinking about it too much, or telling your mother."

He got up and wandered off to the front part of his garden. Rudi followed. For half an hour or so he worked with Andy side by side. He still felt tired and strange but his experience of the afternoon no longer frightened him. It concerned other people far more than it did himself and Mr. Patterson understood it and did not think it odd. When Andy sent him in to supper he went to the house without remembering that an hour ago the idea had struck him with such terror.

At the supper table, Margaret Collingwood suddenly asked James, "Didn't you say this morning that you had met a newcomer in the village?"

"A Yankee," James growled. "Damned interlopers."

"And he said he was going into business with Alec Munro?"

"Alec said so. Should have expected him to have more sense."

"Christine," said Margaret, "tomorrow is Sunday. I think I shall accompany you to church."

Kirstina was roused from her abstraction to look astonished.

Margaret Collingwood had not begun by hating her sister-in-law. She had at first felt nothing beyond the condescension of her class for one beneath her. But when Kirstina brought Murray Fraser to Prospect, Margaret forgave neither the affront to herself nor the gratification of James's malice, and after that she found other grievances. Kirstina had worked for and established her own supremacy in the house. Kirstina had learned to make use of Margaret. Kirstina had become the symbol of the family's new prosperity. Some time before Michael Shea came to Port George Margaret's resentment had grown to a persistent, restless longing to bring her sister-in-law down.

She went to church next day as she had said. Her large stiff figure was enveloped in a dress of tattered blue silk. Her bonnet was tied on above a mass of untidy hair; she wore French gloves that had split at the seams and an Indian shawl that had once been magnificent but was now encrusted with dirt. She presented, as usual, a ludicrous spectacle, but she swept into the Collingwood pew ahead of Kirstina with an air of frigid hauteur and a glare of hostility for anyone bold enough to meet her eyes. Port George was used to her. The children sniggered and nudged each other but their elders merely exchanged glances. There was only one church in the community. The Reverend Emmett Rogerson conducted the Church of England service for a congregation that included Presbyterians like the Munros and Frasers, Kirstina Collingwood, who was Lutheran, the Nonconformist millowner Ferris, and a varying number of Roman Catholics. Michael Shea came with the Munros and Janet whispered to him who Miss Collingwood was.

He was very angry with Kirstina, and her correct, formal bearing and her pale face infuriated him anew. When the service was over he saw to it that the Munros lingered to greet the Collingwood party and that he was presented to Margaret. Kirstina was in a hurry to leave. Michael began to talk with vigor and emphasis of what he and Alec intended in Port George. He took their interest for granted; he spoke of the charm and possibilities of the place, and he appealed to Miss Collingwood for her opinion. Janet and Alec and the vicar were included in the discussion but Michael's voice and commanding figure dominated them all for as long as he chose. They were still standing there twenty minutes after everyone else had left.

Margaret Collingwood drove away in a daze. In Michael Shea she saw a man built on a scale large enough to impress her, one such as she had not encountered since her father died. He seemed to her to have the same brand of careless, overbearing energy as Edward Collingwood had had, the same faculty for compelling attention. Michael Shea was ten years younger than she but that fact passed her by, for she had been trained to be subservient to the man who could excel. She lost sight of her original purpose in going to Port George to seek him out and very shortly she had worked herself into a state of anxiety lest when she saw him again she should be disappointed.

Two days later she had the horse harnessed and drove to pay an unannounced call on Janet Munro. Having arrived there in mid-afternoon, she waited in stiff, ungracious determination until the men came in for tea. Alec was so astonished as to be useless and Janet was already pushed to the point of silent exhaustion, but Michael out of consideration for them obediently talked and, because he was curious about anything that went on at Prospect, Margaret was not wholly unwelcome to him. Her first impression was endorsed. She stayed until the hour forced her to leave, and then she went enslaved.

Thereafter she made no effort to check herself. Michael had moved in to stay with the Munros; Margaret visited them regularly two or three times a week. She appeared in the taproom of the inn; she went every Sunday to church; she strode down to Munro's dock and stood watching the men at work.

At first she merely transferred to Michael the girlish hero worship she had had for her father, but presently the character of her feeling began to change. She wanted to be listened to as well as to listen. She wanted Michael to return her attention, and she wanted him to think her distinguished and to admit that they two were on a plane above the rest of the world. She could remember a time when she had known she was the most admired and courted girl in Upper Canada, and she believed the elements of her success then had been her position as her father's heiress, her birth and her personal attractions. The fortune was gone, but she still had faith in her family's exalted station and she could, if she had a reason, do much for her appearance.

In days gone by Mrs. Raikes had been a very competent lady's maid and now she was called upon again and willingly left the duties imposed by Kirstina. Margaret began to appear in dresses made over from draperies, and from evening cloaks that had once belonged to Estelle. As a girl she had ridden a great deal and had sailed her own boat in the bay. Now she began to ride again, complaining bitterly of her poor mount, but still taking exercise and being seen abroad. Murray Fraser roared with laughter over each new manifestation and Port George was first puzzled and then speculative over the transformation. Within four months of Michael Shea's arrival, Margaret Collingwood was being thought not so much a figure of fun as a handsome, though opinionated, woman.

Michael, meanwhile, was tremendously busy. Alec Munro had contracts to fill and saw no reason to discontinue his regular business. They had therefore decided to build a second dock and to lay the keel of their first ocean ship as early as possible in the new year. Michael went to Toronto to secure extra labor. He was only partially successful, but he started dredging and the first piles were driven and the dock began to advance into the bay. In the evenings he worked at blueprints and figures.

His one pressing anxiety—his relationship with Rudi—had already been relieved. He and Alec had decided that the wooden building on the existing dock, their storeroom and office, needed extending to make working room for them both. The further end of it was torn out and a frame for a twelve-foot extension set up. Since so much had to be finished before winter would halt all activity, Michael told Alec to put the men back to their other work; he was a fair carpenter himself and he would nail the clapboarding in place. He was hard at it next day when his son arrived, accompanied by an immense blue-gray dog.

"Hello, there," said Michael.

"Good morning," answered Rudi. He came a little nearer and sat down with his hands clasped about his knees; he was unsmiling and unnaturally still.

Michael glanced at the boy for a moment and went back to his work. His mouth tightened to a grim line. He had been so sure he was right in believing that Kirstina would not denounce him to his son, and he realized suddenly how much he had counted upon it.

He went on placing and nailing boards, knowing that he had never in his life been more minutely observed. Rudi was not staring to annoy, but his absorption became embarrassing and Michael maintained his indifference with extreme difficulty. Inevitably it was he who weakened first.

He glanced round again and asked, "Is that your dog?"

"No. Argus is Mr. Patterson's dog."

The great brute sat beside the boy with his red tongue lolling out. Michael thought him unlovely and noticed his sardonic, inquisitive expression. Rudi lapsed into silence again and Michael went to pick out another board.

"Mr. Patterson," said Rudi, "is a great friend of my mother's."

"Oh."

"He is an Irishman."

Light dawned on Michael: the old man who had brought him Kirstina's letter. "What does Mr. Patterson do?"

"He works for my mother. His other name is Andy. He says my mother needs looking after."

"Perhaps she does."

Argus got up on his legs and stretched. He ambled over and

snuffled amiably round Michael's ankles. Then he sat down again and thumped his tail on the boards of the dock. Michael looked down at the dog's clownish face and grinned. His tension was eased as he realized that whatever was worrying Rudi was not anything Kirstina had said and would probably pass off. At this same moment Rudi also got up and came near. His hands in his pockets, he stood looking at the boarding, which was now three feet from the ground. "If you had another hammer," he suggested hopefully, "I know how to help."

From then on Michael never knew exactly when Rudi would appear but saw him for at least a part of every day. He understood that Kirstina could be placing no obstacle whatever in the path of the boy's coming and, though that was what he had expected and what he had demanded, he was grateful.

In October, Margaret Collingwood invited him to Prospect. He refused and when she pressed him to say why, answered shortly, "Your brother does not like me."

Margaret knew that this was true and was half relieved at his refusal, for though she wanted him within reach she did not want him where Kirstina and James were. The more she saw of him the more infatuated she became and his indifference both infuriated her by denying her own attractions and delighted her as a proof of his superiority. She was persistently at the Munros'. Janet was no nearer enjoying her company than on the first occasion but she was becoming accustomed to it and told Alec that Miss Collingwood was at least improving in civility.

One afternoon Margaret was standing on the stairs in Munro's house and Michael was alone in the parlor below when Murray Fraser breezed in to join him and announced himself by demanding loudly, "Well? Are you still unseduced?"

Michael's answering laugh showed neither annoyance nor surprise.

"Laugh while you can!" scoffed Murray. "Soon it will be too late. The witch woman of Prospect never slackens her grip."

"I shan't be able to complain of not having been warned."

"Alec and I will come to the keening."

"You and Alec," retorted Michael, "would save yourselves a lot of speculation if you could bear in mind the poor woman's age."

"Full-blown charm, Shea! Well, overblown if you insist, but 'tis you that have the discerning eye."

"Thank you for nothing."

"After all, my friend, you have not much choice. Alec's Clare is a little young and every other spinster from here to Toronto is bespoken."

Margaret Collingwood retreated slowly into Janet's bedroom and closed the door. She was shaking with shocked pride. She lay down on the bed and when Janet came up said she felt faint. After Murray had gone she drove home without letting Michael see her.

The incident did give her pause. For a week she half believed she looked a fool and she did not leave home. Then she reasserted herself. After all, she had never pretended to be younger than she was and she had advantages to offer that had nothing to do with years. Persons in her position were always exposed to jealousy and malice and from Murray Fraser what else could she expect? Michael Shea she did not blame. He was young and handsome and strong: how should he not know his own worth? If he would only come to know hers she would forgive him more than this. She returned again to Port George and immediately the memory of her brief discomfiture was obliterated.

The dredging for the new dock was extensive and Michael was in a hurry to get the last piles in before the snow came. Various odd relics were dug out of the bay. One evening when his men were working late with the November light fading fast, they hauled up Edward Collingwood's lost strongbox. Michael was called over and he yelled for Alec. The box was thoroughly waterlogged, the lock heavy with rust. Alec had it carried to the office and sent an urgent message to Prospect. James Collingwood, Kirstina and Margaret came down. The blacksmith struck off the lock and pried the box open; inside, the canvas bags had rotted from long immersion and the gold coins lay uncovered in three inches of water and mud.

By this time it was dark outside and half the village had assembled; a crowd of people was pushing to get into the small office or peering through the window. Alec methodically counted the coins out on his desk. James and Margaret stood by in a stiff, unnatural silence. Kirstina looked on at a transaction which Michael knew must be awakening memories.

It was ironic that after all the accusations and despair the residue of Edward Collingwood's fortune should amount to only three hundred and twelve gold sovereigns. It was a double irony that this sum, which would to him have been paltry, should look more than adequate now to his son and daughter. James gave five pounds to the men who had found it and at his request the rest was locked up in Alec's safe for the night. Then John Hobart invited all and sundry to the inn for free drinks and everyone streamed out and round the bay. The celebrations continued until late. For the first time in his life James found himself a popular fellow. His health was drunk again and again, and his sister's, and their father's memory was invoked with good feeling. Prompted by Kirstina, he told Hobart that he would bear the cost of the refreshment. Hobart demurred but at length agreed to divide it in half. Murray Fraser arrived late with his two older boys and congratulated Margaret Collingwood in good faith, but the stony glare he received in return marred briefly the friendliness of the gathering.

James and Margaret shared the money equally, and Kirstina persuaded James to bank his half. But Margaret, having got her hands on a lump sum, knew how she wished to spend it. She went to Toronto for the space of two weeks and came back with some smart, up-to-date clothes, a handsome saddle horse and an English pony trap. Almost at once the snow came and the trap was put away until the spring, but she drove herself everywhere in a cutter and was sure her luck had changed for good.

Margaret's initial suspicion that Michael Shea might prove to be Kirstina's lover had never quite faded. She was subtle enough to sense the increase of tension whenever Michael and her sister-in-law were present together and she persistently strove to find some illuminating connection. Whatever there was had to be in the past. In Margaret's opinion James was such a fool that what he had seen or heard in Montreal she could utterly discount. She knew it was useless to question Kirstina for she had done that often already, just as she had many times searched her belongings. Three times she managed to get to Michael's room at the Munros', but she found no old letters, no keepsakes, and no inscriptions in books. Though she was looking specifically for a link with Kirstina, she would have been glad to seize on anything that would give her a handhold to help wring a more intimate relationship from him.

His office, when he was not working in it, was locked up. She visited him there several times, and glanced over the desk with its many drawers and the various stacks of papers. It was too recent and businesslike to be promising but her chance came when she arrived one day in early spring to find Alec and Michael with their head workman in the shed beyond the office, assembling an engine that had come in parts from the Clyde. She heard them talking and instead of continuing through the door she stared around the office with a lift of excited anticipation. Her nostrils inflated and her fingers flexed as she debated what to try first. Michael's coat, flung down carelessly on his chair, appealed to her as being easy and quiet. She went at once to the inside pocket and drew out his note case. Inside were the two notes Kirstina had written: one to Toronto arranging the time of her call, and the other bidding him come to Prospect.

Margaret sighed in deep, satisfied joy. She put the notes back as she had found them and then sat down calmly to consider their meaning. Michael Shea had been Kirstina's lover. But why, if that were finished, had he followed her here, and why had he stayed? She sat with her eyes half closed, thinking of Michael as she knew him, picturing him with Kirstina, with James, with herself, searching for a clue. All at once she saw him as he had been only a day or two before, helping young Rudi with the tiny model of a boat, showing him how to fit it into a bottle and to pull up the masts. Michael had been wholly absorbed; there had been a stillness about him; he had been unconscious of anyone watching and his face had held gentle, proprietary affection.

Michael and Alec came back together from the shed. They were surprised but greeted her, and then Alec excused himself and went out of the building. Michael picked up his coat and put it on. Margaret stood up and came round in front of him. She was excited and her bearing was so ominous that he was warned before she spoke.

"I have found out," she said ringingly. "You were my sister-in-law's lover."

Michael's face remained unmoved. He settled his coat on his shoulders, looking at her steadily all the while. "Did your sister-in-law tell you so?"

"I found it out!"

His hand went to his breast pocket and drew out his note case. He turned it over. "Did you find out from this, or when you went through my room?"

But Margaret had no feeling of shame. Though she would have resented being caught while she was looking, once she had found what she wanted she delighted in the power it gave her. She did not trouble to argue over her spying, only insisted, "It is true!"

"So you say. It seems to me to have singularly little to do with you."

"She is my brother's wife!"

"Exactly."

"I understand now why you came here. You came because of the boy. You were her lover and Rudi is your son. You traced him here and you stayed because you want him back. But she will never give him up! You will never get anything from her!"

Still watching her closely, Michael eased himself to the edge of his desk. Margaret's hands were clenched. She was very pale and her breast rose and fell rapidly. "I understand you!" she cried. "You want your son. Why don't you take him then? Why are you patient? If you told my brother this, he would send her off—or if he kept her he would make her give you the boy!" In the face of his silence she paused a minute and came a step nearer. "You don't want her," she said. "She doesn't care for you. Why should you want her when there are so many other women? When there are women who would give you anything you ask? Who would be glad if you only smiled at them?"

"Take care. You had better stop now."

"Why should I stop? Listen to how I will help you. I will tell my brother and you shall have your son. Isn't that what you want? I will do it for you. I will do more than that."

"My God," Michael said slowly, "I believe you are proposing yourself."

"Yes!" she cried. "Why not? Haven't I enough to offer? Take me and she will be punished!"

Michael stood up. He had known the disclosure would one day come; he had waited for it; but he had wished it made some other way. He wanted no help at this woman's hands and he would have choked her off if it were not already too late. He said coldly, "I am afraid you do not know enough. I have a wife and I am not free to marry."

Margaret's excitement drained out of her and left her very still. She looked at him dully and echoed, "You are married."

"I have a wife. You were misled."

"But Christine—?"

"Whatever you wish to know about your sister-in-law you will have to ask her yourself."

At long last her cheeks colored. "Yes!" she exclaimed. "I will! See how she makes us both suffer!" She snatched her shawl from where it lay over a chair and rushed to the door. There she turned, tugging at the shawl between her hands. "I will make her pay!" she promised. "That at least I will do for you."

She meant at first to go straight to Kirstina with her rage and accusations but by the time she reached Prospect she had changed her mind and went after James instead. He was in the library alone. Margaret stormed in upon him. With a sure instinct for damage she was not circumstantial; she did not say what she had found, or how, or that it was long past. She said that Michael Shea was Kirstina's lover and that Rudi was his son.

James listened utterly bemused and Margaret thought, as she had so often before, how thoroughly stupid he was. She started to tell him all over again. This time he managed a few phrases. "But how do you know?" "I don't understand you!" Then he fell silent.

The idea that Kirstina could be unfaithful to him had never entered his head. She was all that he could wish, the most completely satisfying wife he had ever imagined. Margaret's wildness and ravings offended him deeply. He wanted to repudiate what she had said. Tell her to go to the devil. But he was a man who was not sure enough of himself to resist the suggestion that he had been deceived and his own doubts and lack of confidence told him where he might be found wanting. He began by feeling furious with his sister but little by little he saw how what she said might be true; then he thought it likely; then he was sure that the truth must actually be far more than Margaret knew.

"She met him in the wood?" he asked.

"Yes! And before that in Toronto."

It was too convincing. James could see a long chain of deceit reaching back before his marriage: he had so often been betrayed: it was the fate of his life that he should be betrayed time after time. The dislike and jealousy he had always felt for Michael Shea rose up and choked him; Michael was everything he himself was not. In less than half an hour from Margaret's first words it would have been useless for her to begin again and insist upon the actual truth, that Kirstina and Michael had not met alone since the first week he came; James was no longer capable of believing her.

Very little of his emotion showed. He sat palely at his writing table, his eyes wandering over his sister's angry face and his hands fidgeting with a paper knife.

Kirstina came in at last and found the two of them. She looked from one to the other, her glance inquiring.

With a mendacious assumption of tact, Margaret said to her brother, "I will leave you alone."

James raised his head sharply and begged, "Don't go."

At such proof of dependence Kirstina frowned while Margaret smiled and stayed.

"You tell her," said James. He would not look at his wife.

"I have been with Michael Shea," Margaret announced. "I saw two letters you wrote to him, arranging assignations. I have been telling James."

"Michael Shea never showed you those," Kirstina said.

Margaret spoke triumphantly to her brother. "You see? Then you did write them?"

Kirstina came slowly on through the room and went to the window, where they had to turn to face her. She told herself that she must go carefully, but that she had had a long time to prepare.

"This should be between myself and you, James," she said, "but since you have asked Margaret to stay I will answer you both. Yes, I wrote to Michael Shea. Once when I heard he was in Toronto and once when he came here."

"And you went to meet him!"

"I did. I did not wish to see him, but it was necessary."

"Because he was your lover."

"No. We had not met for nine years. I wanted him to go away."

James looked up. "I don't believe you."

"No," said Kirstina reasonably. "It must be hard to after you have been listening to Margaret. But it is the truth, James. I hate Michael Shea. I do not want him here. I tried to send him away."

"That is a lie. If you had really tried he would have gone. Why didn't he?"

"He wanted his son."

"You see?" cried Margaret again.

Kirstina glanced at her briefly. "What is so terrible? Rudi is Michael's son. He was born five years before I met James. There is no infidelity in that."

James got up and came over to her, flicking the paper knife between his fingers. "Are you utterly shameless? Do you think I would have married you if I had known the boy was illegitimate?"

178

"I think at the time you wanted to marry me, you would not have cared."

"Don't listen to her, James! She will make you forget what she is. She wants to trick you again!"

"Did I trick you, James?"

"She married you and brought her lover here! Isn't that enough? To our very gates! There is nothing for you to do but turn her out— her and her bastard brat!"

Still watching James, Kirstina insisted, "Michael Shea has not been my lover since before Rudi was born. I have done you no injury."

"You have deceived me. I do not trust you. For three years you have made me provide for that man's child. You disgrace the name I gave you. I do not want you here any more."

Kirstina suddenly laughed. "Will you divorce me?"

"I will not have you in my house."

Margaret Collingwood sighed and then viciously broke out, "Now do you understand? Did you think you could make fools of us all? I know what you are, Christine. You glory in your power. You thought you could hold my brother forever. You keep Michael Shea here. You want your victims where you can see them. But now they will both be free. You are punished!"

"Be quiet, Margaret!" James said. "Christine, you had better go to your room."

Kirstina looked at each of them in turn. She saw that after all she would have been wise to have done what she had considered doing months ago and then decided against. She should have told James that Michael had once been her lover, and was persecuting her now. Then she would have been protected. To have had Margaret speak first was disastrous; it meant that now she would have to go much further and use the hold that terrified her—that had terrified her ever since she realized it was within her grasp. Trying still to avoid it she attacked a side issue and said, "You will find it hard to manage without me. Do you remember Prospect before I came?"

"It will not be the same now," said Margaret. "And do you think that counts with us? It is the shame you have brought that we want to be rid of! To think that my father's house should have sheltered a whore and her—"

"Be quiet!" Kirstina warned. "I will not have you say that again of my child."

"Why should I not? What else is he? When he leaves this house he will be known for the little bastard he is!"

"No," Kirstina said. "I think not. I see, James—and you, Margaret— that I shall have to tell you the whole truth. I believe it will be a shock. Rudi is my son and Michael Shea's son, but he is not illegitimate. Michael Shea and I were married."

The queer silence that fell upon them showed her they understood. They were standing so close she felt hemmed in. She was doing what she had planned to do if ever this moment should arise; she had no intention of being driven out; and yet her fear of what she did kept rising in her throat.

"You will ask me for proof," she said. "I cannot give it to you here and now. My copy of the marriage lines I lost in Montreal. But I was married to Michael in Boston, first on board ship by his uncle the captain, and again by a Roman Catholic priest. It was a true marriage. Only I did not intend to deceive you, James. Michael deserted me. When I married you I had every reason to believe he was dead. I learned differently only last year, when he came to Toronto."

"He wanted you back," said Margaret.

"He did. But what I said to you earlier was true. I hate Michael Shea. He has done me untold injury. He is doing this to me even now. I would neither go back to him nor give him his son."

"But you were his wife!"

"I was."

"He could have forced you!"

Kirstina's lip curled. "He did not choose."

James spoke at last. He had been staring at her and his face was noticeably changed. He came up to his desk and leaned upon it and he moistened his lips. "If you are his wife, get out now and go to him."

"No," said Kirstina. "I shall not. And you will not make me. . . . Margaret knows why, already. If you don't know, ask her and she will tell you."

Stiffly, James turned his head. His sister's mouth was tight and she did not speak.

"Very well," Kirstina said, "I will say it. Michael Shea is my husband and his son is legitimate. But your son, James, is . . . what Margaret called the other. If you make me go it is I who will not keep quiet. It is your son who will pay. It is your name and pride that will be absurd."

James pushed himself along to his chair and sat down. Pity mingled with Kirstina's contempt and she softened her voice. "James, I do not want to go. Last summer I chose to stay, although Michael is rich and I am his wife. Doesn't that prove to you that I hate him? Margaret wants you to think evil and she told you what would make you do so. I want only what I have—the asylum you can give me. I want to protect both my sons. I am faithful to the vows I made you. Why should you need to drive me away?"

"Christine, you are much stronger than I."

She came close and stooped, laying her hands over his on the desk. "James, you were good to me. I need your kindness now."

James drew his hands away. "I have no choice," he said. "My name and my son are very important to me." He stood up, hesitated awkwardly, and then went out of the room, refusing to look either woman in the face.

"James is a fool," said his sister, "but he is a stubborn fool. You will not find him so easy now."

Kirstina shrugged. "I will manage. It is you who went out of your way to make this trouble. What do you think it has gained you?"

Margaret could not tell. Sudden despair when she learned Michael was not free had sent her to wreak vengeance on Kirstina. Now she knew both Michael's secret and her own hopelessness; she had pushed too roughly at a house of cards and it had shattered down about her head. She could not go back to Michael and she asked herself bitterly why he had not warned her? If he had, she would have been spared the cruelest part of her defeat. She blamed him for it and at once forgave him, sure that he had refrained only because he had been bewitched. Christine had them all in chains: Michael, herself, and James; Christine forced James to do her bidding and Margaret to keep silent; she denied Michael and still he had not betrayed her.

I love you, Margaret thought of Michael; even now I will set you free; I will destroy her and you will see what she is. But she could not plan clearly and her mind churned with possibilities and with confused longings and hates. Ah, she dreamed, how I will punish you! How I will love to see you punished one day! Then she saw that the most helpless victim of all was the baby, the little Geoffrey, who because of Kirstina was the Collingwoods' illegitimate heir. Tears filled her eyes as she promised that he should never know. In my father's name, she promised, I will keep you safe. You shall be the more cherished and the more beloved because of what she has done. I will make her other child the guarantee that you shall never suffer. Then she remembered that Rudi was also Michael Shea's son, and that Michael Shea was still inviolate.

Kirstina went to bed too worn out even to think over what she had done. She turned down the lamp, closed her eyes and slept. An hour or so later she awoke to see that James had come up and was setting his candle on the table. This was no longer habitual and she was irritated with his lack of consideration. She pretended to sleep and, when she felt him watching her, she said, "James, I'm very tired."

"That will not do tonight," James said, in a tone different from any she had ever heard from him.

She opened her eyes wide. It occurred to her with great swiftness that a weak man could be a very spiteful one and might take strange ways of feeding his self-respect.

"You are not my wife," he said. "You told me you chose to stay in spite of that, and I must keep you to protect my name. But I will say how I am to be paid."

Kirstina sat up in bed. "That is not the way to talk to me."

He attempted to laugh. "You despise me, Christine. I have always known that and I do not care. From you I can get what I want and, since nothing can drive you away, there is no reason why I should not exact all I can get."

"I will not allow you."

"You will do as you are told."

Watching him, she swung her feet to the floor. At once he was at her side, his fingers digging into her shoulders. "Christine, are you going to fight me?"

She met his eyes and felt herself trapped, for she could not subdue him by day and run from him at night. If she struggled she would never forgive herself. She shrugged herself loose and fell back against the pillow.

Hours later, in the gray light of dawn, she knew she should have done otherwise. She could see then what James might become. He had used her violently often, for his emotions were always uncontrolled and wild, but she had never before been taken with cruel and experimental pleasure.

Then, too, she began to think how this time whatever she was called upon to endure she deserved. If Michael Shea had never

182

come back from the dead, both her children would have been legitimate; because he had come back, one of them was not. That was what she had seen months ago. She might hate Michael for it but it was nothing he could help, and he had not willed it to be so.

She, on the other hand, had taken her child's misfortune and used it to force her own will. What fools Margaret and James must be to believe she would use it further, or ever publish it abroad! Yet she had used it as a threat, and for her that was already a deadly sin. It was the betrayal of her unhappy childhood, of every covenant she had ever made with herself. What had she been striving towards if it could be bought only at such a price as this? She lay shivering as much from fear as from exhaustion, and then stilled herself and watched the sky brighten above the trees.

She thought, I had only one thing I could do, and so I have done it. Now I am safe. I have what I want. It is mine because I have made it and know how to keep it.

A tiny thread of doubt remained and reminded her that Michael Shea could still take her away any time he chose to use force. She dismissed it, for she had persuaded herself that that was what he would never do, and that because of such weakness she despised him.

VI

WHEN Margaret Collingwood left him, Michael Shea had been reasonably sure that Kirstina would reply to Margaret's accusations with the truth. He had told himself so often that Kirstina's fault lay in her peculiar blindness: in her inability to imagine what a thing could mean until she came to it. He had believed that when her true situation became known to the Collingwoods it would suddenly become clear to herself and she would fly from Prospect in the same revulsion as years before she had flown from Nordrupp's inn.

When he heard no further word that evening he was worried over her safety and over whether he should have done more to protect her. Early next morning she drove herself down to the shipyard and her cold level gaze told him at once how utterly he had been mistaken. She had come ostensibly to speak to Alec, but she made opportunity to come close to Michael and to say, in a low voice, "James knows the truth. I would have been wiser to have told him before, but I can still make him do as I wish."

He was as much appalled at her white, sleepless face as at her words, and she went on, in the phrase that had become almost a refrain between them, "You have done me all the harm you can. Now will you leave me alone?"

He had no answer and she turned from him without waiting for one. He watched her dicker with Alec and drive herself away.

He saw then, at last, that it was he who had been blind. He had wanted Kirstina; he had believed he understood her and he had let himself be deceived by his own sanguine, idiotic wish to have her come to him of her own accord. No one could have been more farcically wrong. Now he had to admit that she would never come, that he understood her as little as he understood James Collingwood—and it was inconceivable to him how even James could continue to support her as his wife on the terms she must have imposed.

He found himself asking repeatedly, Why? Only a thoroughly immoral woman would have been likely to act as she had done, and he knew from experience that she was not immoral. Then why? Was it pure hatred, or was it fear? What had become of her fierce independence? There she stayed, clinging to the name and position of a man whom she nakedly despised.

He considered leaving Port George. However, as he had told Kirstina before, there was nowhere else he much wanted to go. He disliked the thought of being driven out. And there remained his son. He realized finally that while he wasted time deliberating Alec Munro was bearing the brunt of their enterprise, that his new dock was almost completed and that all the work he could ask for lay to his hand. It seemed to him that after the great foolishness he had committed he was lucky to have this much left, and he started in at his work again with a determinate, unresting energy that demanded success as its daily bread.

Under such impetus the firm of Munro & Shea could but prosper. The lean years that Alec had prophesied came with the late fifties. The railways stole passenger trade, and a brief boom in shipping Lake Ontario wheat to England died with the end of the Crimean War. Other firms, hunting for business, also began building ocean ships but Munro & Shea maintained its lead. Michael named their first clipper the *Sacramento* and had her christened by Clare Munro. When the time came he himself sailed her to New York and Alec was smugly excited over the profit they made.

Their next two ships were disposed of in Montreal and the fourth to a Liverpool firm which sent out a skipper and crew to sail her home. In Boston, Michael hired a marine draftsman of such excellence that even his frequent drinking bouts hardly explained why his former employers had let him go. Roger Gaines drew ships that looked as though they might fly but whose delicate, integrated lines had the resilient strength of steel. When he was drunk he mourned with epic despair over the passing of sail; sober, he had a sour respect for engines and stubbornly urged their adoption. Alec and Michael both came sufficiently under his influence to begin planning largely in terms of steam and iron, though they still turned out the trawlers and fishing smacks that were a reliable sideline. In the winter months they kept the master carpenters at work in the sheds but sent their own teams into the back country to cut lumber and keep up their supplies.

With the expansion of the business workmen began coming to

Port George from Toronto and Kingston, even from Rochester and Oswego across the border. New wooden houses went up all along the road and down the little lanes. A second bridge replaced the ferry across the mouth of the George and more houses went up on the other side. Ferris's flour mill and the sawmill worked overtime and a man from Toronto started a tannery farther up the river. The population doubled and still continued to increase.

Almost suddenly, it seemed, the forest had receded for good, leaving the countryside open and rolling, with shade trees clustered about the houses and only small woods dotting the larger farms farther out. At Prospect there remained a fair stand of timber and Kirstina would not allow any more cut. Murray Fraser had cleared eighty per cent of his acreage and had easily sold all that it could produce. Saturday became market day in Port George, to which farmers from ten miles drove in, but every day there was noise and bustle on the road and Alec Munro put in a thick cedar hedge about his house "to keep the folk from peering in." In 1858 the whole varied congregation got together and raised a hall beside St. Peter's Church; next, they held a meeting in the hall and decided to build a school. The same year saw the coming of a Methodist preacher who held services in Ferris's mill until a new chapel went up. With two houses of worship, the new school, three major industries and constant altercation over road-mending in summer and snow-clearing in winter, Port George had acquired the status of a town.

A reflection of this growth was the way in which local interest in Prospect House faded. With so much that was new and vital going on, Port George had no time to gossip about Edward Collingwood's twenty-year-old megalomania and the topic gradually departed from conversation. When newcomers asked about the vast house on the bluff, old Port Georgians shrugged them off with a deprecatory explanation, and turned the discussion to the shipyards and the career of Michael Shea. They made it very plain that he was now the great man of the place.

Michael played the part that was expected of him. Murray Fraser's voice was the loudest on the school council but it was Michael Shea who sent up building materials and workmen from the yard and who, when more money was needed to engage a first-rate master and to buy books, provided it from his own pocket. It was he who went to Toronto and made representations so that a platform and shed were built at the Port George railroad stop. It was he who headed the list of subscribers when one of Ferris's men lost an arm in the mill machinery, and who saw to it that the man received a stretch of cleared land as well as the money.

For three years he continued to live with the Munros; then he built himself a house on the bluff opposite Prospect. His windows overlooked the bay and the village; when he stepped out in the morning he could see the dock and his ships building. His house was made of the pleasant red brick that was beginning to be common in Toronto and thereabout; it was square, comfortable and not too large; behind it was a stable where he kept two horses. He found a couple fresh out from England to look after him: the man was a groom and the wife a fair housekeeper and cook. The garden about his house was devoid of shade but Janet Munro came up day after day with cuttings and slips which she carefully planted and watered.

Because it had no mistress his house could not become a true social center, but it did become a gathering place for the men. Each evening one or more would drop by and stay to talk: Murray Fraser or Alec, Roger Gaines, Ferris, Emmett Rogerson, or David Hughes, the new schoolmaster; often they would drift down later to Hobart's inn and the meeting would swell to twelve or fifteen men, wrangling happily over their achievements and their expectations. "Biggest little town this side of Toronto," Hobart would say, in bland disregard of the claims of Hamilton and Niagara and points west. Even Alec Munro let the statement pass, afraid lest by caviling at good fortune he might end it; and indeed, after so rapid an advance, it was still possible Port George might outstrip all its rivals.

From time to time Michael heard from San Francisco. He had still some money invested there and his partner, John Surrey, wrote urging him to come out again to see for himself the progress that had been made. He was never seriously tempted to go. In Port George he had found a place that suited him. Sixty years old itself, the community had its roots in the older cultures of Scotland and England, and yet at the same time it was on the outskirts of the wilderness. Here he could enjoy both good company and good talk; if he wanted sport there were wild fowl in all the marshes, or he could pack up and go inland to hunt deer. He came to appreciate that indirectly the worst injury Kirstina had done him was to condemn him to live alone, but in spite of that his life was full and interesting and, on the whole, he liked it.

As Rudi grew older and went to the new school, he acquired a host of friends. He went off to the woods to set snares with the Fraser boys and he went fishing with young Adam Ferris. He brought them all to Michael's house and they sprawled there in the library, or in the garden in summer, complaining of their schoolwork and their parents' demands and asking for tales of the Far West. Each one was bound for a life of adventure and had made Michael Shea a hero; he encouraged them to come and was seldom bored by their company. Rudi's other friend was still Clare Munro. Their continued association much amused Michael and he would not have Alec and Janet interfere.

"What is wrong?" he asked. "If they keep it up long enough is there any reason why they should not pair off in the end?"

"He still says he wants to go to sea!" protested Janet.

"He could start worse. I went to sea myself."

Janet admired him too much to say more. She was, besides, quite at a loss to know how to control her daughter. Clare went her own way with complete unconcern for the wishes of anyone but Rudi and occasionally of her father and Michael Shea. She was a tall, thin girl, pale except when she browned in the summer. Her lank, dark hair fell on her shoulders and her enormous gray eyes were her one good feature. Janet thought privately that it was as well her daughter would inherit money and supposed that if she discouraged Rudi Brandt it was unlikely anyone else would ever find Clare attractive.

Murray Fraser's second son was apprenticed in the shipyard. When Rudi was fourteen Michael asked if in a year or so he would choose to do the same, but it was the sea and not the ships that attracted Rudi. He dreamed of salt water and badgered Michael to let him make his first voyage.

"Even just up the Lake, sir. So that I could get a start."

"Ask your mother," said Michael, sure that Kirstina would never agree. Rudi came back next day with her written consent to let him go anywhere Mr. Shea considered wise.

Two weeks later Michael sent him off on a trawler that was to be delivered on Lake Erie. Rudi was delirious with joy. His mother came down to see him sail and brought with her the young stepbrother whom Michael had hitherto seen only in church. Clare stood by, pale under her tan with jealousy and excitement. Later she followed Michael back to his house, muttering sullenly, "Why did you send him, Uncle Shea, when you know I can't go?"

"Perhaps because I enjoy having you to myself."

"You know I don't like you to flirt when I'm cross."

He smiled at her impudence and her sulks and invited her to stay to dinner. "Only remember, young Clare, it isn't becoming in a plain little piece like yourself to be too autocratic."

"I shall probably improve," said Clare complacently. "And if I were pretty my mother would not let me go about alone."

Michael sent her home early. That afternoon was the first time in months that he had seen Kirstina close to, and she had looked worn and tired, and even when she kissed Rudi good-by her face had remained impassive. It was years since she had made a practice of coming to the village for anything but to transact business, and she no longer visited even the Frasers at home.

His mind went back to one evening in the week after he had moved into his new house. He was living quite alone then, for he had not yet found the English couple. It was early spring and the weather was cold and the ground still soggy from the thaw. He had had guests and had seen the last of them leave when there was another rap at his door and he opened and saw Margaret Collingwood. She was in riding dress and she was wet from a drizzling rain; her horse was tied up at his gate. He could not do less than to ask her in. She went through into the library, where a light was burning. When he followed she was prowling about, touching and peering at all that was there.

"I knew it was your house," she said. "I watched all the time you were building. Why didn't you invite me to the housewarming?"

Her face was very white and somehow malevolent under the piles of dark, graying hair, yet he knew that she meant no harm to him. She picked up a book and fingered its cover. "How absurd is a bachelor's house! When I heard, I made sure you were to be married. Are you taking a bride, Michael?"

"You know very well that I am not."

"Yes," she agreed, "you have a wife. Why don't you divorce her?"

She put down the book and began to wander again. Michael stood before the fireplace and watched. He remembered how he had always disliked her voice: it was too high and light for her size. Suddenly she looked round and came towards him. "If you don't, you will always be alone. Don't you mind being lonely?"

"Margaret, why not sit down and let me give you a glass of wine?"

She gave a little shrug and pout. "You are trying to put me off and

I don't like to be put off. I have been waiting behind your stable most of the evening."

"Have you?"

"You had so many people here. I saw Alec leave and old Rogerson and Ferris and Fraser. I waited again and I rode right into the garden and looked through the window. I saw this room before you let me in. I had to be careful because I didn't want to be seen."

"I am sorry you had so much trouble."

She shrugged again and went and sat down in a corner of the sofa. "Don't be tiff!" she complained. "I wanted to talk to you. I would like that glass of wine, now."

There was a decanter still standing on a tray. He found a fresh glass and filled it and poured another for himself. She invited him to sit down beside her but he sat instead in the chair opposite.

"Now you look comfortable," Margaret said. "I did not feel I was welcome." She took a little sip from her glass. "Christine hates you," she said. "I suppose you know that."

"Margaret, have you come only to discuss what does not concern you?"

She exclaimed "No!" as if she were indignant. "It does concern me! I am so sorry for you. She is wicked to ruin your life."

Michael set his teeth. She rushed on in speech.

"You want a home—anyone can see that. You want a wife and children you can acknowledge as your own. You are getting on in the world and you need a hostess. Christine is robbing you of so much. I want to give it back."

"Margaret—"

"I was not brave enough two years ago. I did not see then what I ought to do. Michael, why should you not marry? I don't mean that you must get a divorce. Who is there to know?" She was leaning forward, her face thrust out like a mask. Her glass was held in her two hands. Suddenly she bent her head and drained it.

Michael said, with slow incredulity, "Are you suggesting I should make a bigamous marriage?"

"It is what she did, and you have not interfered."

"I suppose you have worked out how completely I would be in your power."

She dropped the glass; it rolled aside on the rug. She got up and came quickly and knelt beside him. "I only want you to have what you have lost! I would not mind. I would do it for you and never

give you away. Look at me! I am still young enough to have a child.
I love you." She reared up close. "Don't you hate her?" she cried.
"Surely you must hate her. She is your wife and she is living with
James!"

Although she was speaking to him so urgently, her gaze never
met his but slid past his shoulder. He stared at her, fascinated and
disgusted. Then he pushed himself out of the chair and moved away.

"Margaret, get up. You must put an end to this nonsense."

She stayed where she was, peering at him with the sly, sidelong
look. She said, "It is she! You are still in love with her."

"Get up!"

Automatically she started to get to her feet. When she was standing she broke out, "What a fool you are! Can't you see what she is?"
Suddenly she wailed at him, "You and James! You are both fools! I
hate you both!"

His dislike of her became distilled and concentrated. He said,
"You are completely mistaken. Kirstina is nothing to me now. I do
not even wish to remarry."

"But I want you, Michael!"

He drew his breath. "If you were a sane woman you would beg
me to forget you ever came here tonight."

Something in her face changed. "Why do you say that? Of course
I am sane!"

"You will not be if you go on indulging yourself like this! Have
you any idea how you seem—a woman of your age?"

"Michael, don't be cruel. I love you. One day I will show you
what she is. Then you will understand."

"None of this has anything to do with my wife."

He said the words with unintentional grimness. Margaret smiled;
then she began to titter. "Your wife! She is my brother James's wife!
You have had no wife for years! Oh, what a fool you are! How you
love her! If you did not love her you would have gone away." She
rocked where she stood and collapsed into the chair he had left.
Slowly she grew calmer and nodded to herself. "You will see," she
said. "You and James are quite wrong about her. She is a very wicked
woman. You don't believe me but one day you will see." For a little
while she was broodingly silent, then she sighed. "I think now I will
go. It was a waste of my time, wasn't it? And yet I spent so long
making ready."

Michael stood rigidly waiting for her to get up and leave. When she had started, she paused again at the library door and asked, "Are we quite alone in the house?"

"Yes."

"Then I am compromised!"

Again he drew a long breath.

"If my father were alive he would force you to do as I wish."

"If you mean," he said, "that your father would beg me to ravish you, I doubt that. The one thing you can do is to go home and not think of this any more."

He would have been happier if she had become angry or had even struck him, but she looked meltingly, as if he should later regret turning her away.

It was a horrid incident, that left him very uneasy, and it made plain to him once and for all that he did not hate Kirstina; that however bitter he might be against her, he loathed to think of her in the same house with that vile and unbalanced woman. Today, seeing her again, he knew that through the years even his bitterness and resentment had faded. Kirstina was a part of Rudi. She was piteously mistaken. He was sorry for her, and he was afraid for her.

Kirstina's second child Geoffrey had always seemed to her to belong far more to the Collingwoods than to herself. For years he was given over entirely into Margaret's care, and Margaret pampered and indulged him and was delighted with his excitable temper and furiously stubborn will. He was very bold and resented his aunt's watchfulness; if he was thwarted at all he raged at her until he made himself sick.

One day when he was six he was in front of the house playing at jumping from the steps. Margaret sat near repeatedly warning him to be careful and because of this he became progressively more daring. He jumped three steps, then four steps several times over, then five; then he climbed to the sixth and leaped outward and landed ignominiously on his knees in the drive. Margaret ran to pick him up but he was on his feet before she reached him and he turned on her, kicking wildly at her legs and screaming and clawing her hands.

Kirstina was upstairs in her bedroom and the noise brought her out on the balcony. She had never before seen the child in quite such a state and she stood transfixed. Then she shouted, "Geoffrey! Stop that screaming at once!"

Both the child and his aunt looked up, each as startled as the other. Kirstina disappeared, came quickly down the stairs and out.

"Tell your Aunt Margaret that you are sorry."

Geoffrey looked from her to Margaret and then back. "I shan't."

"Christine, he was hurt," said Margaret, as furious at the interference as at being taken by surprise.

Kirstina answered coldly, "That is no excuse at all. No child of mine is going to kick and scream like a wild thing."

"I shall kick her when I want to," said Geoffrey. "Aunt Margaret doesn't mind when I scream."

Kirstina eyed him quietly and then took him up to his room and spanked him. Afterwards, tearful and subdued, he let her attend to his scraped knees, looking at her all the while with immense respect.

From that hour he deserted Margaret and attached himself to his mother. He worked fanatically hard to please her, becoming studiously polite to Margaret and James and even to Mrs. Raikes. He stopped tormenting the animals; he ate the food he was given and did promptly as he was told. Kirstina paid him no more attention than she had before, but he found that a relief after Margaret's cloying devotion and when his mother did praise him he basked in content. Within a space of weeks he had changed from a spoiled, whining baby into a sensible, well-mannered little boy. Andy Patterson chuckled over the transformation and Rudi hailed it with heartfelt relief.

But to Kirstina, Geoffrey's allegiance was only one more problem to add to those that were already too many. It was one more grievance for Margaret to hold against her, one more bone of contention with James. Her life had degenerated long before into a wearying, piecemeal struggle.

At first she had believed she would be able to reinstate herself with James, but this hope had been lost when she was finally driven to shut him out of her room at night. Since then at Prospect it had been he and Margaret in league against her; only as long as her energy and strength were the greater was it still she who prevailed. She had made the estate productive and rich. She disposed of crops and livestock as and when she chose. She forced James to pay the men's wages and to spend on improving the land. She insisted he make Margaret share the expense of repairing the house. She brought in a doctor for Estelle. Sometimes she fought over points that were completely unimportant to her: she changed the furniture in the drawing room because Margaret wished it to stay as it was, and for the same reason she moved the portrait of Edward Collingwood from the dining room to the hall. After each victory she found she could enjoy watching both brother's and sister's looks of baffled, ugly defeat.

She was often terrified to see the woman she had become and it hurt her to remember how once she had been so proud of her hardness and her strength. She remembered the long-ago bargain she had driven with Nordrupp, the way she had hounded Michael during their brief months of marriage, the way she had risked her child's safety by running off with him to Montreal. Not all her striving called for regret, but she knew now that every time she had paid too dearly for an advantage, she had been drawing nearer to the day when she would commit unforgivable wrong to secure her place at Prospect. And, though even the night after that happened she had recognized her sin, not for a long time had she realized all that would follow from it.

She had robbed James of the pride that had been his only support and forced him to live with a corroding shame. The weapon she had used against him had been the illegitimacy of his son. She could not plead ignorance nor lack of understanding, nor tell herself that the thing had been done in the heat of the moment. She had intended it, and carried it through. Her only excuse lay in the peculiar blindness— the inability to forecast the consequences of her actions—which Michael had descried in her; of this she herself was unaware.

Where her hatred of Michael had gone she did not know. All the news she had of him came to her through Rudi. It was not too hard for her now to understand why he had stayed away so long and built up a life in the West. That must have been the life of which every young man dreamed—of which his son and his son's friends were now already dreaming—and all he had had to call him back from it had been the disagreeable young wife who had first driven him off. He had committed no crime, but only the mistake of not suspecting Johanna Warre, and of that mistake he as well as she had been a victim. When she considered all he had done since, she saw that he had become just such a man as she would always have admired, and she wondered how it was possible that in the beginning she had never been willing to wait, or to trust him to achieve his own ends in his own way.

She could not blame him even for his present abhorrence of her. He had built his house where each time she looked from her window she was forced to see it. He had made sure she should never forget what she had done. But he was kind to Rudi, and he was kind to her also in that he did not betray her.

Neither Margaret Collingwood nor James would hear of Geoffrey's going to the school in the village, and they insisted on teaching him themselves. Since he was told repeatedly that if he learned fast he would quickly outstrip Rudi in the common children's school, and as he was very jealous of his brother, he devoured everything he was given. Until then, Geoffrey had embodied to James only Edward Collingwood's appearance and his own nervousness and delicacy, and, much as he resented Kirstina, he had wished she had given more of herself to their child. But to have his son shining as a scholar appealed to him and he began to see Geoffrey perpetuating his own bookish tastes and making a great name. Naturally he hurried the boy along and it was lucky that Geoffrey had a precocious intelligence and an astonishing memory; under concentrated coaching he was reading Cicero and beginning his Greek when Rudi was still casually imbibing his first Latin verbs.

In the spring before Rudi first went to Lake Erie, Geoffrey was only eight, but he was beginning to chafe against the restrictions and pressure of his regime. He was irritated and unhappy when Margaret attempted to fondle him. He had tantrums during which he threw books at her and shouted to his father to let him alone. He had nightmares. Day after day he was expected to spend long hours shut up in the library at his studies. James would never realize that a child might need more rest and sunlight and air, and when Kirstina remonstrated he told her patronizingly that it was he who could best foster his son's interests. But one day when the long library windows were open, Geoffrey looked up from his book and saw his mother by the barn; in the space of seconds he had jumped out and come running to her, bursting into hysterical tears as he arrived. James could not understand. Kirstina said grimly that she did only too well, and for the first time she felt that this child, like Rudi, was her own to protect.

She refused to allow more lessons and for a while kept him with her as much as possible outdoors; then she enlisted Rudi's help. It was in keeping with Geoffrey's jealousy that he admired his brother greatly and wanted to do everything he did, and Rudi took him fishing and taught him to swim. Then came the day when Rudi was to set sail. Geoffrey had been to Port George many times before but he had never dreamed it contained anything so engrossing and alive as the shipyard, and all the while his mother had him there he was looking about him with sharp, observant eyes. When they went home again, Prospect already seemed to him very dull.

Late in the summer, after Rudi was back, Michael Shea realized that James Collingwood's son had now attached himself to Rudi's and Clare's circle. Geoffrey was years too young and Clare and the Frasers had no use for him; they called him a baby and told him to go on home. When they teased him too unmercifully Rudi came to his rescue, and then Geoffrey rounded on his brother. He was never grateful for any help he was given and felt insulted that it was offered. He insisted on going everywhere the others went, and doing everything they did, and so presently it became a game with them to try to wear him out. They took him on expeditions from which he returned with his face pinched and shadowed with fatigue, but he was always ready for more. When he was desperately outdistanced he would fall back on the one advantage he possessed, and boast shrilly of his superior learning. The Frasers scoffed and told him that would have to be proved. As a result Geoffrey fought his way through all opposition at home, and turned up at the village school when it opened in the fall. His grounding with James was uneven but his brilliance was never in doubt. David Hughes, the master, was thoroughly perplexed and put him in his top class, where he triumphantly began scoring points off Jock Fraser and Rudi.

"What else was I to do?" young Hughes asked Michael. "Are they a very gifted family?"

"Half mad."

"If the boy keeps it up he'll be a genius. It's all for effect, of course. If there were no kudos attached I doubt if I'd get anything from him at all."

Margaret insisted that Geoffrey ride her horse to school, "to mark him off from the common children," and that, together with his scholastic triumphs, gave him a certain consequence, so that his companions began to show him a guarded, half-humorous respect.

So also did Michael Shea. The dislike he had expected to feel for the child never materialized. Geoffrey was so cocksure, so stubborn and so indubitably himself. "Rudi is not my real brother," he would explain. "It is I who will have Prospect." And again, "This is a nice house that you have, but it is not so large as ours. Prospect is a mansion." He wandered in and out of Michael's house as freely as the other children, and seemed to enjoy talking to a man who had some claim to the position next in importance to the Collingwoods' in Port George.

One day he recounted at length how his father was always in the library, with the shutters half closed, and every now and then was ill. "He says it is the food, but my Aunt Margaret says it is because he is a fool. She says he makes himself sick and it wouldn't happen if he took a firm stand. My mother gives him special things to eat. . . . But he is always sick after they have been quarreling. He was very sick indeed when my mother wouldn't let him go on teaching me. My Aunt Margaret says my father always does as he is told. He was afraid of his own father. It is because I am like his father that he doesn't like me."

Another time, after looking at Michael very curiously, Geoffrey said, "My Aunt Margaret says she has been in your house. She asked me about you."

"She did?"

"Do you know my mother too?"

"Yes."

Geoffrey nodded. "I thought you must. Do you like my Aunt Margaret?"

"No."

"Neither do I, and she hates my mother. She would like to kill her. My mother is not afraid of anyone. . . . Do you know that Aunt Margaret watches you from the summerhouse? . . . She goes there every day and watches and watches and watches. I used to go with her. I liked to look through the glasses. You can see the dock. I saw Rudi there, and you, but I didn't know then it was you. You can see this house, too—even the flowers in the garden. If you didn't draw the curtains at night you could see right into the rooms. But Aunt Margaret always wanted me to sit on her lap. I don't go any more."

"No," said Michael slowly, "you are too old for that kind of spying."

Geoffrey explored Port George as if it were a new world—which, indeed, for him it was. "I have been to the Munros' house," he said, "and I have been to the Frasers' house and I have been to the Ferrises' house." He had been sitting on Michael's library floor, reading, but now he had closed his book and was in earnest thought. It was late afternoon and rather dark, and he spoke as if he had had something on his mind for a long time. "Mr. and Mrs. Munro are married and Mr. and Mrs. Fraser are married and so are Mr. and Mrs. Ferris."

"Well, yes?"

"None of them are at all like my father and mother. My father and mother don't like each other. Sometimes they don't even talk to each other. . . . I have asked Rudi about it. . . . I would like my mother to be happy."

Michael waited, and the interval was long. Then, "Once I saw my mother cry. It was in the middle of the night. I woke up. My Aunt Margaret had been out and she was all dripping wet. She was in my mother's room shouting. My mother shouted too. She said, 'You filthy woman! Get out!' Then she saw me and came and put me back in bed. She was crying."

Suddenly the boy jumped to his feet, his face working with passion. "Don't you tell that to anyone! Don't you tell Rudi! I never told anyone before! I never meant to tell you that! It was a long time ago! . . ." His hands were clenched tight and his voice became shrill. "My mother is not as my Aunt Margaret says! My mother is good!"

He was quieted at last by Michael's calm. His shoulders went down and his hands relaxed. He said, "I don't suppose you would tell." Michael answered, "No, I would never tell."

He thought that the most revealing thing about the incident was the hint of how much more was left unsaid, and it occurred to him that Geoffrey's usual talk was nothing but a froth of gossip: he gabbled happily enough over that, but what he felt deeply he was not able to put into words; when he tried to do so he had an instant sense of betrayal.

Towards the end of the winter Rudi began to talk of nothing but the voyages he would make next summer. He was to have a berth on a trading schooner. He might get as near the Atlantic as Montreal; he knew he would call at Kingston and Oswego and Rochester. Geoffrey hated to hear him talk about it. In a babyish fit of sulks he would exclaim, "Who wants to go on any old ships!" and Rudi invariably fired up.

"Mr. Shea was a sailor!"

"That was on the real sea!"

"If you were on the real sea you'd be seasick!"

"I would not be."

"You would."

"I bet I get on the real sea before you do!"

"Don't be silly, Geoffrey. I am a sailor already."

This was exactly what Geoffrey could not forgive. He had no

earthly desire to be on any ship and was besides very much afraid he might be sick, but he could not bear that Rudi should have any field in which he triumphed alone.

"I shan't wait till I'm fourteen before I make my first voyage," he said.

"Mr. Shea will make you wait."

"Mr. Shea doesn't own all the boats on the Lake."

"Now you're talking like a baby. If you tried to go before he let you someone would be sure to tell him and he'd fetch you back."

It began to seem to Geoffrey that unless he could beat Rudi at this one thing life would not be worth living. He had always before done what he said he would do, and the fact that this time he had not at first meant what he said faded from his mind. All he could think was that he had to find himself a ship and get away on her before anyone knew.

Late in April he disappeared. At nightfall one day Rudi came back from Prospect to the village to inquire if he were with any of their friends. No one had seen him. Few suggestions were forthcoming. He was too old to get lost in the woods unless he had gone very far afield and no one could think of any likely way in which he could have been drowned. It was Michael who first guessed that he might have gone on board the trader that had sailed from the harbor that morning. He remembered the ship was to call at Toronto and supposed that if Geoffrey were on board they would hear next day and get him back by train. But they could not take that solution for granted and a search party was organized to scour the woods up the river. Rudi went back to Prospect with the news and set out again to help search. He brought old Mr. Patterson with him.

Next afternoon Michael received the message he expected, but the captain of the trader reported he would not risk sending the young gentleman home alone: he seemed a slippery fish and he would deliver him when he called back in ten days.

So Geoffrey would make his voyage after all! Michael grinned as he refolded the note. He was on the point of sending a man with it to Prospect when he stopped and considered. He looked out of his office window up at the great house and he thought suddenly that no such opportunity was likely to come to him again. His curiosity had been riding him far too long; now was the time to find out for himself. He tucked the note in his pocket and went out, hailing a man from the yard to go and warn the search party to come home. Then he mounted his horse and rode off to Prospect.

When he arrived at the house Mrs. Raikes opened the door and he asked for Mrs. Collingwood.

"In the drawing room, sir. They are about to have tea."

She meant Kirstina and Margaret and Estelle. Michael followed her across the hall. She threw open the door and he went in. The room was bright with the afternoon sun. Margaret was standing by the spinet, drumming her fingers on its lid. Kirstina sat in a low chair. Beyond her, near the fire, Estelle was placidly stitching at a sampler on her knee. She did not so much as lift her head, but both Kirstina and Margaret turned to the door and stayed immobile.

Michael said, "Geoffrey is safe. I have had a message about him from Toronto."

The tension did not go out of the room, but its character somehow changed. The door behind him softly closed. Margaret's body sagged and she leaned on the spinet; then she recovered herself and came forward. "How good of you to come and tell us yourself! Isn't that kind, Christine?"

Kirstina was looking at him without expression. She said, "No doubt everyone else was out searching."

"Not quite everyone," Michael said, "but I decided to come. This is the note I had. You will want to read it." She took it from him and read and then remarked, "Geoffrey is a spoiled, headstrong child. He will have to be well punished for giving such anxiety."

Margaret said acidly, "Christine is the most unfeeling mother. If you can believe it, last night she went to bed and slept."

Kirstina looked at Michael. "Rudi told me what you supposed had happened. I thought it very likely."

She did not say anything further and he knew that what she intended was for him to leave at once. Since he had come in she had not once glanced at the tea things on the table at her side. She had laid the note in her lap where her hands were folded.

But Margaret hurried on in speech. "Christine, have you no courtesy at all? Sit down, Michael. Now that you are here you won't go without some tea!" She crossed over to the fireplace and pulled the bell for Mrs. Raikes.

Kirstina made no move until he sat down in the chair opposite her. Then he saw her face change, and she said, "But of course you must stay."

She turned and pulled the tea table a little closer. As if it were the most natural occasion in the world, she began to pour. Michael's gaze wandered for an instant to the strange figure of the little old lady, still busy with her embroidery frame and quite unaware of anyone present. He had not thought Kirstina observed him but at once she explained, "Estelle is Geoffrey's grandmother. You must not mind her ignoring you. She seldom notices anyone but the children." As she spoke she turned and went on, "Estelle, dear, put away your sewing now. It is teatime." Estelle looked up and smiled. Michael saw with a shock how smooth her face was, unlined and unmarked, yet the skin was stretched tightly across the tiny bones. She was fastidiously dressed and her white hair was beautifully neat. With a smile of childlike pleasure she put down her work and came and took her plate and cup from Kirstina's hands. She arranged them carefully on a table by her chair and sat down. Then she lifted the cup and saucer again and very daintily began to drink.

"Estelle is like a good little girl," Rudi had said once. "My mother always dresses her herself." Michael had an illusion of fantasy, as if he were looking on at something that was not often to be seen.

But beside him Margaret's voice was ugly. "I don't wonder you stare. If I had my way she would be shut upstairs. The creature has been a lunatic ever since my father died."

"She was shut away for a good many years before that," Kirstina said.

Margaret shrugged. "My father never bore gladly with fools. No one would think you did, either, Christine, judging by the way you treat James." On mentioning her brother's name, she started up. "James!" she repeated. "No one has told James! Why didn't you remember him, Christine?" With a sharp flicker of excitement, she glanced from her sister-in-law to Michael. "Of course he must be told," she said, and hurried from the room.

"You are going to be very satisfied," Kirstina said. "No doubt you wanted to see us as we are."

He could feel the heat of her anger. The skin about her mouth was pinched with the effort of reining herself in. He wondered if it was unforgivable of him to have come and to have stayed when she desired him to go.

The door was flung open. James Collingwood directed one ugly glare at Kirstina and rounded on Michael. He was shaking with fury and his voice was high and tense. "How dare you come to my house?"

Kirstina spoke in utter, cold contempt. "Sit down, James. There is nothing you can do and not the least need for you to get angry."

"Christine, if you think I am going to allow this—!"

"Mr. Shea has come out of charity," she said, "to tell you that your son is alive. No doubt he will go when he is ready, but you will not make him go before."

It was a vicious exchange. Michael listened with a chill of incredulity. Estelle's pleading voice broke in. "Christine, dear, don't be angry. You hurt poor James."

"He has only himself to thank. Don't be a fool, James. Sit down."

James was watching her, still with sullen malevolence, but he seemed puzzled. He glanced indecisively at Michael and then moved to a sofa and slumped down upon it.

"You too, Margaret," continued Kirstina. "Then we shall all be together. I am sure you want to see Mr. Shea."

Michael turned his head. Margaret was leaning against the door she had closed after James came in; she was watching Kirstina with a look of thwarted, unashamed hatred such as he had never before seen. Suddenly he thought, It is true that they would both like to kill her; but they are afraid of her and they cannot find the means.

Margaret stood away from the door and came to sit by her brother. Michael had them together then. It was ludicrous that both of them now dismissed Kirstina from their minds and devoted their attention to him, James's eyes glittering with resentment, Margaret's hot and devouring. But Margaret said nothing more to him. She stared, sunk into herself, concentrated upon her own emotion.

Meanwhile, Kirstina talked. "I have been wanting to see you for some time. Rudi tells me you have promised him a berth on a ship when he is sixteen. Are you sure that that is best for him?"

Well, he thought, he is her son and mine: why should we not together discuss his career? But he knew why she did it. He knew that he as well as the Collingwoods was being shown his place.

"It depends," he said, "on whether you wish him to go to sea at all."

"There is no future for a sailor on the Lakes."

"The best I could do for Rudi would be to send him to California, to a friend of mine there."

Her eyelids flickered and he knew he had dealt blow for blow. But it was the truth, and he had considered it often before. John

Surrey's ships sailed to the Orient and back, and John Surrey's wealth would one day be divided.

"I would let Rudi go," she said, "if it was for his own good."

"Then when the time comes we must talk of it again. I might have a few requirements of my own."

Again the little flicker. She passed away from the subject. She spoke of Geoffrey and his incredible behavior, of the bad winter they had had, of his half-finished ship. She even forced James to make one or two civil comments. When Michael got up to leave she accompanied him, still talking conventionally of this and that, until they stood outside the door. Her eyes were as inimical as ever and she stood there as if she were barring his return. He thought how, when she went in, she would be faced with those two whom she must hold at bay.

"If that should happen again," James said, "I will not answer for what I shall do."

"I did not invite him here. No one invited him—unless it was Margaret. Did you, Margaret?"

"Why don't you go to him?" James asked.

"Margaret would never let me go."

"Do you want to, then, now?"

"Of course she wants to!" jeered Margaret. "Look at yourself—and then look at him!"

"Christine, dear, don't! Please don't . . ." pleaded Estelle, her small face loose and shaking with fright.

Kirstina had fought too many of these battles not to know how this one would end. She could always defeat James because she wore him out first, and when he failed Margaret deserted him in disgust. He kept it up this time until they had had their evening meal. Then he was seized with cramps and became violently ill. That also was part of the regular pattern. When it happened he turned to Kirstina because she knew what to do for him, but he spat at her between intervals of pain. The house was in an uproar until he was exhausted enough to sleep. Margaret, raging and contemptuous, paced up and down the halls.

Rudi came in. He was tired and very much disturbed because Michael Shea had been in the house.

"What did they talk about?" Margaret repeated after him. "Why, naturally, about you."

Estelle was whimpering in her room, and when he went past she called to him. Later he went to his mother and said accusingly, "You have made Estelle cry. What happened this afternoon?"

For the first time in her life, unable to find any other defense, Kirstina lost her temper with him, and he flared back and then rushed away, shouting, "Why do you make us all so unhappy?"

Margaret asked then, "Have you never realized what Rudi will feel when he finds you out?"

Kirstina stared at her in horror and was lost in a morass of self-loathing. Earlier that day she had been sick with anger against Michael; now she was sick because of the risks she ran. She dared not wait to be attacked again. She had to make some attempt to save the little she had.

She went out to the barn and found Andy and told him to harness the horse. He asked her, "What are you after now?"

"Let me alone, Andy! Haven't I enough to bear without you asking me too?" Then she was at once repentant and said, "Forgive me. I believe one day they will have me as mad as they are themselves."

His kind eyes watched her while he did as he had been asked. "Why should I blame you?" he said. "Don't I know the trouble you are in?"

That night the village was tired after the search and so for once Michael was alone. She reached his house with no one hailing her. His man opened the door and Michael came out of the library asking, "Who is it?"

She felt then that she should never have come. Her throat worked and she was faint, but she could not leave now. When he said, "Will you come in here?" she went before him into the room he had left.

Michael closed the door and came away from it. She watched him closely and saw that he looked gravely inquiring and no more. She said, "I came to tell you . . . that you must never do that again."

"Were you so much afraid?"

"Yes."

He still held the book he had been carrying when he came out, his finger marking his place. Now he laid it away on his desk. He looked up at her again and said, "I have been thinking, since I left you, that if I had ever guessed it was so bad, I would have understood how much you hated me. I never understood that.

"Kirstina, why didn't you come to me years ago? I would have provided for you. In spite of anything I had said, I would have let you go away alone. You loathe that ghastly place. There is nothing there for you. You even sent the boy to me as much as you could. Why did you never say?"

"You mean, in the beginning, if I had come to you and said I could not bear it . . . you would not have forced me to stay as your wife?"

"Never."

"Nor taken Rudi?"

"Not for all the time."

Her earlier faintness swept back. There was a chair beside her and she moved to it quickly and sat down.

Michael turned away from her, staring at the window before which the curtains were drawn. "Until this afternoon," he said, "I did not really believe it could be hate. At first I used to think it was perversity and greed, because you would not surrender anything you had. I thought somehow—somewhere—you must have found compensation, and I despised you because you were able to make yourself live in wretchedness. I never knew it was open hell, or that you walked in it knowingly because you would not come to me."

She said dully, "I don't understand you. Nothing can have made you change that opinion today. I showed you exactly what I am."

"I did not have to change it today. Although I never understood, it is a long time since I resented you. Since then I have been sorry for you and marveled at you, and I have admired your stubbornness and your courage. But not till today did I see all you had fought . . . and I wish you had had less pride."

He was looking at her steadily now. Kirstina was heavy with the weight of her despair. She got up and came close to him, near the window. She leaned against the wall. She said, "It is true that I hated you once, and that I was afraid of losing what I had. But that did not last. It only lasted until I saw to what it had brought me. . . . Once he knew the truth, James no longer wanted me. I forced him to keep me because of Geoffrey—because of the disgrace I said that I would bring on a child. You know, as James did not, how great a shame it was for me to use that threat but I used it willfully and knowingly, and if I have paid for it, I deserved to pay. . . . There has been no pride in anything I have done. I have fought those two at Prospect until I have become like them, and I have made their house a place from which I would be glad to save my sons. . . . When I sent them to you it was as much to defend them from myself as from anyone else."

"Yet you were angry with me this afternoon."

"I was angry because I was tracked down. Because I could not hide any more."

They were so close together that she could see the recognition of truth come into his eyes. He moved away and sat down in the chair behind his desk and for a moment leaned his head on his hands. Then he looked up at her and said, "All that we have wasted!"

"What do you mean?"

"This is what I knew—what I was sure would one day come—but I believed that when you saw it yourself repulsion would drive you away from Prospect rather than bind you to it. I waited for that. I was a fool. I should have taken you by force."

"If you had, I would have hated you forever."

That also he had known. He sat looking at her. In the lamplight she was pale. Her head was outlined against the dark red of the curtains. They had each of them injured the other beyond repair, and yet already that lay far in the past.

Kirstina suddenly moved. Her hands clenched and her body taut, she came into the middle of the room. "Why don't you say something?" she cried. "Don't you realize what I have told you? Why don't you say, I hate you now—even if I did not before? Don't sit there! I know how much wrong I did you! Why not say what you think?"

She shouted at him much as her son Geoffrey had once done, and in the same place. Michael stood up, and when he put his hands on her shoulders she flinched. "Don't touch me! I won't have you touch me!" He remained still and, as Geoffrey had done, she slowly became quiet.

He said, "I want to be sure that you do understand what I think. I don't hate you now and I never could again. It is a long time since I was in love with you. But you are the person I care for most in the world. I know you best. Whether it brought me happiness or not, I would still wish to look after you."

It seemed to him that quite suddenly the blue eyes became black. She trembled and swayed forward against him, and as he caught her she said at last, "Michael, hold me. . . . Please hold me."

He remembered that what he had always wanted was for her to need him but even as he felt her within his arms he was sharply aware of his own helplessness. He wondered if she also knew how much could not now be made good.

Presently they sat down. The fire burned quietly and the room was warm and dim.

"I have brought you nothing but harm," Kirstina said, "and yet I used to believe that that was all you had brought me. Even now . . ." She hesitated and paused. "Michael?"

"Yes?"

"Even now . . . there is Geoffrey. If I were to leave him, he would be alone with them."

"I know." He reached out and covered her hands in her lap with one of his, almost exultant because she too understood, and knew that you could not go on running away forever: the time came when you had to abide by what you had done. Geoffrey belonged to them both; as they had created his weakness, they could not now disown it with impunity.

"If he were still a baby," she said—"or if they would let him go—" but she let the sentence drop and did not finish it. James Collingwood's son could never be left to his father and to his aunt as they were now, and as they would be if he were left to them.

Michael said to her, "Once we each had a choice, and each of us chose wrongly. Perhaps it is only justice that this time we have no choice at all."

She was filled with gratitude to hear him thus couple them together. They began to talk a little, slowly, of the things they might have done and had not.

"If you had never gone away!" she said.

"If I had not stayed away so long . . ."

"If we had not been so young . . ."

It was a litany that could have gone on forever, that would go on forever in their minds. Eventually she had to say, "It is late, and I must go."

He kissed her once before she left, holding her as she had begged him to hold her. He came out with her and put her up into the pony trap.

As she drove in at the gates of Prospect, a figure disengaged itself from the shadows as Margaret Collingwood stood in the drive. Kirstina was forced to stop. "I know where you have been," said Margaret. "That was what he came for this afternoon." There was more than jealousy in the evil gloating of her tone, and there was madness in the way she must have stood waiting for hours.

The change that came to Prospect was marked and sudden and the children bloomed under it. Kirstina could see that at first they were mystified. Rudi as well as Geoffrey scurried about to please her, as if to ensure that the shadows would not return. Gradually they began to take the improvement for granted. There came the day when Rudi brought Clare Munro to his home and that was the start of an invasion, for thereafter the whole troop of children came and Prospect, from being taboo, became one of their natural haunts. From June on, Rudi was away, and Geoffrey played host with regal generosity.

That year the land prospered. There was more under cultivation than ever before. All the crops were rich and there was no blight; Kirstina looked out over fields that were green and rippled like silk under the breeze. One after another the fruits ripened and the children turned out to pick. There were four young calves in the pasture and two litters of young pigs. Andy Patterson looked over his animals with contented eyes. "A good year," he said often, "a good year. Not one of them but is straight and well-grown." His dog was very grizzled now; they walked about together in perfect amity, and whenever Kirstina came out she would presently find them at her side.

Even in the house there was peace. Mrs. Raikes amiably did as she was told. James was led into no sudden rages. Estelle wandered about unalarmed and played her tinkling tunes on the spinet. Each one's confidence had expanded. No one was desperately afraid.

Kirstina knew how much of this must be the reflection of the change in herself, and she marveled at it. She was not forgiven, for she would never forgive herself. The wrong she had done was with her daily. But, now, she did not believe it could only breed more wrong.

James watched her with increasing wonder. He was nearing forty and looked much older than his years; he stooped and had a bad color, but he was still expert in the art of self-deception. He would never have resented Michael Shea if he could have believed Kirstina greatly preferred himself, and her new gentleness allowed him to believe whatever he pleased. He could pretend that she would not let him sleep with her from principle alone, and he could respect such a scruple so long as it implied no slight to himself. The change in her had come after Michael Shea had invaded the house, after which —if Margaret was to be believed—Kirstina had gone to him.

His tortuous mind wound in and out until he had persuaded himself that what she wanted was his protection and he resolved that he too could show himself generous. He began once more to seek her company. He would come out of his library to join her when she was with the children in the garden. He would walk with her over the fields and praise what she was having done. Instead of waiting for her to ask for money he made an effort to remember when it would be needed and to offer it himself. To a casual observer they might have been a normal and contented couple.

Only Margaret Collingwood took no part in the new life. Margaret hated Kirstina always and now, even more, she hated James for his fresh desertion. The house became unendurable to her and, though she slept within it, for whole days on end she went out to the summer-house and sat there where no one came, where there was nothing to hear but the faint sound of the water below and the voices of the birds. She did not look through her glasses, but sat staring, not moving for long stretches of time. She went in to her meals when she knew the others would be gone.

The summer nights were warm. Kirstina and James and often Geoffrey too would sit late out of doors or in the library with the windows pushed open. Margaret took to wandering about the estate after dark. She walked fast and very silently. With a silk scarf thrown over her head she would appear suddenly by Andy's little house, and then the dog Argus rumbled with anger and howled for minutes after she had moved away. She would go down to the gates and even out into the road beyond, along towards the Frasers' farm or towards the river, where there were new houses she had never seen. Murray Fraser came upon her there one night. "Sitting at the side of the road," he told Michael. "She rose up and startled the horse out of his senses. She was all in white, with a white thing over her head. For a moment I was fashed about my own wits!" He paused a moment and then added, "You know, she's not quite right. She should be shut up."

Murray was delighted with Kirstina. For years he had had to listen to Alec Munro prophesying that the Collingwoods were bound to win in the end, that no woman could fight eternally against such odds; and, for a long time, looking at Kirstina's set, inimical face in church and when she drove to market, at the fashion in which she fled his or any other friendly advances, Murray had felt forced to agree. But now at last she was justifying his original faith in her and he was jubilant. "There is a woman!" he declared. "Didn't I tell you so before? The pride of her, now, and her two fine sons! And a finer farm than my own she has—which I'd allow no other man to say."

Alec, listening judicially, agreed that Mrs. Collingwood had a free look again. "And very friendly she can be, too. She was in to see Janet and they had a nice crack together."

"Did you hear him?" demanded Murray indignantly later of Michael Shea. "For a Scotsman the man has no sensibility at all. Janet Munro is a kind woman and so is my Ellen, but Christine Collingwood could set a man's bones on fire. She ought to be a widow."

"What good would that do you?"

Murray looked sideways, with a slow, appraising eye. "My friend, if you don't know that there's no one to match her with here but yourself, why should I tell you? I'm fifty-two. I would have to guess your age and I know you're as continent as a monk, but if Christine Collingwood were a widow I'd arrange the marriage myself and give her away in church."

Kirstina thought it wisest to ignore Margaret entirely. No one warned her except Andy Patterson, who said to her, "Hatred is an ill thing on which to turn your back." Kirstina looked where he did and saw Margaret walking across the lawn. As always she had the feeling that he knew more than he would ever tell and she asked, "What harm can she do me now?"

"Any that is within mortal power. For the mad there is God's pity, but I have seen her sit in her spying place with only evil behind her white face, and I cannot pity her."

"But what can I do?"

"You can watch. You will be forgetting to do it because you are not afraid. But you can watch and it is I that will be watching too."

The months of summer wore to an end and Rudi came home, very bronzed and taller than herself. She was proud of him for that and delighted that he was shy when she had to reach up to be kissed. He sat talking and telling her and James of his adventures, telling Geoffrey also when frantic curiosity drove Geoffrey to come and listen. He had been to Montreal and not been able to recall anything about it. He had bought his mother a length of silk there, and he had brought Estelle a fan and Geoffrey a knife; he had even brought a handkerchief for Mrs. Raikes and a French book for James and a picture for Mr. Patterson.

"Why a picture?" his mother asked.

"To put in his little house. He will like it. It is a fine picture of a ship."

It was in fact what Andy had always wanted.

"What did you bring Clare?" Geoffrey asked.

Rudi grinned. "You'll have to ask her after she has got it."

He went to Michael and talked there almost as much, but home had become so pleasant that he was less inclined to stray away, and he discovered also that Michael was pushing him to stay with his mother.

"In a year or so you'll be off for good. She won't try to keep you then. You must give her all you can now."

Rudi listened without any feeling of strangeness. He had grown up with the knowledge of his parentage. It had become a part of him and he was at ease with it. He was not quite sure when he had first realized what his legal status must be; it had not bothered him then and it did not now. Naturally the last thing to occur to him was that his parents might have been married, but he knew them both and he knew they loved him. He did stay a great deal with Kirstina and he told her what Michael had said.

In a way that she had not anticipated, Kirstina discovered that she was recovering a little of her one-time compassion for James. For so long she had refused to admit that there was anything in him that was not despicable, and she had injured him deeply and repeatedly. Was it to be wondered at that he, who had been poor in spirit at the start, should under such treatment have become vicious and mean? In her effort to atone she was charitableness itself, so that one day he said to her, quite suddenly, "I have never given you any reason to be kind to me. I am almost afraid to ask you now why you are?"

She answered with equal sincerity, "I am so much ashamed of the time when I was not."

"The best thing I ever did was to induce you to marry me, and I never thought I should find the courage for that. But even at the beginning I didn't treat you well, and God knows what possessed me later."

Kirstina said slowly, "I believe *I* did."

"What do you mean?"

"We brought out the worst that was in us, James. We should have realized that we were caught in a situation that we could not help, and not have mistreated each other."

"But now you have forgiven me?"

"Now I am sorry for what I did, and I should like to think I had your friendship again."

He admired her tranquillity and her moderation and he became devoted. Kirstina knew she would never understand him: her own nature was too positive and too dependent upon action. She did as she was moved to do and then afterwards considered what was done. James wavered and accommodated himself and reflected what he found in the person momentarily closest to him. If she dispensed no malice he could not return it to her.

A few weeks later, in the middle of November, he drove her to the village, where they were caught in a shower of icy rain. It was several hours before they returned home and James by then had contracted a severe chill. Kirstina put him to bed and moved a small stove into his room. Nothing was ever easy for him; after two restless, uncomfortable days he began to run a high fever; the third night Kirstina came in to see how he did and found him by the open window, his teeth chattering with cold.

There was a doctor now in Port George, an elderly man who had come out with his wife from England. He had been to Prospect once already when Kirstina had had him to see Estelle. On that occasion James had glowered at him and had made him thoroughly unwelcome. This time when Dr. Ross stepped into the house he felt the atmosphere was changed, but he was not impressed with James's condition. He examined him conscientiously and inquired into his past history. Then he shook his head and told Kirstina, "Not a strong constitution. These cases can degenerate suddenly and you don't want him with a congestion."

James began to cough and complained that his chest hurt. He refused to make the effort to eat. Within twenty-four hours he was delirious and the old doctor came back to say with no further doubt, "Congestion—and of both lungs, I am afraid." It was not a doctor's business so much as one for continual nursing, of which Kirstina bore the brunt, with Mrs. Raikes and Rudi to relieve her. James became desperately ill and was all the while in acute pain. He knew no one and raved in incoherent, wild phrases. He became exhausted, and had sudden lucid intervals when they were sure he was going to die.

As soon as he was seriously ill Margaret reappeared in a comparatively rational mood. She hovered in the corridor outside his door and wanted to help and tried to get into his room. Kirstina at first

212

did not see why she should not, but Margaret's presence drove James into a frenzy. Even when he did not know her his excitement rose as she came near. After leaving her with him for an hour one day, Kirstina returned to find him struggling to get out of bed. He screamed, "Christine! Christine! Get me away from her! Keep me safe!" Kirstina thereafter banished Margaret from his room but asked her to help with the incessant carrying and fetching. Margaret showed patience; she stayed hour after hour at her post. Once she said, "He is dying. I know he is dying. I want to be there."

But the constitution the doctor had disparaged held on until one night James slept without pain and woke with a clear understanding. He was horribly weak. The winter would be over before he could be about again, but there was no reason now to fear that he would not see the spring. Kirstina needed rest herself and was glad to get uninterrupted sleep and to take her meals at proper hours. The first time James sat up, when she brought in a tray, he said to her in a flat, reflective tone, "You should have let me die. Then you would have been quite free."

Now that he was getting stronger he did not maintain the same violent aversion to his sister. Margaret was still attentive and quite prepared to sit in his room or to give him his food. She was apt to fall into blank silences, staring at him as if he were not there, but when he could persuade her to read to him he found her company pleasant enough.

Almost as soon as he was allowed more varied food he frightened them all by having a severe gastric attack. Kirstina was puzzled but the doctor, when he was appealed to, reminded her, "It's a chronic condition, ma'am—didn't you tell me since he was a child? Go slowly, but you can't expect to keep him on slops forever." She became doubly careful.

In spite of that, within a few days he had a second attack worse than the first. He complained of burning pain in his stomach and vomited repeatedly. None of the usual remedies helped, and after hours of pain he lapsed into a coma. Kirstina was more distressed than she had been in his long illness: this seemed to her so unnecessary and cruel. He was slow in rallying again and apprehension weighed him back. The third attack came two weeks later. He had eaten only eggs and a milk dish, but frightful pain clawed at him shortly afterwards, and he clung to her and cried out. His stomach and throat were on fire and when she gave him barley water he

retched in agony. His weakness made his suffering the more terrible
to watch, until his breathing became shallow and irregular and he
collapsed. He was still alive when Rudi arrived with Doctor Ross and
they struggled to put warmth into him and to bring him back, but in
half an hour more he was dead.

James Collingwood was buried in St. Peter's churchyard beside
his father, on December twenty-third. Almost all Port George was
there; no one escaped feeling the futile sadness of his life and the
people were sober and shocked. Kirstina was still too bewildered to
understand her position. Michael Shea came up to her and said
quietly, "I will not come until you send me word." She realized that
this was something she would think about soon.

She drove home to Prospect. Mrs. Raikes, with unusual initiative,
went at once and made tea. Kirstina sat in the drawing room and
looked at those about her: Geoffrey large-eyed and nervously excited, Estelle frightened, still crying gently as she had all through the
service. Rudi stood by the fireplace, as quiet as Kirstina herself. She
was aware that he had borne half the burden of the last few days,
that she had leaned on him because he had invited her to and because he had known all that needed to be done.

When she had drunk her hot tea, she went up to her room. She
was appallingly tired and she longed to be alone. She sat down on
the bed and took off her bonnet and laid it behind her.

The door opened and Margaret came in. Kirstina looked at her in
weary exasperation. She could not recall that Margaret had spoken
a word to her since James died—she had not withdrawn herself entirely but had sat wherever Kirstina and the children were, watching
them from the corner of her eye. Now she swept into the room. She
crossed to the window and turned there. Her eyes were excited and
she looked over Kirstina's head to the wall beyond. She did not speak
at once; she stood still, breathing audibly, until she began, "I saw you
speak to Michael Shea. You think now that you will go to him."

Kirstina did not move.

Margaret said, "You shall not go. You shall never go. I will stop
you." She paused as if she waited for protest. Getting none, she went
on, "You don't believe I can, do you? You think you are safe. You
think now you can leave this house and be together with him. . . .
But that is not so. You are never going to him. You are going to stay
here. . . . I can stop you leaving because I know how James died."

214

Yes, she is mad, Kirstina thought. Something will have to be done with her. She is mad and her madness is not the same as Estelle's.

Aloud she said only, "Yes. I also know how James died."

Margaret began to smile. Her upper lip rose over the thin line of her teeth and she asked, very softly, "Do you, Christine? . . . Are you quite sure you know?"

The hidden meaning in her voice was unmistakable. Kirstina grew pale and grew still and her hands tightened in her lap. She looked up into the dreadful woman's face and the black, excited eyes.

Margaret said, "Mr. Patterson uses arsenic in his sheep-dip. . . . I have known that for a long time."

The silence in the room became thick and pressed down. Kirstina stifled in it. She saw that this thing might be true. As yet it was only in her mind, but it might be true. Margaret had hated James because he had turned from her. She might have killed him for that— killed him painfully, making two attempts before the last. She would not have pitied him: she had stood in the room and watched him while he died.

In an agony of her own she said, "How cruel you must be. . . . You poisoned him."

Margaret came close to her. "James left me. I hated him. No one will know I killed him."

"Everyone will know. You have told me."

Shockingly, Margaret began to titter. She caught hold of the bed-post and swayed about, laughing. "You are stupid, Christine! I don't have to be afraid. James was my brother. Why should I have killed him? . . . If they find out they will think it was you. . . . Can't you see that? They will think it was you because of Michael Shea!"

"No one would believe that!"

"Tell them, and find out! Or go to Michael Shea, and I will tell. There is only you and I, Christine. You will never dare to tell. So you will not go, ever. Michael will be punished, too. I had to kill James for what he did, but there is a much easier way to punish you. . . ." She was quiet, contemplative as she considered what she had done. "Arsenic stays in the body," she said. "It is even in the bones." Without glancing at Kirstina again she walked away out of the room.

Kirstina was left with the feeling that nothing had happened and yet that everything had. She had been talking with a madwoman— a madwoman who was also a murderess. Or was that not true? Was there really poison in James's poor body? Margaret was mad. Margaret had wanted him dead and he had died: there might be no more to it than that.

But in her own mind she was sure that there was. "Mr. Patterson uses arsenic. . . . I have known it for a long time. . . . It is even in the bones." The woman had taken it and used it and James had died. There had been his terrible thirst—that had been different from his attacks before these last ones. And there had been no spasms, only steady, burning pain. I did not know what to do for him, she thought, and she felt deathly sick.

She was not afraid as Margaret expected her to be afraid. It was she, Kirstina, who would be believed. Only, Margaret would speak— would shout—all she knew. There would be people to hear, and who would have to ask questions about the things they heard.

For so long she had struggled so hard to be safe; when she had preserved nothing else at Prospect she had still preserved her silence, and in these last months she had learned to enjoy esteem and friendliness again. Now, after this, there would be nothing she would any longer be able to hide. It would all be there, for everyone to see. She thought, They will accept my word, but when they go back and find out what I am they will say, "Perhaps she did not do this—but she is a woman who could have done it." Then they would look at her and at Michael, and at her two sons. Margaret had used one threat against her and inflicted another, and she so dreaded what she saw must come that she lacked the courage to send for Michael at once, and put off doing it from day to day.

Margaret went through the house a swaggering queen. With no opposition she gave orders and sat herself in James's place at table. She put her arms about Geoffrey and told him that now he must love her again. Rudi was furious with her. He saw her taking advantage of his mother's fatigue and he made several attempts to put her in her place. Margaret retaliated by further arrogance and by innuendoes that made him long to burst every bond of restraint.

In his own mind he was disturbed because he felt he could relieve at least one part of his mother's trouble, but he did not know how to do it and he worried lest he should make a mistake. He waited until after the New Year had arrived. Then, when he was sitting alone with her in the drawing room, he asked her quietly, "How soon will my father be able to come?" and before her bewilderment had had time to mount he went on, "You do not have to tell me that Michael Shea is my father. I have always known."

216

It was difficult for her even to whisper, "How do you know?"

"I was in the wood by the gate that first day."

He knelt beside her chair, trying to explain. All his love for her was made plain and all his idolization of Michael. She could not fail to see that what counted with him was that he was their son, and tears poured down her cheeks. "You should have known! I should have told you long ago!"

"But there was nothing more to tell."

"Yes, there was." She began to tell him now, finding it easier as she went along. When she had quite finished he stayed quietly holding her hands until he asked, "Then my name is really Shea, like his?"

"Yes."

His thoughts ran on. "Geoffrey—?"

"My marriage to Geoffrey's father was no real marriage at all."

He waited a long time before he spoke again. "Geoffrey must never know that," he said. "It would matter to him."

When he left her she found that he had steeled her resolution. In the past she had never counted the cost of what she wanted, and they had all paid in turn: Michael, and Rudi, and poor James. Now she would have to find the courage they had deserved of her. Geoffrey she would try to protect insofar as she could; perhaps, sooner or later, even if Margaret had not acted, he would have had to learn to live with the truth.

She felt as if a powder train lay ready to her hand, but already, while she delayed firing it, she was tired of her fears and tired of being bound by weakness; Rudi, who had no heroics but instead kindness and fortitude, made her ashamed.

At length she went to her writing table and wrote two notes, to Michael and to Murray Fraser, asking them to come that evening. She called in the hired man and sent him off with the notes, and she had a great sense of relief, knowing that no matter what came of it now the thing was done.

They ate supper and then she told Mrs. Raikes whom she was expecting. While she was standing in the hall Margaret came rushing back.

"You have sent for Michael Shea!" she cried.

Kirstina was deliberately calm. "I have sent for him and for Murray Fraser. I am going to tell them both what you did."

"They will not believe you!"

"I think they will."

"They will not believe you! You fool! James was poisoned. They will take up his body and they will find the poison. They will know you did it. James loved me. They know James loved me! It was you who did it!"

At the shouting Rudi ran out of the drawing room, crying, "What is it?" He put his arm about his mother and turned on Margaret. "Be quiet!"

"You will see!" cried Margaret. "They will all see now! I will tell them what you are, you greedy whore! You tricked poor James. You wanted James to die. You waited for him to die. I will tell about you. They will believe me. Michael will believe me. I said I would show him. Now he will see!"

Her screaming voice filled the house. White with horror, Rudi stepped forward against her, but she struck out her arm and swept him back. Her eyes on Kirstina's face, she leaned towards her and shouted, "Are you afraid? . . . Are you afraid now?" She started for the front door.

"Rudi!" implored Kirstina.

He had already moved. He shouldered Margaret aside and stood with his back against the lock, but she flung herself at him, fighting to get out. She got a grip on the handle, and began to pull the door open, even with all his weight against it. She thrust her body into the opening. He let the door swing back and tried to grapple with her again, but already she was out on the steps and running away.

"Let her go," Kirstina said. "Let her go."

He turned back. His mother leaned against the wall and he was shocked to see her face. She said, "This is just the beginning . . . and it was only you who heard."

Michael Shea had dined with the Frasers and he and Murray started for Prospect together. They were within sight of the gates when Margaret Collingwood ran out and along the road away from them. She was wearing neither shawl nor cloak and she ran blindly, her feet making no noise in the thin snow.

Both men pushed their horses forward. Murray reached her first and leaped down. He caught her arm.

Michael also dismounted. He looked into the woman's face and then met Murray's eyes. Margaret glanced from one to the other. It was not until Michael took her other arm and they started to urge her back to the house that she tried to pull away.

She struggled with them as they went up the drive. She shouted, "I want to tell! . . . Stop! Let me go! I know what she has done! . . . She killed him! She killed him! Listen! I want to tell! . . ."

Michael spoke only once. "What has she done at the house?"

Murray said, "We knew this. We should have acted months ago."

As they came out beyond the woods her struggles became more violent. Murray swore and said, "Don't let her get away!" She twisted herself and pulled. Suddenly she doubled forward and flung up again and broke loose. She ran off, straight across the front of the house, toward the cliff edge.

Murray yelled, "Go on into the house! I will see to her!" He tore after her, running as hard as he could, but there were clouds and Margaret's dress was dark, and as soon as she was within the trees again he lost her. He swore wildly, casting around him and wishing he had a light. Andy Patterson came up behind him with his dog.

"She went up the cliff path, Mr. Fraser. Have a care to yourself, now, in the dark."

They followed the path, keeping away from the edge, not touching the handrail. The dog went ahead, growling deeply in his throat. Andy's hand was on his back. Murray came behind.

The trees ended just before the summerhouse. They stopped and they could not see her up there. Then they saw her below. She stood on the outside edge, between the house and the cliff.

She watched them coming, two men with the dog snuffing the ground, and her hair prickled on her neck. She shrieked at them, "Why do you come for me? I didn't do it! Leave me alone!" They came on cautiously, afraid of startling her. She shook with terror and moved back. "Can't you see? It is she you want—not I! She killed James. She poisoned him. I didn't do it! She wanted Michael Shea! She loves Michael Shea! You don't want me! You want her!" Murray was only six feet away. Andy stood with him, the dog crouching and growling under his hand. "She did it!" screamed Margaret. "Christine did it! Don't come for me! You want her!"

Andy lifted his hand from the dog's back and the beast leaped ahead. Margaret flung up her hands and turned to run. Then she was clawing the air and the snow as she went down screaming, her body sliding between the jutting rocks and trees to the ice and water below.

Neither man moved. They stood staring at where she had been. The dog snuffed at the edge and began to howl.

After a long time, Murray said, "Why did you loose the dog?"

Andy did not answer. Murray looked at him and then looked away. "I thought . . . we might have saved her. . . . You heard what she said?" he asked.

"Two of us heard, Mr. Fraser. She was an ill thing. She killed her poor brother."

"That was not what she said."

"Will you be thinking it was the other one, then?"

Murray went on staring ahead. Too much that he did not want came crowding into his mind. At his side Andy said, "It will have to be the one or the other, Mr. Fraser. It will have to be the sister or the wife."

Murray said, "She is . . . she is a strong woman."

"She is that. She would not have been afraid."

"Mr. Patterson . . . was James poisoned?"

"I'm thinking it is likely. But go on and ask yourself. It would have been easy for her. Mr. James turned to her like a baby. It would have been easy to set herself free. And she is a strong woman, as you said, and sometimes a hard one. Do you believe then that it was she who made him die?"

"No," Murray said slowly. "No."

"Then why should anyone else believe it?"

Andy's chin was outthrust. He was not shaken by what he had done. He looked to where the dog was still standing and said, "That one was the murderess, Mr. Fraser. She would have done more harm yet."

The dog came back to them, and Murray nodded. They turned and began to go down again beside the trees.

In the house Michael held Kirstina. He understood her horror and her dread of what would come, and he felt a desolation of his own. "I wanted you so safe," he said. He would have married her again and brought her and her two sons into his house. They would have had the peace and the time they had wanted. There would have been no more waste. There would have been friends and good will and contentment. These were the things for which she had always yearned, and which this time again she would not have.

"We will go away," he said, but she answered, "No. We will stay."

Suddenly he was close to laughter. He would always understand her now. She was stubborn and demanding and brave. What she most wanted she took, and she paid for it in her own coin. She longed for peace and yet could never willingly let go. But it was from the fears she turned her back on that she derived her strength, and her fears were his guarantee that she would always need him.

"I love you," he said. "We will stay and you shall lose nothing you want to hold." He began to wonder whether this fight that they would wage together might not be better than the tranquil retreat he had planned, and he told her so, assuring her that it would turn out well. "This time I will be here to look after you, and you will forget to be so much afraid."

It was the howling of the dog that first roused them. They were in the drawing room and they went together to the window that looked on the back. The moon had come out between the clouds and the snow was bright. After a while, black against the snow, they saw the two men and the dog coming back alone.